A BEWITCHING RENDEZVOUS

Almost leisurely, he leaned forward and bent to kiss me. I could have escaped that kiss. All I had to do was lean back on my pillows. When I did not, his arms came around me and gathered me close. It took my breath away.

"How strange this is, this love," he said. "I have never felt anything like it before. Oh, I'll not lie to you. I had my calf love, my affairs. But even in the heat of passion, I knew it would not last. This time, this time it will. Your mother named you truly. You are Delilah. You must be to bewitch me so."

"You are mad," I breathed. "I am so ordinary. And I'm too tall, and I'm not at all beauti—"

I was not allowed to finish, for he was kissing me again—all over my face, my throat, my mouth—while his hands caressed me until there wasn't a coherent thought in my head.

"Never let me hear you say anything so silly again," he growled in my ear. . . .

Dear Reader,

When this book first saw the light in 1981, when I started writing Regencies, it was called *The Covington Inheritance*. This version is very different. Some of the characters have changed, and more than just their names. The story is told now by the heroine, Lila Douglas, and a lot of new things happen in that old castle in Scotland facing the North Sea. There is a brand-new, surprising ending as well. Please, no peeking! It will ruin the mystery for you—and the love story.

I hope you have fun reading *The Scottish Legacy*, as much fun as I had writing it for you.

The Scottish Legacy

Barbara Hazard

A SIGNET BOOK

SIGNET
Published by New American Library, a division of
Penguin Putnam Inc., 375 Hudson Street,
New York, New York 10014, U.S.A.
Penguin Books Ltd, 27 Wrights Lane,
London W8 5TZ, England
Penguin Books Australia Ltd,
Ringwood, Victoria, Australia
Penguin Books Canada Ltd, 10 Alcorn Avenue,
Toronto, Ontario, Canada M4V 3B2
Penguin Book (N.Z.) Ltd, 182–190 Wairau Road,
Auckland 10, New Zealand

Penguin Books Ltd, Registered Offices:
Harmondsworth, Middlesex, England

Published by Signet, an imprint of New American Library, a division of
Penguin Putnam Inc. Originally published in a very different version in a
Signet edition under the title *The Covington Inheritance*.

First Printing (Revised Edition), December 1999
10 9 8 7 6 5 4 3 2 1

In loving memory of
Linda Conant Markham
Kindred spirit, constant friend

Prologue

It was very late and the candles were burning low when at last the old woman straightened up and abandoned her quill to massage her twisted, tired fingers. As she did so, she stared at the letters she had spent all evening writing, and a wicked smile of satisfaction crept over her face. Her raucous chuckle of complete enjoyment caused the old bulldog who was sleeping at her feet to snort before he settled his head back on his paws and began to snore again.

"Do be quiet, Excalibur," she said tartly, pushing him a little with her foot to reinforce her command. The dog paid no attention. Obese and almost blind, he had been her companion for so many years he knew this was not an order he had to obey. He was very old, but then, so was she. On her head she sported the powdered wig of an earlier time. Its high pompadour and dangling side curls made a mockery of her wrinkled face and sunken lips, as well as the dark age spots she had not even bothered to try and hide. Still as slender as a girl, she wore a man's dressing gown of scarlet velvet with a moth-eaten fur collar that had belonged to her father. On her fingers and wrists, at her throat and set in her earlobes, were all manner of jewels. They had not been cleaned in some time, but still they caught the light of the candelabra set on the mahogany writing desk. When one candle sputtered and she reached up to extinguish it, a huge ruby ring glowed a brilliant red.

The room the woman was in was as unusual as she was. It

was very large and filled with a variety of furniture, placed with complete disregard for period or style, so that priceless antiques sat next to rough country pieces. Although nominally a drawing room, one end was dominated by a huge four-poster draped in faded purple hangings heavy with tarnished gold braid. In addition to the bed, there were sofas and chairs and stools, as well as tables and étagères filled with the trivia of earlier generations. Every surface was crowded; one large Queen Anne table held a pair of antique dueling pistols, several books and papers, two fragile French figurines, and an irreplaceable Chinese porcelain bowl containing a moldy stuffed owl. The floors of the apartment were covered with a number of carpets laid one over the other. Some were priceless Orientals, some worn drugget more suitable to servants' quarters. The mantel over the fireplace held still more ornaments, and occupying the place of honor on the wall above it was a large oil of an elderly man dressed in the clothes of the mid 1700s. There was a distinct family resemblance between the room's present occupant and the elderly gentleman in the portrait. Perhaps it was the deep set of the dark eyes or the arrogant beak of a nose, or perhaps it was the haughty expression of the aristocrat who bowed deeply to no man save his king. On a wing chair near the fire, several gowns had been thrown carelessly, as if the lady had had trouble deciding what to wear before she put on the velvet robe for comfort. Certainly she did not need it for warmth, for in spite of the drafts that occasionally stirred the draperies, and the fierce wind that could be heard moaning outside the long windows that marched down one side of the room, it was very hot.

The old woman picked up the last letter she had written and read it through again, nodding in satisfaction as she did so. "Yes, this will fetch 'em," she muttered to herself, and as the old dog pricked up his ears, she added, "And then we shall see. Oh, yes, Excalibur, then we shall see."

She rose unsteadily and gripped the writing desk for a moment until she was sure of her balance. Then, leaning on an ebony cane with a chased silver head, she moved slowly toward the fireplace. After she had poured a glass of wine from one of the decanters placed on a table there, she held it up to the fire-light to admire the ruby color that echoed many of her jewels. Her father had been fond of rubies. With the tip of her cane she pushed the discarded gowns to the floor and sank into the chair to stare at the dying fire. Idly she wondered if it would be worthwhile to summon Crowell to build it up again. She knew it was very late. She should sleep, but sleep came hard these days. Some nights she did not even close her eyes, but spent the time wandering aimlessly around the room fingering her me-mentoes and sipping the wine her doctor had forbidden her to touch anymore. When he had issued that order, she had scowled and he hurried to say, "To speak plainly, ma'am, it will kill you. So, no more wine or brandy or I cannot be responsible for the consequences."

At that she had retorted, "And if I abstain, do you promise me a complete recovery from my maladies? The chance to live many more years?"

When the doctor had no reply, she shrugged. "Let us be hon-est and admit I have but little time left. I am, as you know, well over eighty and I have lived recklessly. What good can it pos-sibly do to give up one of the few comforts of my remaining days?"

Matthew Ward shook his head but he said no more. He had been her personal physician for several years and he knew that once her mind was made up it was impossible to change it. There had only been one man who had been able to do that, and he had been in his grave for forty years.

The old woman finished her wine and grimaced at the sud-den pain in her stomach. Yes, there was very little time left. She had known it for weeks, and that was the reason she had spent the evening painfully writing her seven letters. Spenser could address them in the morning, but she had not cared to dictate the contents to her secretary-companion. This was to be her se-cret. She wished to relish it alone.

Making a sudden resolve, she put down her glass with a snap. Until she finished this task she had set for herself, she would drink sparingly, no matter how her body cried out for the dulling of pain the liquor always provided. For what she was about to do was not just a whim, it was important. Very important. And when a successful conclusion had been reached, why, then, she would be grateful to go to her grave and peace at last.

She struggled to her feet and stood for a moment looking up at the harsh face in the portrait above her. Then, nodding her head, she prepared for bed. When she was under the covers, she closed her eyes and sighed, and as if the letter writing had eased her mind and her pain for this evening at least, she slipped easily into a deep slumber. In a short time both Lady Cecily Douglas and her old dog were snoring gently. The fire died down, and the only other sounds to be heard were those of the wind which continued to moan around the house, and the spaced, incessant thunder of the breakers as they rolled in from the North Sea to crash against the base of the cliff far below.

Chapter One

I came to Grimshead one bitterly cold February evening. The journey had been long and arduous, made more so by the company of my cousin Cecilia who had traveled with me. Since our mothers were not friendly, I had only met her two years earlier when I had gone to London for the Season. She was not out then, and I had thought her a silly, vain girl. Now, at eighteen, she seemed much the same. When we had first set out she had chatted gaily—and incessantly—of her family, her clothes, and her beaux, but as our way north grew progressively more rugged, and the countryside more lonely, she had ceased to prattle. On this final day of our journey, it was too cold even to snow, and the sky had barely lightened. The widely scattered villages we passed through had seemed empty. There were no children at play, no barking dogs to snap at the wheels of the coach, no laden farm carts to pass. If it had not been for the occasional plume of smoke from a chimney, it would have seemed as if no one lived in the tightly shuttered gray stone cottages with the dreary, empty garden plots. It was all very desolate, very wild.

I felt Cecilia shudder as she said, "Surely this miserable journey is a warning of some unpleasantness that lies ahead. I wish I had not come, indeed, I do."

Her light voice was dark with foreboding. In the six days we had been traveling, I had discovered Cecilia tended toward the dramatic. "We can hardly know what lies ahead," I said, as calmly as I could. Cecilia sighed and turned her shoulder to stare out the window. It had been clean at first light, but now it was begrimed with spattered mud and gave but a poor view of the world beyond it.

No doubt that was just as well, I thought as I stared from my own window. For a moment I pictured the bright sunny breakfast room at my home, and felt some doubt and apprehension, too.

But I have been most remiss. My name is Lila Douglas. Well, to be entirely open, it is really Delilah Douglas. Delilah *Mary*, if you can imagine anything so incongruous. My mother had told me she had been determined her daughter would have a biblical name. There was no such nonsense about my brother's name. No, that fortunate infant was christened Robert James after his grandfather. My father was named James Robert after his, and so it had been for generations. Neat, wasn't it? Avoiding all the confusion that two Jameses or two Roberts would have entailed? But such was not my luck. As soon as I was old enough to realize how inappropriate my name was, I had insisted on being called Lila. I did this by refusing to answer to any other name. My mother said such stubbornness showed a willful nature, but my father only laughed.

He had not laughed however when he received the letter from his aunt, Lady Cecily Douglas. No, then his face had turned red, and he had sputtered as he said, "I have never heard such impertinence! How *dare* she? Here, Janet, just listen to this!"

We were in the breakfast room at the time, and we both listened amazed as he read the letter in a voice full of loathing. At the end, he threw it down on the table and rose to pace the room, muttering to himself.

"Bad lot, indeed! Not worthy of her money! I'm sure I don't know how she can judge whether we're a bad lot or not; she hasn't had anything to do with us for years. Buried up there in Scotland in that ancient pile of stone my grandfather so foolishly left her, along with his fortune, never answering my letters or inquiries about her health. Why, Janet, do you remember last year when I sent her a dozen bottles of the best Madeira? And did I hear a word of thanks? No, I did not. And here she has the colossal gall to imply that far from sending the wine from a proper family concern for her welfare, I was trying to bribe her into leaving her fortune to me! Well, I can tell you I'm glad she is not here in this room, the miserable old cat, for I should give her a piece of my mind she wouldn't soon forget!"

Neither my mother nor I said anything to that sweeping statement. We both knew he would do no such thing. In fact, the reason he was upset was because he most certainly had sent the wine with the intention of remaining in his aunt's good graces.

"Still, I suppose we must comply with her wish to have Lila and Robert visit alone. There is a great deal of money at stake here. I would not have them forfeit it because of her insults to us. No, indeed."

"Must we go?" I asked. "I admit this royal summons does not make me all eagerness to meet my great-aunt. And surely Scotland in February will not be a pleasant locale."

"Of course you are not required to go, Lila," my father replied. "But you may be sure all the others will be making plans to leave immediately. I'd not have you and Robert left out of her will simply because you could not bother to make the journey."

"All what others?" I asked, pouring my mother another cup of tea. "The only relative I know is Roger, Lord Danvers, and his wife. Oh yes, there is Aunt Mary's daughter, Cecilia. You remember, Mama. We met her in London two Aprils ago."

"You may be sure *she'll* be there," my mother said with a sniff. "Your aunt will see to that."

My father took his seat again, looking thoughtful. "Yes, of course both Roger and little Cecilia will go north. I've often thought it so very obvious of Mary to practically name her daughter after my aunt; I'm sure the old lady saw through the ploy. But there are some second cousins as well. Cecily had two brothers and a sister. One brother, Anthony, had only a single issue, a son, Hector. He died childless. Then there was my father, Robert, who had me and your aunts Mary and Rose. But there was also Emily Douglas, Lady Cecily's older sister. She married a man named Aubry Russell and they had two children, Gloriana and Donald. Gloriana married the Earl of Byford. They had one son, who, if I remember correctly, inherited a great fortune from his father's side. I am sure I don't know why he would need any of Aunt Cecily's. And of course Donald had a son, too. I'm sure you must have met him. Alastair Russell is well known in the *ton,* I believe."

I made no comment. Instead I said, "I must admit I am confused. Why does the lady want to skip a generation in the disposal of her fortune? Whatever did you all do to give her such a dislike of you?"

My father looked confused. "I've no idea," he admitted. "I only met her once when I was a green lad. My father did say there was bad feeling between Aunt Cecily and the rest of the family, perhaps because they felt cheated when the old man left her all his fortune, and she but a mere woman. And now we see the result—disastrous!"

He chanced to glance up then to find his mere women regarding him seriously, and he coughed as he picked up the letter again. "But I have only mentioned six relatives, you and Robert, Roger and Cecilia, and Grant St. Williams, the new earl, and his cousin Alastair. Yet here she writes of seven. Can it be her mind is becoming addled with age? Or do you think she includes Roger's wife Sylvia?"

"Rest assured, Lady Danvers will strive to be first to arrive," my mother said tartly. Then, turning to me, she added, "Do say you will go, Lila! If nothing else it will be a change for you. It has been such a dreary winter, and the Season is still many weeks away. No doubt Robert will travel directly from London, but you may go in your father's coach with Cecilia. I'm sure with your maids to accompany you, it would be considered proper."

"Of course I will go," I told them calmly. And there in the cheerful room with its table covered with damask and silver and plate, the chafing dishes steaming gently on the sideboard, I had looked forward to it. Now, I was not so sure.

I saw Cecilia had leaned back against the squabs, her face white with strain and I hoped I was not going to arrive with a sick girl on my hands.

"Are you all right, coz?" I asked.

Cecilia barely glanced at me before she whispered, "I do not like Scotland. It is so frightening—so lonely. Oh, why did Mama make me come?"

Relieved that it was only apprehension, I tried for a rallying tone as I said, "It is only that we are unused to such scenery. See there, through the mist. I believe that is what is called a tor; it is very mountainous, is it not? And just think, all around us are the famous glens of Scotland, where the clans hid before they came out to fight, behind their lairds and swirling bagpipes. How very interesting it all is, for so much history has been made here."

I saw my words had only caused Cecilia more unease, for now she peered out the window as if she expected to see a band of kilted savages stalking the carriage and getting ready to attack, swinging their cudgels and screaming their war cries. I thought her very childish although I had to admit I had seldom seen a prettier miss. She had a slight, girlish figure, and her heart-shaped face with its normally rose-tinged cheeks, gentle mouth, and melting brown eyes, was framed by clouds of chestnut hair. Until she spoke, she was captivating; when she did, it became obvious no one, after all, is perfect. And then I scolded myself mentally for such an uncharitable thought.

An early winter dusk had fallen before we turned at last into a long, unkempt drive. As we passed the sagging iron gates, I saw a deserted stone gatehouse. No lamps were lit there, and as the carriage lumbered slowly up the drive, some leafless branches scraped the sides. Cecilia, who had been dozing in her corner, woke with a start.

"What . . . what was that?" she asked fearfully.

"Nothing but an overgrown branch, coz. See, we are almost there," I told her as I stared out the window. Between the sleety rain and the early darkness there was little to see, and I was glad when we swept around a half circle and stopped before a set of stone steps. As I climbed down on the groom's arm, I squeezed it and said, "Bless you, Henry, and John Coachman as well. We've done it!"

"There are no lights," Cecilia whispered as she followed me from the coach. Behind her our maids were busy gathering up our possessions. "Perhaps we have come to the wrong place; see, no one is expecting us."

The groom touched his cap. "Beg pardon, miss, this is Grimshead, all right. There was a sign at the gates."

I gave the male servants orders about the baggage and told them I would make arrangements for their comfort before I led my little group up the stone steps. Grimshead loomed above us, dark and cold, and, I had to admit, extremely unwelcoming. I tried not to let my own doubt show as I talked of warm fires, comfortable beds, a hot supper.

No one answered our knock. "Oh dear," Cecilia whispered. "I am so afraid!"

It seemed an age before the door creaked open very slowly. All at once I was tempted to laugh. Cecilia had read a Gothic tale to me whenever the state of the roads permitted it, and her story was set in just such a place as Grimshead appeared to be. Would the butler be the same crippled retainer with the ghastly cackle, I wondered? But the old man who opened the door almost grudgingly and peered out at us stood tall and straight.

"Good evening," I said, moving forward and dragging a reluctant Cecilia with me since she would not release my arm. "I am Lila Douglas. This is my cousin, Cecilia Worthington. I believe we are expected?"

The old man held his candle higher for a moment. Just when I thought he was about to refuse us admittance, he opened the door wider. Eager to escape the cold rain, I swept by him, beckoning to the others to follow me.

The servant did not speak, and I looked around curiously. The hall we had entered was massive. You could not even see the ceiling in the gloom for outside of the candle the servant held, there were no other lights. At one end of the hall a small fire burned in a fireplace large enough to hold an ox, and I could make out some tables and chairs placed there. On one side of the hall, a wide staircase with a heavily carved bannister stretched upward to the next floor. Aware of the silence then, I turned back to the servant.

"Perhaps Lady Cecily was not expecting us to arrive so late, . . . er? What is your name, if you please?"

"I'm Crowell, miss," came the sullen answer. "The butler."

"Very well, Crowell. If it is not convenient for us to see our great-aunt this evening, we shall pay our respects in the morning."

"Not bloody likely ye will," the butler muttered almost to himself. Just then a woman's voice came from the shadows at the back of the hall, demanding to know who was there.

A middle-aged woman dressed in black with her graying hair scraped back in a tight bun came toward us holding a single candle high. From its unpleasant odor, I could tell it was made of tallow, not beeswax.

"This here be Miss Spenser," the man who had admitted us said. He sounded relieved. "She's Lady Cecily's companion-like."

I held out my hand and smiled. "I am delighted to make your acquaintance, Miss Spenser. We have been on the road a long time today, and we are tired and hungry. Since I understand our great-aunt cannot receive us tonight, perhaps it would be best if we went immediately to our rooms. A light supper will be all that is required, and of course, food and accommodations for our servants."

"Oh dear," this Miss Spenser said, one thin white hand going to her cheek. I couldn't help but think of a frightened rabbit, her gray eyes were so magnified behind a pair of thick glasses. "Oh dear me! I don't know when Lady Cecily will receive you. As for food, I'll have to see . . ."

Stunned by this uncivil reception, I was delighted when a door opened to our right and light streamed out to illuminate the stone flags we stood on, and our little party of travelers.

"Can it be another contingent of relatives has arrived?" a drawling, lazy voice inquired. My breathing became uneven, and my heart began to beat erratically. Mentally I called myself every kind of fool, for it was not as if I was surprised Alastair Russell was there.

"Ah, I see I was correct," the gentleman said. "Do come into the library, er, cousins. It is the only fairly warm room in this decrepit old pile of rock they call a castle."

Miss Spenser wrung her hands. As I moved past her I heard her whisper, "So many candles! So much coal!"

As I entered the library I said over my shoulder, "Perhaps you should summon the housekeeper, Miss Spenser. I am concerned with the welfare of our servants. I assume we are too late for dinner?"

"You would be most untruthful to call what we had to eat this day 'dinner,' " Alastair Russell said as he led us toward the fire. "Grant, I am desolated to disturb you, but I fear you must give up your chair. These ladies are in need of warmth."

Even as he spoke, the other gentleman in the room was rising to bow to us. "I am Grant St. Williams," he said. "And this, of course, is Alastair Russell." He turned a little and added, "You really must not assume that everyone automatically knows who you are, cousin. This is not London, after all."

"Please do not remind me," Russell drawled. "I miss it terribly already."

As they spoke, I studied the Earl of Byford carefully. He was very tall, with dark hair and craggy features. Next to his handsome cousin, he seemed almost rough-hewn, as if the sculptor who had fashioned him had been called away before he could apply the finishing touches. And unlike his cousin, who was attired in faultless evening clothes, he wore buckskin breeches and a dark riding coat. There was a slight family resemblance between the two even though Russell had golden hair and curiously intense green eyes. I saw Lord Byford was studying me as carefully as I had studied him, and I smiled to myself as I dropped him a curtsy.

After introducing myself and Cecilia, who was now all smiles and blushes as Russell seated her, I held out my hands to the fire and said lightly, "How good that feels! We have been traveling for six days, although it seems even longer. Now, if only Miss Spenser does not forget to feed us. We are ravenous."

M'lord grimaced. "Unfortunately, in this house you will find you are often ravenous. However, tonight you may leave the matter in my hands."

He strode to the door and called, "Here there, Crowell, bustle about, man! Some food for the ladies and a pot of tea as well as wine."

I could hear the servant mumbling as he went away and then Alastair Russell claimed my attention. "Traveling is so tedious, is it not?" he drawled. "I had no idea it would take us so long to reach Grimshead, even behind Byford's teams. But I underestimated the state of the roads in this backward part of the world. I cannot imagine why any civilized person would choose to live here on the North Sea, especially in the winter."

"But, Alastair," the earl said as he rejoined us near the fire, "you have so often said that about an estate located only a few miles from London."

Russell nodded calmly. "It is true I find the country an abomination. May I tell you ladies how delighted I am to have your company? We have seen no one but servants since our arrival yesterday."

"Is Great-Aunt Cecily ill, sir?" Cecilia asked, her eyes wide.

"We have been informed Her Royal Highness will see none of us until the entire party is assembled," Alastair said. His words were light, bantering, but I thought his expression somewhat grim. "I hope that will not take long, but I intend to make my visit as short as possible. There is nothing to do here. Nothing."

"But now our cousins have arrived, we can play cards, perhaps explore the countryside if the weather ever improves. Do you ride, cousins?" the earl asked mildly.

As we all conversed, I wondered why I felt so uneasy. It was as if I sensed there were undercurrents in the room, undercurrents I did not understand. Then I told myself I was imagining things, no doubt because I was so tired.

Just then the butler brought in a tray. At the earl's direction, he set it on a table near the fire. It was not much of a meal, just some bread and cheese and a bowl of apples, but the wine that accompanied it was excellent, and the hot tea refreshing. After two glasses of the wine, my cousin Cecilia became very chatty and when I saw her trying to hide a yawn behind her napkin, I rose and excused us both. I could tell by her pout, Cecilia did not want to leave the gentlemen, but she was forced to curtsy and follow me.

I was very conscious of their gaze as we made our way to the staircase, where the butler waited to escort us.

Chapter Two

When I entered the room that was to be mine, I found my maid busy unpacking my trunk. I looked around, shocked as well as a little amused. The room was large and well furnished, but the bedhangings were ripped in places, and they, like the draperies, had faded with age. The rug before the fire had a hole in it, and with the exception of a table Polly had obviously dusted, all the furniture looked sadly neglected. The handsome antique pier glass set in one corner was so clouded it was impossible to see yourself in it. I thought perhaps it was just as well candles were dispensed with such a sparing hand. Dim light was certainly kinder to the decor.

"This room's a disgrace, Miss Lila, that's what I say. But don't you worry. I'll see to it tomorrow," Polly said as she shook out one of my gowns. "There's no use asking the servants here to help. They're all of them elderly, and from what I can gather, under no supervision. There isn't even a housekeeper. That Miss Spenser seems to be in charge."

She sniffed and went on, "I've never seen such dust, why, there's even cobwebs! Your mother would be horrified."

I laughed as she came to help me out of my clothes. To be truthful, I was so tired from traveling I didn't much care about the condition of the room. I could see the bed had been made up with fresh sheets and that was all that mattered. Well, almost all, I reminded myself as I asked Polly to try and persuade someone that four coals did not produce a blazing fire.

It was not very long before I was tucked in bed, and although I had been afraid the wind and the sound of those crashing breakers would keep me awake, I dropped off to sleep almost at once.

The next morning I woke before Polly brought me my chocolate, and for a while I snuggled under the warm blankets and reviewed my situation. I had arrived at my great-aunt's stronghold, as I was beginning to consider it, and besides my cousin Cecilia, Alastair Russell and the Earl of Byford were also in residence. For a moment, I allowed myself to think of Mr. Russell, something I had not done up to now. I had met the gentleman the previous spring in London, although I doubted he remembered the occasion that had been so very momentous to me. I can still remember how my breath had caught in my throat as the evening's hostess introduced us, how my heart had pounded so I was sure everyone could see it beating through the thin silk of my gown. I had never believed in love at first sight, but then I knew I had been proved wrong. He was so handsome, his blond hair so dazzling in the candlelight, and he was so beautifully clad. But it was more than that. It was his eyes that caught me, held me. They were a clear green, lucid, direct. I could not take my own eyes from them as I curtsied. And Mr. Russell? Alas, he had only smiled the slightest bit, bowed ever so casually, and left my side as soon as he could contrive it. And I, sensible, clearheaded, practical Lila Douglas, well past the age of girlish fancies, had fallen deeply in love. It had been most unlike me and there had been nothing I could do to stop it. For the rest of the Season I worshipped my second cousin from afar, and I put myself to sleep at night inventing possible future meetings when the scales would fall from the gentleman's eyes and he would see, as I had, that ours would be a union made in heaven. But no such happy ending occurred. In fact, we never exchanged another word before the Douglas family retired to Oxfordshire and I was left with only a memory. But perhaps it would be different, now we were here, thrown together by an old woman's whim. Perhaps as he got to know me better, he would fall in love, too. Perhaps . . .

Sighing, I rang the bell for Polly. As I did so, the embroidered cord came away in my hand, and it successfully diverted me from further daydreaming.

I chose to wear a warm gown of sky blue woolsey that morning, and I am not ashamed to admit I did not have to be coaxed to don a pair of warm woolen stockings as well.

I discovered Grant St. Williams when I entered the breakfast room. He seated me, remarking our cousin Alastair never left his room before eleven, and it appeared Miss Worthington was of like mind. As I ate the oatmeal and single slice of toast that was provided, I put Mr. Russell from my mind to concentrate on the earl.

"I am surprised I have not met you in London, sir," I said before I sipped my tea.

He looked as if he were surprised by my comment. "I have been traveling abroad for some time," he said. "But even if I had been in town, I doubt we would have met. I seldom attend society's amusements. Indeed, if I did not have to take my seat in Parliament, I would sell my house there, and spend all my time in the country.

"But of course I have horrified you with my choice of the better locale, have I not? I know how you ladies adore London—the shopping, the parties, the balls."

His voice held a hint of superiority and I stiffened. Still, I reminded myself he was entitled to his opinion. "It can be delightful in London after a hard winter," I only said. "But I do envy you the chance to travel. It is something I have always wanted to do. Tell me, if you would be so kind, what countries have you seen?"

The rest of our meager meal passed quickly as the earl regaled me with tales of the former colonies and Canada, even those parts of Europe Napoleon did not control. We did not leave the breakfast room until Crowell came in to clear the table. His sniff told us clearly we were upsetting his routine.

"Charming creature, isn't he? So obsequious," the earl murmured as he held the door for me. I couldn't resist a smile.

"But he is not the crippled old retainer with the ghastly laugh so often found in Gothic tales that I expected," I said. "And no, m'lord, I am not addicted to such literature. Cecilia is, however. I hope she slept well. She is a fearful girl, and the waves were very loud last night. I wonder if they always pound against the rocks that way."

Before he could reply, the knocker on the front door beat a loud tattoo. As the earl went to answer it, he said over his shoulder, "If we wait for Crowell to come, whoever is there may leave in frustration. We can't have that."

As soon as the door was open and I saw my brother Robert standing outside, a bewildered expression on his fresh young face, I cried out and went to hug and kiss him for I had not seen him since Christmastime.

"Stop that, Lila," he growled in my ear. I could tell he was embarrassed because the earl was there, so I did not tease him. Instead, I introduced the two men gravely.

As Robert made a careful bow, he said, "I'm delighted to find someone else is here, m'lord, at the end of the world. Seems as if I've been traveling forever. I left the stage some miles back and I was sure I was fated to ride forever, never reaching my destination. And coming up that long, overgrown drive—well! I can see we are to have a real adventure here."

He looked so pleased at the prospect, I had to laugh. Bobby, as I used to call him before he threatened me with bodily harm, was only just turned twenty-one, and newly let loose on the town. He had yet to acquire the sophisticated patina so many men had. In a way, I wished he never would.

Crowell shuffled in then, mumbling about another visitor, but he took him away to show him to his room and agreed to see to his baggage when it came later by carter.

Left to ourselves, the earl and I explored the ground floor, which was one dark, neglected room after another. Most of the furniture was covered in dust sheets, the draperies pulled tightly closed. As we retired to the library, I wondered why Lady Cecily chose to live with such ugliness when she had a fortune at her disposal. But perhaps she was a miser?

Cecilia joined us in the library shortly thereafter, and she positively glowed when Robert appeared and she was able to make the acquaintance of yet another eligible gentleman. To my disappointment, Alastair Russell did not come down till after eleven. I saw Robert trying very hard not to stare at the picture of sartorial splendor he presented: boots by Hobey, coat by Stulz, breeches by Goren, and cravat by Mr. Russell's own accomplished hand. I told myself the pace of my heartbeats changed only marginally, and congratulated myself on my self-control.

There was still some time before the luncheon the earl had ordered, and he suggested we all take a stroll through the grounds. The sun was shining, although fitfully, for the sky was full of scudding clouds. After our wraps had been brought to us, we went out into the gardens, or what appeared to have been gardens at one time or another. Cecilia was in a fret about the wind, and it was true there was a strong breeze from the north-east. It had a salty tang to it, and it went right through the thickest clothing. I was warm enough in the fur-lined cloak my mother had lent me for the journey, but Cecilia said she must return to the house. I was sorry when Alastair agreed to escort her. Indeed, some of the day's brilliance disappeared with them.

"I wonder why Great-Aunt put us all on the side of the house that faces the North Sea," I said, freeing my cloak from a bramble bush and determined to forget him. "Surely a room facing the drive and the park would be more comfortable this time of year?"

"But it is so healthful, cousin," Byford assured me. "Why, you may always have the benefit of fresh air without the danger of opening your window. Haven't you noticed how the drafts stir the draperies almost continually, and help fan those very inadequate fires as well?"

I was not required to answer, although my brother burst into laughter, for just then we rounded a windbreak of stunted firs and I was forced to concentrate on taming my suddenly unruly skirts. Robert took my arm and hurried me down a sloping lawn that led to a low stone wall. The earl followed us at a more leisurely pace.

"My word," I said faintly, my words snatched away by the wind as I stared over the edge. Far, far below massive waves rolled in toward huge ledges, where they were tossed upward on impact into a cascade of foam and turbulence. The spectacle was accompanied by the tremendous booming I had heard all last evening. Beside me, Robert leaned far over and I reached out to grasp his coat, afraid the wind might snatch him away and dash him on those glistening black rocks below.

"I say, this is something like, isn't it, Lila?" he yelled, for it was impossible to speak normally over the sound of the surf.

I shivered as I watched yet another breaker roll in to do battle with the earth. It seemed to me as if all that ferocious, restless energy was determined to undermine the very ground on which we stood. An errant strand of my hair blew across my face, and I smoothed it back with a trembling hand. The earl must have noticed, for he took my arm and said to Robert, "It's very exciting I'm sure, but your sister is cold. We'll go in now."

Without waiting to see if Robert agreed, he led me away from the precipice. I was relieved. It was an awesome sight, but I admit I was frightened by the majestic, relentless power.

We found Alastair and Cecilia in the library reading. I excused myself to tidy my windswept hair.

When at last the gong sounded for luncheon and we went toward the dining room, Robert noticed the closed doors leading from the hall and said, "Is that the drawing room? Why don't we use it instead of the library?"

"Because that is our dear Great-Aunt Cecily's lair," Alastair replied. "Miss Spenser says it is her bedroom, sitting room, and receiving room—when, that is, she condescends to receive. Let us hope our Danvers cousins are not far behind us. I, for one, am all impatience to meet our most unusual hostess."

His tone was light, but I noticed the earl give him an intent, speculative look, and I wondered at it.

We had barely begun our luncheon when a commotion could be heard in the hall, and a woman's sharp voice raised in command.

"Your wish appears to be granted, Alastair," Byford remarked. "Perhaps you will be sorry you voiced it, before long."

My brother looked a question at me, but he did not say anything. He knew he was beneath the notice of his two male cousins, for who was he, after all, but a young man of no distinction when set beside an earl and that leader of fashion, Alastair Russell?

The Danvers joined us only moments later. Roger Danvers, a plump young man in his late twenties, smiled and said how pleased he was to see us, but his wife glared at each one of us in turn. Robert kicked me under the table, but I was careful not to catch his eye.

"Well," Lady Danvers said as she took her seat and stared at the small portion of baked eggs Crowell was serving her. "We are quite a large group, are we not? I did not expect so many. And how comes it that I have never met some of you before?"

Her tone seemed to imply there was something disreputable about relatives one had never met, as if they had been up to something she would not approve of all these years. She glared at us again, which caused Cecilia to drop her fork and Robert to blush. I gave her an indifferent nod, while Alastair and Byford ignored her.

"I suppose you've all been very busy, worming your way into Great-Aunt Cecily's good graces?" she asked next, taking three scones and a large dollop of butter from Crowell's tray.

"Sylvia, dearest!" her husband said weakly. Alastair Russell raised his quizzing glass to inspect the lady carefully. The rest of us were dumbstruck at her temerity.

She managed a slight blush. "Well, why beat about the bush?" she asked in her strident voice. "Why not come right out with it?"

"Perhaps because it might be considered—oh, only by the *highest* sticklers in the *haut ton,* of course—to be in rather bad taste?" Russell asked gently. Somehow a shiver ran up my arms. I wondered at it. There had been no threat in his voice.

"I do not believe in subterfuge. That is why we are all here, is it not, to try to gain sole possession of a very large inheritance? But I do find it most suspicious that you are all come before us. Most suspicious, indeed."

"You may be calm, Lady Danvers," Grant St. Williams remarked in his deep voice. "Lady Cecily has said she will see no one until the entire party is assembled. So you see," he added as the lady's expression brightened, "no one has stolen a march on you. You and your husband will have exactly the same opportunities as the rest."

"I can tell you do not approve of my honesty, sir," Lady Danvers said. "I must say I am sure I don't know why you are even here. With all your wealth, you can have no need of any more. Greedy, I call it."

Her look at the gentleman was belligerent, and since he was rigid with anger and her husband had succumbed to a coughing fit behind his handkerchief, I hastened to say, "No one here has even spoken of the inheritance, Sylvia. And as far as we know, Lady Cecily may live for several more years. Indeed, I for one hope she does."

"Do you, Delilah?" she asked in a stunned voice.

I hate you, I thought. You are a horrid, disagreeable, nasty woman with the manners of a goat. I was aware that both the earl and Alastair Russell were staring at me with arrested expressions, for they had not known my real name until just then. And I was aware, as I had always been, that my ordinary face and hair and much too tall figure were in no way deserving of the name my mother had given me.

"I should think that at your age and in your circumstances, the inheritance would be vastly important," Sylvia Danvers continued, and I clenched my hands in my lap and swallowed to control my anger. At twenty-four I was only a year older than my cousin's wife, and hardly considered myself on the shelf.

Turning to Cecilia, I said, "We had the most interesting walk this morning, Cecy, after you and cousin Alastair left us. You must both go and see the view over the North Sea as we did. The castle is built on a cliff and you are able to stare down at the breakers. It is most impressive."

Cecilia shuddered, but she did not speak for fear Lady Dan-

vers would turn her guns her way. My heart lightened when
Alastair raised his glass to me in a silent toast before he said,
"It sounds frightening. I have always had a fear of heights. I am
not sure my health is up to the excitement."

Lord Byford wiped his lips and put down his napkin, his
composure regained as he said, "Do try to forget your consequence as London's finest exquisite, Alastair. The view is the
most interesting thing here. I'll even escort you to the precipice
so I can lend you my support if you are overcome by weakness."

For a moment I thought a dangerous light flashed in Russell's eyes, but it was gone so quickly I was sure I must have
imagined it. Lady Danvers had discovered the comfits dish and
was now blessedly silent as she selected all the best sweets. Her
husband looked relieved but I felt my disgust rise as she gob-
bled, her plump cheeks wobbling with her efforts. What a terrible woman Sylvia Danvers was, I thought. If she did not have
us all at dagger-drawing in a day I would be surprised.

I saw Cecilia was looking at me, pleading silently with me to
remove her from this situation, and I rose and excused us both.

As soon as we reached the hall, she whispered, "How are we
to bear that awful woman? Surely she is dangerous for I can tell
she'll let nothing stand in the way of getting Lord Danvers
named heir. Oh, I wish my mama had not insisted I come and
try for it, too. I don't want the money, I don't, I don't!"

As we settled down in the library with our needlework, I
said, "Then all you have to do is tell Sylvia so and be as indifferent to Lady Cecily as you can manage."

"But . . . but Mama will be so angry if I do not make a push
to be the favorite," Cecilia wailed, dropping her tapestry to
wring her hands.

I pushed down the feeling of impatience that always came
when I was forced to reason with my cousin, and said, "I think
the only sensible way to behave is to pretend there is no inheritance at stake here. And please, do help me draw Sylvia's bow.
I'm afraid Lord Byford and Mr. Russell will kill her if we don't.
Did you see the way they looked at her?"

"I couldn't. I'm not brave, like you are, Lila. I envy you but I intend to keep my mouth shut around that lady at all times."

"In that case you'll starve to death in short order," I said as I measured out a length of dark green thread. "There's little enough to eat here, and if you don't nip in and get your share before Sylvia, there'll be nothing at all."

I chuckled, but Cecilia only shivered and said starvation would be preferable to having the lady's attention focused on her.

Perhaps it was the unpleasantness at the luncheon table that caused each member of the party to go their separate ways that afternoon. Lord Byford took Robert off for a long ride, and Sylvia Danvers insisted on inspecting every room in the house carefully. Going to the hall once to tell Crowell we would need more coal, I noticed Miss Spenser following them around, her hands clasped tightly before her, and her habitual frown marring her brow.

To my chagrin, Alastair Russell only stayed in the library long enough to select a book; he disappeared then to his room and was not seen again until dinner. Cecilia and I had the library to ourselves, which soon had her in chattering good spirits. I had little to do but listen and nod and exclaim. And secretly, brood. Brood about my looks, my height, my name, and the unfairness of life in general.

Chapter Three

I sat at the old dressing table in my room while Polly brushed my hair into smooth waves and fastened on my mother's pearl set, lent for the occasion. The maid had managed to steady the table by propping up a rickety leg with a piece of board; indeed, the entire room looked a great deal better after her earnest attention. I was quick to tell her so, and we both laughed when she related the trials she had undergone to wrest another hod of coal from Miss Spenser.

As I went down the stairs in response to the dinner gong, I wondered why I had chosen to wear my most becoming gown. It was made of velvet in the newly popular Wellington brown shade and featured creamy lace at the low neckline and puffed sleeves. But I did not have to wonder long. I knew I wore it because it fit me so well, and because it showed off my figure and the skin my mother had told me was my best feature, pearly and flawless.

I was the last to arrive in the dining room, and Lord Byford, this evening attired in formal dress, led me to my seat. As he did so, I saw him openly admiring my bare shoulder, and I pretended not to notice. I saw Robert had struggled to turn himself out in a style that would not disgust his male relatives. To my eye, he had only succeeded in making himself look very young. He had brushed his brown hair into what he no doubt considered windswept fashion, but his fresh, open face helped divert attention from it and from his poorly tied cravat and wrinkled coat as well.

He seated Cecilia Worthington with a flourish, and she blushed. Tonight she was wearing a gossamer gown of palest blue with sapphire combs set in her chestnut curls and she drew every masculine eye. Mentally I shrugged. So much for perfect skin.

When I dared look at Alastair, I saw he was impeccable as always, although the sardonic twist of his well-shaped mouth somewhat marred the picture he made.

Sylvia Danvers was already tapping an impatient finger on the table. Tonight she was resplendent in a gown of maroon Pekin satin and the beautiful set of rubies her husband had given her on their betrothal. That gentleman, so eagerly going around the table to greet everyone individually, was decked out in a pale gray coat and tight satin pantaloons. He also wore a waistcoat of scarlet silk, embroidered with peacocks, vines, and flowers which unfortunately called attention to the vast expanse it covered. As he beamed and bowed to me I did not have the slightest desire to smile at his dandyism, for he was so eager to be liked, much like a puppy that gambols about you, begging to be petted.

At last Crowell shuffled in with the soup tureen, followed by the oldest footman I had ever seen, and dinner commenced. Conversation was general and innocuous, for which I was sure everyone felt a vast relief. And when Sylvia Danvers had not insulted anyone for two entire courses, even Cecilia dared to contribute her mite. Byford and Robert told about their ride and the surrounding countryside, Alastair discoursed on the London theater, and Lord Danvers told several long, boring stories about their journey north. I suspected his wife was only quiet because she was so busy eating.

When the table was cleared at last, and I was wondering if I, as the eldest lady present, or Sylvia as the only married one, should give the signal for the ladies to adjourn, the dining room doors opened to reveal Miss Spenser. She stood there as we all stared at her, and her nervousness was obvious from the way she swallowed quickly before she spoke.

"Er . . . I beg your pardon, ladies and gentlemen," she said in a strained, high voice. She coughed before she continued, "Now that everyone has arrived at Grimshead, Lady Cecily has instructed me to tell you she will receive you after dinner, for brandy or any other refreshment you might wish."

Before anyone could question her, she fled like a frightened mouse, and Crowell shut the doors behind her.

"How very unusual," Alastair drawled, his long, beautifully manicured fingers playing with the stem of his wineglass. "I wonder why our dear great-aunt did not join us for dinner?"

Lady Danvers scraped up the last of her trifle. "Why would she want to?" she demanded. "She probably dined very well in her own rooms, leaving us to eat the sparsest meal I have ever seen. Imagine, only two removes for each course." She reached down her lap and drew out a small enameled box, which she opened with a flourish to take out a sweetmeat. "I, at least, will not starve," she declared.

I looked around and caught Lord Byford's eye. There was an unholy look of delight in it, and I had to look away quickly lest I disgrace myself by laughing out loud.

Robert and Cecilia were whispering, their heads close together. I saw my brother was speaking rapidly, and I knew from the excited look on his face, he was looking forward to the coming confrontation. Cecilia, on the other hand, looked petrified. I could read nothing in Alastair Russell's contained face except indifference. Then Roger Danvers said, "Perhaps this evening, cousins, we should all retire to Lady Cecily's rooms immediately, instead of lingering over our port."

"What port?" Byford inquired, as he rose and beckoned to the rest of us. "Come, children, shall we obey Lady Cecily's command?"

We left the dining room together, preceded by Crowell and his single candle. No one spoke now. The only sound was that of our footsteps on the flagstones of the hall, which was lit, as was customary, by the very inadequate fire in its huge fireplace.

When Crowell had knocked and opened the door to our great-aunt's room, I knew I was not the only one who gasped in surprise. The crowded room we entered was fantastic, dominated as it was by the large bed at one end. It was also very warm, so warm it was as if we had stepped into a conservatory. But all eyes went immediately to the figure of the thin old lady seated in a large wing chair before the fire. Miss Spenser hovered behind her.

From her powdered wig to her overornate gown of stiff white brocade, worn over the hoops of the last century, she looked like a caricature of a young girl dressed for her presentation at court, except she wore more rubies and diamonds and pearls than I had ever seen on one person. The bracelets alone covered almost her entire forearms. She sat motionless, only her black eyes darting over us where we stood in a *tableau vivant* at the door. Nobody moved until she raised her hand and crooked an imperious finger, beckoning us all to the chairs that were set in a semicircle near her.

Byford spoke first, bowing as he did so. "Good evening, Lady Cecily. I am Grant St. Williams, at your service, ma'am."

Our hostess peered at him. "Yes, yes of course you are. Emily's descendant. She always did have a high-handed way about her. I might have known you would take over the party."

Byford's eyebrows came together in a quick frown before he said mildly, "I am unable to defend my grandmother, ma'am, for I never knew her." But Lady Cecily had turned away.

"Let me see if I can guess your identity," she began. "You, there, sir," she said, pointing her cane at Alastair Russell's elegant figure as he made her a deep bow, "you are also of Emily's stock, are you not? Neither of you seem to have inherited any Douglas features at all. Well, your grandmother might have been opinionated, but she was nothing out of the ordinary way, I can assure you, for all her airs. No wonder she didn't have the strength to pass on her own family traits. Weak, spineless, and simple."

I could see Alastair was about to reply, but she said abruptly,

"Sit down!" and both of Emily Douglas's hapless grandsons subsided without demur.

"You two, there, yes, you, Tweedledum and Tweedledee. Or Lord and Lady Danvers, I'll be bound. Roger, is it not? Your mother was Rose Douglas before her marriage?" Lord Danvers nodded, his little eyes popping in amazement and his cheeks reddened, while his wife smiled and said, "We are so pleased to meet you at last, Lady Cecily. I am so sorry we could not entice you to attend our wedding." Her voice was so warm and soothing the rest of us stared at her in amazement.

"Bah," her hostess returned before she said, "Miss Cecilia Worthington; you're a pretty thing. At least your hair has a tint of Douglas to it. Mine was a more brilliant red, like my father's although you can't tell from his portrait." She sighed and stared at the painting over the mantel for a moment before she turned back to Cecilia. "Your mother is a fool, girl. I hope you are not one, too." She paused, but Cecilia was incapable of speech. I could see her tremble and prayed she would not faint as the old woman went on, "Why she thought to turn me up sweet by naming you for me—well, almost for me—I shall never understand. Does she think I am as silly as she is?" Still Cecilia did not reply, and she waved her hand in dismissal. "Silly, and dumb as well, I see.

"And you last two; yes, I can see the family resemblance between you. You are Delilah and Robert Douglas. My father was James Robert, of course, as you are Robert James. Time will tell if you are worthy to carry his name. Be sure you will never equal him."

Robert bowed to her and I said, "Good evening, ma'am." To be truthful I found my great-aunt more amusing than intimidating. It was easy to see she was trying to startle us, to test our mettle as it were.

"I see I do not frighten you, girl."

"Not at all, m'lady," I replied.

"Good for you. How very strange it is that of all of you here, only you and your brother bear the Douglas name." She turned to Robert and added, "You must marry at once, boy, and produce a great many children as soon as you can, else the name will die out. Marry a good, strong breeder of a woman and get her with child."

Robert blushed a deep, painful red, but she ignored him and said, "Mr. Russell, if you will be so kind as to pour me a glass of port." There was a small sound from Miss Spenser which she ignored. "The rest of you gentlemen, help yourselves. The ladies will probably muddle their insides with negus or cordials. I myself drink like a man, as my father taught me. I can vouch for the port. I keep a good cellar."

"So I have noticed," Alastair said as he moved to do her bidding. There was a large tray of bottles and glasses on a table to the side of the group, and he poured her a glass of port as she had requested. His movements seemed to break the spell, and we ladies settled ourselves as the men moved to the table. I asked Robert to bring both Cecilia and myself a glass of wine, since I could see she was still incapable of speech.

As Alastair stepped up to hand the port to our hostess, he stepped on a dog that lay asleep at her feet, half hidden by her skirts. The dog yelped in pain, and Alastair drew back in surprise as an old English bulldog staggered to its feet and moved away.

"I beg your pardon, m'lady," he said, his usual drawl absent.

"You did not step on me, sir. Better you apologize to Excalibur."

"What a dear doggie," Sylvia Danvers purred, although I could have sworn she hadn't taken her eyes from Lady Cecily's jewelry since she entered the room.

"Excalibur is old and blind and of no earthly use to anyone. The sooner he dies, the better," came Lady Cecily's retort. "No doubt you are all thinking the same of me. And I would be the first to agree with you. But come, if you have all been served, sit down. I have a surprise for you."

She chuckled as she grasped the embroidered bellpull by her side. I saw Alastair move back to the table to pour himself a snifter of brandy. I thought his face unreadable now, although it seemed paler than usual. Lord Byford obviously did not care to sit, for he lounged against a large table, somewhat removed from the rest of us, his glass in hand and his expression stern. Sylvia Danvers popped a sweetmeat into her mouth as she accepted a glass of liqueur from her husband, whose fat face was damp with perspiration from the heat of the room. When Crowell appeared at the door, Lady Cecily nodded to him without speaking and he turned away.

I took a welcome sip of my wine as I wondered why Lady Cecily looked so pleased and excited. She certainly hadn't appeared to like any of us with the exception of Robert, and he only as future sire of many little Douglas males. And perhaps she liked me as well, I mused as I sent Cecilia an encouraging smile, but only because I refused to let her fluster me. Everyone else has earned only her sarcasm and her insults, including Lord Byford. Briefly I wondered how he had liked that.

My thoughts were interrupted by the surly voice of the butler, and we all looked to the door.

"Mr. Douglas-Moore, m'lady," he said and a man stepped into the room and moved toward us. He was of no great height, but he was strongly built with powerful hands and muscular legs that could be plainly seen in his tight pantaloons. He had a broad face with a large nose, and bushy brows over a pair of light hazel eyes. But surely his most arresting feature was his brilliant red hair. No one spoke as he came up to us and bowed, his thin mouth twisted in a sneer.

"Douglas-Moore?" Mr. Russell asked, his snifter halted halfway to his lips.

"The very same, sir," the man replied. He had an uncultured accent. "M'lady," he added, bowing to Lady Cecily. She sipped her port, her eyes over the rim of her glass darting from one to the other of us, gauging our reactions to her surprise. She smiled in delight when she saw our stunned faces, and nodded.

"Get yourself a drink, sir," she said, then added, "You are all amazed, are you not? Mr. Douglas-Moore is the grandson of my brother Anthony. His father was Hector Douglas."

"But . . . but Hector Douglas never married," Lord Danvers burst out. "How is this possible?"

"More easily than you think, my dear *legitimate* relative," Lady Cecily said. "He is a bastard, of course."

Over by the drinks table, the gentleman's neck reddened, but he did not speak. "There are many Douglas by-blows around; why my father himself had several besides his legal issue. Now, there was a man for you! Spenser here is a descendant of one of 'em, but her mother was lucky enough to marry before she was born, thereby sparing her the shame."

We all looked at Miss Spenser, who was wringing her hands and looking miserable to be singled out and stared at, in such a way, too. I was angry my great-aunt had embarrassed her, singling her out for our ridicule, and the tiny bit of admiration I had felt for the old lady's spirit faded away.

"Mr. Douglas-Moore is the son of a Marjorie Moore, who was a barmaid in Edinburgh. He has a look of my father, don't you agree?" Lady Cecily said, waving her glass at the portrait of the gentleman who seemed to sneer down at us from his lofty perch. "I see no reason why I should not consider him as one of my heirs, if I want to."

Sylvia Danvers choked and raised her handkerchief to her lips, so stunned by this information that the comfit she had been about to eat fell to the rug.

The newest member of the party returned to the group and took the only vacant seat, near Cecilia Worthington. She paled and turned slightly away from him and Lady Cecily chuckled. "It's not contagious, goose! But come, another glass of port? Spenser, fill my glass, and none of those meager tots you generally try to give me, mind. We are having a family reunion tonight."

Her companion obeyed without a word as the earl said, "You live in Edinburgh, sir?"

The stranger nodded, his lips still sneering. I thought the late Lord Douglas must have been an ugly man, if this by-blow of his son was anything to go by. Lady Cecily, who seemed determined to hold center stage, interrupted my thoughts.

"I should tell you all that I have already made a will, *dear* relatives, but I have summoned my solicitor to come here in two weeks' time. By then, I am sure I will be able to decide which one of you should inherit my fortune. Of course, if I die before then, not a one of you will see a penny, for I have left it elsewhere. I suggest you pray fervently for my continued good health. In the meantime, I shall ask to see each one of you alone so I might get to know you better."

She paused, then added, "If I should decide none of you is worthy of the fortune, I shall let my former will stand. I assure you we are talking about a fortune here."

I saw Sylvia Danvers trying to hide her glee under a thoughtful smile. Cecilia was still pale, but she seemed to have regained her composure, now that the conversation had turned away from her.

"I am so looking forward to your visits," the old lady chortled. "I haven't had this much fun in years!"

The earl went to get another drink. Over his shoulder, he said, "Of course we are delighted to be a source of amusement to you, m'lady." His voice was carefully expressionless.

"Come now, Grant, it will do you good," our great-aunt said. "You are thirty-two, I believe? Had your own way for years no doubt, and were left enough money so that you are probably thoroughly spoiled. Do you good to dance to someone else's tune for a change."

The earl returned to his perch by the table, stepping around the old bulldog who was wandering among the guests, sniffing at their feet, as if bewildered by all these strangers in a room generally populated only by his mistress and himself.

"How disappointing if I should refuse to dance. Or any of the others, ma'am," Byford remarked.

"You would not be so cruel. And as for you others, I know you are all here for one reason only. I do not mislead myself thinking it was deep family concern that brought you so far north in the winter. Certainly not!"

She chuckled and shook her finger at us. I looked away from her gloating, painted face and started.

"Look at the dog!" I exclaimed. "Whatever can be wrong with him?"

Indeed, the old bulldog was behaving very strangely. He moved backward and forward in some agitation, pausing now and then to shake and tremble, and then he began to whine and toss his old blind head in distress. "Oh, dear," Cecilia said, pulling her blue skirts aside as he staggered near her. Suddenly he halted, gave a loud bark, and fell to the carpet. He lay there, his sides heaving for a moment before he was abruptly, ominously, still.

"Excalibur!" Lady Cecily said, struggling to her feet. Her glass fell unheeded to the carpet. Miss Spenser was at her side immediately, holding her arm as she tried to reach her dog. The earl was before her, and he knelt and put his hand on the old bulldog's side.

"He is dead, m'lady," he said quietly, a faint frown creasing his forehead.

"Dead? Excalibur? No, no!" she cried.

"Sit down, m'lady, do," Miss Spenser urged. "There is nothing you can do to help him, and it will distress you."

"Of course I am distressed," Lady Cecily snapped, tears running down her wrinkled cheeks. "I've had Excalibur for so many years; you remember, Spenser, when he came here as a puppy? Oh, I did not mean for him to die when I spoke earlier about his uselessness!"

She sank back in the wing chair and took the handkerchief Miss Spenser produced, to bury her face in it. I looked around at the others. Alastair Russell was also holding his handkerchief to his nose, an expression of profound distaste on his face at the scene he had just witnessed. Cecilia looked horrified; Mr. Douglas-Moore, bored; Robert, perplexed; and Roger Danvers was patting his wife's hand and saying, "There, there, my dear." His wife did not appear unduly upset even though the dog had expired practically at her feet. Instead, she lifted her glass to gulp the last of her liqueur. Suddenly the earl rose and stared at each of us in turn.

"I say," Robert exclaimed in bewilderment, "the dog acted as if he had been poisoned. But why would that be?"

Byford turned quickly to glare at him and I wondered he

would look so dangerous. My brother seemed to feel something more was called for, for he hurried to add, "But he did! He behaved just like a dog of mine who got into some poison, put down for the rats in the barns. You remember, don't you, Lila? Snuff? My favorite bird dog?"

I nodded as Alastair said, "Poisoned? Nonsense!"

"It's not nonsense at all. The boy is right," Mr. Douglas-Moore contributed. "I've seen rats act just like that." He smiled as if he had enjoyed the spectacle, and I shivered.

I saw Robert was about to speak again, but one glance at Byford's glowering face silenced him. Instead, it was Alastair who said, "I do think we might have the . . . the unfortunate animal removed, don't you? So distressing to be talking about him this way while he lies at our feet."

Byford beckoned to Robert. "Come, you can help me carry him outside. Alastair is right. There's no need to discuss this now."

No one said anything as the two men carefully lifted the old dog and carried him from the room, although Lady Cecily wiped her eyes again and sighed. I saw Miss Spenser pat her shoulder and the way the old lady twitched impatiently to get away from her concern.

It was a few minutes before the two men returned. I thought Robert looked pale and subdued, miserable, even, as if the earl had taken him sharply to task while they were out of the room. Suddenly I was angry. What right had he to reprimand Robert? And besides, maybe the dog had been poisoned. Setting my glass down on the table beside me, I said, "But if the dog was poisoned, as both my brother and Mr. Douglas-Moore believe, who could have done it? And for what purpose?"

Now I was the recipient of one of the earl's intimidating glares, but I was not fazed. Indeed, I lifted my chin at him in defiance.

"Yes, that is what I cannot understand," Lady Cecily said, her voice stronger now that her pet was not lying before her. "None of you knew I had a dog until this evening, but Excalibur could not have gotten into any poison by himself. He never leaves—oh, dear, left—this room except to be taken out for short walks. Spenser!"

The lady spoken to jerked, one hand going to her throat.

"Did Excalibur get into anything this afternoon when you took him out?"

"No, m'lady. We only went a short distance down the drive and he was leashed. As soon as he had . . . er, finished, I brought him right back to you."

Lady Cecily nodded as if that was what she had expected to hear.

Byford moved to the center of the room after giving me another dark look. "Since you are all determined to speak of the incident, let me say I do not think the dog was the intended victim."

"Not the victim? Surely you are mistaken, Grant," Alastair interrupted. "The animal hardly went about sipping from our glasses, and that is all that has been served in this room. Besides, we are all in excellent health—so far."

Beside me, Cecilia gave a little cry and stared down at her glass in horror.

"That will do, Alastair," the earl said harshly. "There is no need to upset the ladies any further, and surely we can do without hysterics, don't you think? The poison was not in the drinks. Think—was there anything else consumed in this room this evening?"

I had been wondering about this, and now, without thinking, I blurted out, "Lady Danvers. Her comfits box."

The earl bowed to me a little. "An excellent deduction, cousin. Or did you see, as I did, Lady Danvers drop one of her sweetmeats to the floor? I suspect that the dog, in wandering around after Alastair stepped on him, found it, and ate it."

"But . . . but . . ." Lord Danvers sputtered, while his wife sat frozen, her eyes wide with shock, "that means that you believe someone was trying to kill Sylvia."

"I have to believe it, sir, but for what reason it was done, I have no idea."

We were all staring at the lady and thinking our own thoughts and so it came as a complete surprise when Roger Danvers gave a moan and fell heavily to the floor. The earl was at his side in a moment. Lady Danvers stared down at her husband where he lay at her feet, her fat hands going to her mouth in horror.

"Dear God, he has been poisoned as well," Cecilia cried, before she began to sob hysterically.

"Nonsense! The man has only fainted," Byford assured us as he loosened the gentleman's scarlet waistcoat and cravat. "Does someone have salts? A vinaigrette?"

Miss Spenser hurried to fetch these articles from Lady Cecily's bedside table while I attempted to calm Cecilia. I was forced to shake her hard several times before she became quiet, only the occasional sob or hiccup remaining to show her agitation. I noticed Sylvia Danvers made no move to go to her husband to help him until he moaned and struggled to sit up several minutes later. When he appeared content to remain seated on the floor, she leaned forward and hissed, "Do rise, Roger! Whatever must Lady Cecily think of such unmanliness?"

I stared at the lady in disgust. It was obvious all she cared about was that Roger not cause Lady Cecily to dislike him, lest she leave her fortune elsewhere. No wonder someone wanted to do away with her.

I looked up to see the earl shaking his head, the same disgust I felt plain on his face. Then he helped Lord Danvers to his seat, the gentleman apologizing profusely for his momentary weakness. Alastair brought him a glass of brandy.

"Do not drink it; it might be poisoned!" Cecilia cried in a high, nervous voice.

The irony of Alastair's bow was not lost on her, and she turned scarlet. Mr. Douglas-Moore turned to her and said, "Do try not to be so silly, girl. Of course the gentleman is not trying to poison the fat man."

"Thank you," Alastair said, glancing at him distastefully. "One is of course gratified to have such a vote of confidence, even from one such as you."

The two men glared at each other and suddenly Lady Cecily said sternly, "Go away!"

"I beg your pardon, ma'am?" Alastair said, for once so startled he forgot his customary drawl.

"I want all of you to go away. I am tired and upset, and I do not think I can bear to hear any more of these dramatics. Oh, do go away! Leave me!"

This last was said in a querulous, elderly whine, and we all rose immediately. Byford spoke for the group when he said— although I did wish he did not take over every situation, quite as if someone had placed him in charge—"Of course, m'lady. We will leave you now to rest, and hope you feel better tomorrow."

Lady Cecily made no sign she had heard him. She had struggled to her feet, and now, grasping her cane, she allowed Miss Spenser to support her as she made her way toward the bed. She looked very old to me then, frail and confused.

Nobody ventured to bid her good night as we filed from the room and made our way toward the fire burning on the hearth at the end of the hall.

"Allow me to congratulate you, Lady Danvers," Alastair said, fully recovered from his momentary lapse. "I am sure I could never behave so phlegmatically if I suspected someone was trying to kill me. I am all admiration for your self-control and fortitude. But then, they do say the woman is the stronger of the species, do they not?"

Lady Danvers stared at him. "How else should I possibly behave? Of course I do not believe Byford's explanation, for I have never heard anything more absurd in my entire life. Why on earth would someone want to kill *me*?"

There was a pause while we all, with the exception of the lady's husband, began to count the reasons, and then Byford said, "We must hope you are right, m'lady. But just to be on the safe side, I would not eat any more of those sweetmeats if I were you."

"No, no, of course she shall not," Lord Danvers was quick to assure him.

His wife pouted, but finally she said, "Very well, if you insist, but you will see it was all a mistake. That Spenser woman undoubtedly let the dog eat something he should not when she had him out this afternoon, and now, of course, does not dare admit it. I think this suspicion there is a murderer about shows a lamentable lack of stability in the family. I intend to rise above such speculation and sensationalism."

Thus chastised, we remained uneasily around the fire, no one making a move to adjourn to the library to discuss the events of the evening further. Lady Danvers took her husband a little apart and began to lecture him in quick, querulous whispers. Cecilia seemed to have decided that remaining glued to my side was the safest place for her to be, and Douglas-Moore lounged at his ease in a chair that allowed him to watch us all. I tried to catch Alastair's eye but he was intent on removing an imaginary piece of lint from his sleeve. Only Grant St. Williams nodded to me before he looked at my brother. I saw Robert was pacing up and down the hall, his quick footsteps and excited expression showing he was pondering the problem. I knew he considered the whole thing a terrific lark, no doubt the best thing that had happened to him in months, and he was already planning how he would astound his friends with the adventure when he returned to town. I wanted to smile at such boyish enthusiasm until I remembered that if Lord Byford was correct, there was a murderer in the house, and we were all of us in a great deal of danger.

Chapter Four

~~~~~~~~

The next morning I was surprised to receive a visit from Annie Deems, Cecilia's maid. Watched by my own disapproving Polly, the girl stood near the foot of the bed, clasping her hands under her apron as she begged me to be sure and let her mistress know when I was ready to go down to breakfast, so Miss Worthington could accompany me.

"Didn't sleep a wink, miss, not a wink, she didn't," Annie elaborated. "Miss Cecilia 'as a very sensitive nature wot *feels* things, if ye takes my meanin', miss. Poor lady, that frightened she is, and so am I! Murder! 'Oo would o' thought it?"

I didn't think the girl was at all frightened. Why should she be? No one was interested in disposing of her, so all this was as good as a play to her. I made my voice cold as I ordered her to control herself, for there was nothing to worry about, adding that the best thing she could do for her mistress was to remain calm and not encourage her to dramatize the situation. I could tell I was a terrible disappointment to Annie Deems and she was glad she wasn't my maid. I was glad she wasn't, too.

I felt heavy this morning, heavy and depressed although I couldn't put a reason to it. To realize that I was to be treated to my cousin Cecilia's company throughout the waking hours, and bored by her endless conjectures about the situation, did nothing to lighten my mood. When we went down together at last, and Cecilia hung on my arm, looking about her fearfully, it was all I could do not to call her an idiot.

As we entered the dining room, Crowell bowed and informed us in a gloomy voice that Miss Spenser had had to send for the doctor first thing. Cecilia gave a little cry and sank into a chair, which I was sure was just the reaction the old butler had hoped for.

From the end of the table, Mr. Douglas-Moore said thickly through a mouthful of ham, "No need to take a pet, missy. The old lady's not feeling up to snuff after last evening, but there's naught amiss with her but the usual—old age and too much port."

He sniffed and I poured Cecilia a cup of strong tea before I began to discuss the weather with Mr. Douglas-Moore. I could tell by the incredulous look on Cecilia's face, and the way she ate her breakfast turned half away, with her face averted, that she questioned the wisdom of my even noticing the man. After all, he was not the type young ladies of quality should even know existed, never mind chat with about a possible snowfall and the kind of attractions his native city provided.

After breakfast, Cecilia begged me to walk up and down the main hall with her, for she had something to discuss with me privately. Taking my arm again, she asked if I thought it would do any good for her to write to her mother and beg she might be allowed to return home. Since she knew as well as I did her mama would firmly order her to remain where she was until Great-Aunt Cecily's new will had been signed, with, it was hoped, her as the sole beneficiary, I reminded her that by the time any letter reached Middlesex and an answer returned, we would probably be starting home anyway. Cecilia nodded at this wisdom, but I could tell she thought me most prosaic, without a romantic bone in my body, and considered it awful that I must be so calm and sensible all the time.

Just as I was about to suggest we retire to the library and a morning of needlework, there was a knock on the front door and we waited curiously to see who it might be. Crowell admitted a middle-aged man carrying a black bag, obviously Lady Cecily's physician. He bowed to both of us, but before anyone could speak, Miss Spenser came out of Lady Cecily's room to greet him. She brushed by us rudely in her haste to reach the doctor's side and I hoped our hostess had not taken a turn for the worse. I thought Miss Spenser seemed strangely agitated this morning; there was an unhealthy flush on her face as she took the doctor's hat and her gray eyes were large and distended behind their thick glasses. But the doctor did not seem to see anything amiss as he inquired after her health and was finally introduced to us as Dr. Matthew Ward.

Although he had a pleasant face under his graying hair, you would not have called him a handsome or dignified man. He looked as if he rarely got enough sleep, his black coat was poorly pressed and his cravat darned. I thought Mrs. Ward a poor wife to send her husband out looking so shabby. We had only a minute to talk before Miss Spenser took his arm and led him away, promising to come and tell us his report of Lady Cecily's health as soon as he had examined her.

When we entered the library we found my brother standing before the window dressed in riding clothes, and the Earl of Byford calmly reading a newspaper before the fire. I noticed he had arranged for the grate to be heaped with coal and admired his mastery of the situation. He rose and bowed to us and when Cecilia was quick to announce the doctor's arrival, he folded his paper and excused himself.

"Why are you still indoors, Bobb—er, Robert?" I asked as I sat down and opened my workbasket. "I see the sun is shining. I was sure you had gone for a gallop long ago."

"Go out, Lila?" he asked, his eyes wide. "Why, I might miss something if I did."

"I hardly think we are going to be continually assaulted by dying dogs, fainting husbands, or suspected murderers, my dear," I said dryly.

"But how can we be sure?" Cecilia contributed. "Do stay here with us, Cousin Robert. I feel so much safer with you to protect us."

The two youngest members of the party soon had their heads together in the window seat, and as I bent to my needlework I did not have to wonder why I felt about a hundred years older than either of them.

"I have been thinking," Cecilia began, speaking loud enough to include me. "It occurs to me that perhaps Lord Danvers is using this visit to do away with his wife. What do you think?"

"What an excellent theory!" Robert agreed. "I'm sure if I had the misfortune to be married to the lady, I would have tried the same, and long before this, too."

"And of course it would be easier for him to put the poison in her candy than anyone else," Cecilia pointed out, obviously proud of her reasoning.

Almost sorry to toss cold water on this conjecture, I said, "But what of his faint? Surely that was real, not playacting."

"Well, perhaps he fainted because he was so disappointed his foul deed miscarried," Cecilia persisted, loath to abandon this promising culprit.

"And then there's the way he keeps calling the lady 'dearest,' " Robert said darkly. "Trying it on much too rich, don't you agree?"

Since the Danvers themselves came in just then, we were unable to say aye or nay to his suggestion. Sylvia took it upon herself to give me a critique of my handwork, telling me several ways I might have improved it if only I had had the benefit of her counsel before I was so far along, while her husband engaged the young people in sprightly conversation, teasing Robert about his life in London, and congratulating Cecilia on her pretty gown. I saw both of them exchanging glances for the remainder of the morning, especially whenever Roger Danvers addressed his wife as 'my love.' " They were very obvious, I thought, glad the Danvers were neither of them needlewitted.

As I plied my needle, I let my mind wander away from the trivial conversation in the library to consider my relationship with Alastair Russell. Not that there was one, I thought bleakly as I tied off my thread. Indeed, I seemed little closer to him than I had been in London, for although we now conversed whenever we were together, I had yet to spend a moment alone with the man. If only I could somehow wean Cecilia from her con-

stant attendance, why then, perhaps I could maneuver him into
a tête-à-tête. Looking up, I saw Cecilia in the window seat, a
stray sunbeam turning her cloud of chestnut hair to vibrant
light, her pretty face alive with laughter at one of my brother's
jests, and my spirits plummeted. Still, I told myself stoutly as I
took another stitch, she is a silly little thing. Could any gentleman prefer that to reasoned common sense? Alas, I was afraid
they not only could, but would, with a great deal of enthusiasm.

Mr. Russell did not join us that morning, nor did Mr. Douglas-
Moore. The earl did not return either. Eventually Miss Spenser
came to tell us that the doctor had insisted Lady Cecily remain
quietly in bed for at least a day, and had forbidden her to have
company. She added the lady must be feeling very low, for
when the doctor scolded her for indulging in not one, but two
glasses of port which she knew very well she should not drink,
Lady Cecily had not even told him to stop being an old woman
for she would do exactly as she pleased.

When we went in to lunch, Alastair was there, studiously ignoring Mr. Douglas-Moore. I did not think Alastair looked
well. His face was unusually pale and although he was dressed
with his customary complement of fobs and chains and rings,
he seldom spoke to any of us and appeared to be lost in thought.
I had the headache, and I told myself that even if it were rude
of me, I was not going to spend the afternoon with my female
cousins, not after spending the morning enduring Cecilia's art-
less chatter and Sylvia's superior lectures.

The Earl of Byford had taken his customary chair at the foot
of the table. I saw him watching everyone in turn, and wondered what he made of Alastair's pallor, the suppressed excitement of Robert and Cecilia, and the constant flow of chatter
that Lord Danvers treated us to. Only Mr. Douglas-Moore and
Lady Danvers appeared normal, both of them concentrating on
their plates to the exclusion of everything else. But when Mr.
Douglas-Moore put his hand over his wineglass when Crowell
would have filled it, the earl asked why.

"I dinna touch spirits, sir," the man said, staring with disapproval at our brimming glasses.

"But last night, surely you drank wine, did you not?"

"I take only Adam's ale, the only drink man should permit himself. I certainly dinna approve of all this swilling of spirits the rest o' you indulge in. Disgusting, I call it."

His face had turned very red, and Alastair looked at him and said, "Can it be that *you,* you of all people, are one of those chapel goers? A Methodist, even?"

"And what if I am?" Douglas-Moore asked belligerently. "I ken the ways o' the devil, the evil that waits to engulf the unwary, aye, an' the snare that . . ."

"Oh, spare us, please," Alastair muttered, lifting his wineglass and sipping defiantly. "That the bastard among us should be a religious fanatic, is surely beyond belief."

Mr. Douglas-Moore started to rise, but one glance at the earl's face changed his mind. "That will do, Alastair," Byford said harshly. "At least let us try to keep our opinions to ourselves. There is enough trouble in this house without stirring the cauldron to a boil."

"I see you still hold to your ridiculous suspicions, m'lord," Sylvia Danvers said as she took another biscuit. "However, since you are right to preach self-control and the need to preserve harmony, I shall not argue the point. We will, however, see who has the right of it in the end."

The earl made no reply, which I thought very wise after a glance at the harsh set planes of his face, his tight lips.

It seemed a very long time before I was free to excuse myself, and ignoring the pleading in Cecilia's eyes, I ran up to my room. I intended to be gone long before she came to find me, and so I scrambled into my hooded fur cape and a pair of warm mittens and hurried to leave the house.

There were a great many clouds massing in a sky that looked as if a storm was brewing, but at the moment there was intermittent sunlight and little wind. I walked slowly through the gardens taking deep breaths of the salty air, careful to keep out of sight of any of the castle windows. My headache felt better already.

The sound of the surf was strangely muted today, and I considered going around to the front to admire the breakers. Somehow I could not bring myself to do so. I was walking down a brick path between two overgrown hedges, thinking the gardens might be very attractive if anyone were to take the trouble to care for them, when I came to a crossing and ran straight into Grant St. Williams.

For a moment I was so startled I gasped in fright and he reached out to steady me. "I am sorry I alarmed you, cousin," he said as I tried to regain my poise. "I didn't realize anyone else was around."

I attempted a smile. I noticed the path he had been on led only to an old gardener's shed. What had he been doing there, I wondered even as I assured him I was quite all right now and could stand alone.

Although he continued to stare down at me, he let me go, his rugged face thoughtful. I would have turned away except he said abruptly, "Do me the honor of walking a way with me, if you please. There is something I would like to discuss."

Curious, I agreed and we began to retrace my steps. "Shall we stroll down the drive?" he asked. "We'll have some privacy there."

My curiosity was thoroughly piqued now, and I nodded. He did not seem to be in any hurry to converse for we had gone quite a distance before I was forced to put my hand on his arm to stop him. "This is an unusual request for me, sir, but do you think you could go more slowly?" I asked. "I have to run to keep up with you."

He smiled and apologized, saying he continually forgot his height, and as if this reminded him of the purpose of the outing, he began to speak. "I had not meant to mention it, but I find I must, if only to warn you. One must trust someone, after all," he said, tucking my hand in his arm and commencing our walk again at a much slower pace. "Tell me what you thought of last evening, cousin. Do you believe, as Lady Danvers does, that it was all an accident? That the companion let the dog get into something on its walk?"

"I am not sure, sir. Of course, it could have happened, but

somehow I find it hard to believe Miss Spenser would not notice. And I do not think her a liar. And yet, it is impossible to believe that anyone would be trying to kill Sylvia Danvers. I am sure we would all *like* to, several times a day, but who among us would murder her just because she is annoying?"

"Yes, you can argue the case both ways," he agreed. "The dog was poisoned, by the way. Dr. Ward had a look at the body this morning. He said there was little doubt of it, but he put it down to a dismissed servant who might have had a grudge against Lady Cecily, or a small boy's prank. She is not much liked in the neighborhood from what I can gather."

"But you don't believe that, do you?" I asked, hearing the doubt in his voice as I stared up at his dark, frowning face.

"No, I think the candy was meant for Lady Danvers, but for the life of me, I cannot imagine why. She only arrived yesterday at noon, and I did not see her after luncheon. Do you have any idea what she and Roger did until they joined us all for dinner?"

I admitted I did not and offered to try and find out before he continued, "Abrasive and maddening as she is, I find it hard to believe she could enrage someone so on a few hours' acquaintance that they would immediately try to poison her."

Remembering Cecilia's theory of the morning, I said, "Of course her husband knows her very well, and I suspect he is firmly under the cat's foot . . ."

Byford nodded. "And has the best possible reason to want to be rid of her. But why would he do it here? To throw discredit on the rest of us? There are other ways of disposing of an unsatisfactory wife, ways that would seem completely innocent."

"What ways?" I asked, imagining what my mother would have to say about this unsuitable conversation.

"Well, you can arrange a carriage accident, or see to it the lady's saddle is not properly cinched before she goes for a gallop, or you can have her set upon by thieves while returning alone from a party . . ." He stopped. "What am I thinking of, to be telling you these things?"

"I have no idea, m'lord," I said as demurely as I could. We

had reached the end of the drive, with its sagging gates and empty gatehouse, and we turned and prepared to retrace our steps.

"What I most wanted to tell you was that I think you should be on your guard, that we, all of us, should be on our guard."

Suddenly he stopped in the middle of the drive and turned me to face him, his strong hands bruising my upper arms where he grasped them so tightly. "And what the devil were you doing, wandering around that garden by yourself? Suppose there *is* a murderer, and suppose he came across you there, completely alone in a deserted spot, unable to call for help? I thought you had more sense."

For a moment, when he had pulled me to him so harshly I had been terrified, for I had suddenly remembered I did not know very much about this man who was my second cousin, and we were indeed in the deserted spot he mentioned, where no one would hear me if I screamed. Angry he had frightened me, I pulled away from him, trying to keep him from seeing my fear.

"You are right, m'lord. For all I know, *you* might be the murderer."

I wished I might recall those hasty words when I saw his face darken. Then he said bleakly, "I might be, indeed—or anyone else at Grimshead, right down to the lowliest servant." I shivered at his angry tone as he went on, "And you yourself, dear Cousin Lila, might be the murderess. After all, poison is often a woman's choice of weapon. But I don't fear you for I am stronger than you are and armed as well. Do not go out again by yourself, and lock your door when you are alone in your room. Although I have no proof, I suspect the situation is dangerous. You must promise to take more care."

I would have liked to ask him what business my welfare was of his, but I saw the wisdom of his words, and not wanting to provoke him further, agreed meekly.

"You know, of course, that you have condemned me to the endless chatter of our cousin, Cecilia, sir. But stay. Perhaps I should remain in a group at all times. She did say she was afraid of Sylvia, that she was a dangerous woman. I cannot imagine Cecilia as the guilty party, but then, anything is possible."

The earl had no reply to this ridiculous comment. As we resumed walking, he said, "If you want fresh air, recruit your brother as an escort. I would offer my services, but now that you suspect me, I am sure I would be denied with a royal snub."

I thought it best to follow his lead and ignore this provocative statement. Instead I remarked on the poverty of the household.

"If great-aunt has such an enormous fortune, why does she allow the household to be run so poorly?" I asked. "What a farce it would be if it turned out she is only one step from the workhouse."

"Have no fear of that. There is a fortune. A very considerable fortune besides her jewelry." He paused and I wondered how he had come by that information. "I think it likely she is only parsimonious, as many elderly people are, regardless of their circumstances."

For a moment we continued up the drive in silence. Byford had not taken my arm again and I wondered why I was regretting this. I had liked striding along beside him with my hand tucked safe, for he was very tall and even with my height I had felt dainty and feminine beside him. Somehow, being next to a man well over six feet was very pleasant; I wondered what it would be like to dance with him. Then I remembered Alastair was almost as tall, and infinitely more handsome.

"Shall I tell you who I think it is, coz?" he asked, and at my eager nod, added, "Surely the prime suspect must be Douglas-Moore."

"A Methodist murderer, m'lord?" I asked, pretending horror.

He grinned down at me, and I was surprised at how glad I was his wrath had disappeared.

"Never mind the man's religion. We only have his word for his piety. But do consider. Here he is, thrown into a bevy of legitimate heirs while he alone is a by-blow. He must hate us. And suppose he thought if he did away with us, he could gain control of Lady Cecily's fortune? Remember, she did say she thought him like her father, and she obviously adored that man."

"But to plan in cold blood to kill so many people," I said, my hand creeping up to my throat in horror. "That would be an act of madness!"

"Murderers *are* madmen."

"Or madwomen," I said slowly. "Yes, I can see where he might be suspect, and only by reason of his birth. How unfair it is. It is not his fault, poor man."

"The only thing that bothers me is when he could have done it. He was not present at dinner, and he did not even meet the woman until we were all assembled in Lady Cecily's room. And then he never went near her."

"That's true enough," I agreed. "There is another possibility. Suppose there is one among us legitimate heirs who thinks killing off some of the others will give him or her a better chance to inherit the whole? But I have to ask myself, why Lady Danvers? She inherits only through her husband; why not kill him, instead of her?"

"That is an excellent point, coz," the earl congratulated me. "I suspected you had an intelligent mind. Would more women were like you."

We had reached the last bend in the drive. Ahead of us we could see Grimshead through the dark, bare tree branches. The earl paused again. "I most sincerely hope you will keep all such observations to yourself, however. I would ask you to trust me for I do trust you, you see, but that would be unfair. You must guard against giving the murderer—if there is one—any clue you might be on his trail. Promise me you will be careful."

I looked up at his intent face, saw the concern there, and could only whisper that promise. For a moment we stood there staring at each other. I wanted to look away, but I could not and I wondered why. The moment was too long, there were too many currents here, too much that hadn't been spoken. But what was the Earl of Byford to me? Only a newly met second cousin I was sure I would see little of once our stay was ended.

He seemed to have come to the same conclusion, for he

"It is not immodest! It is all the crack," I heard Cecilia say indignantly and my dreams went away in an instant. I sighed.

"All the crack for a married woman, perhaps, although I myself certainly wouldn't wear it," Sylvia retorted. Fortunately, before Cecilia could think to tell her how ridiculous she would look in the low-cut gown of palest yellow muslin, she went on, "It is not at all suitable for a girl who has not even made her come-out. I am surprised your mother allows it."

As I turned reluctantly to try and prevent a major argument, Alastair came in, his handsome face petulant. "I do not know how I am to endure the boredom," he said, sinking into an armchair and gracefully crossing his legs while one hand shaded his eyes. "Surely even a fortune cannot be worth it. I am almost tempted to return to town at once."

Diverted, Sylvia leaned forward, her face eager. "Perhaps that would be best, sir," she said. "Yes, I think you should leave. Tomorrow? Early?"

Alastair dropped his hand and sent her a glance of complete loathing. She flushed, for once embarrassed to be caught, her greed so obvious. And then the others came in.

Byford had found a chessboard and he challenged Robert to a match. They were soon settled by the window, intent on their game. Roger Danvers stood before the fire, his hands behind his back under his coattails as he rocked to and fro on his heels, and even Douglas-Moore took a seat near a candelabrum so he might read one of the week-old newspapers. The candles turned his red hair to flame.

After a few moments when Roger and Sylvia monopolized the conversation, I could see my cousin Cecilia pouting. I suspected she did not like being ignored by a roomful of gentlemen, for even Alastair had retreated behind his hand again, deep in thought. I took a seat somewhat apart from the others, feeling sad. But surely Alastair had only meant he was bored by the gentlemen here, I told myself stoutly. He did not mean my conversation bored him. I was not driving him back to town. Of course not.

I saw Cecilia had risen and gone to the bookcases. She was

not a great reader; I doubted she would find anything light enough to amuse her. But perhaps she was well aware how fragile and ethereal she looked against the old leather bindings? How the pale yellow gown moved as she bent to get a closer look at a title?

The Danvers had stopped speaking, and for a moment there was only the sound of the fire snapping in the grate, and the muffled sound of the surf. Then Cecilia gave a sudden piercing scream and, putting her hands to her heart, collapsed on the floor.

"Dear God!" Alastair exclaimed, jumping to his feet and looking around wildly, all his ennui gone in an instant. I saw Roger Danvers had paled and his wife was gasping in shock as I hurried to kneel beside Cecilia. Robert and Byford were right behind me. I could see Cecilia's breath stirring her gown, so my first fears, that she had died, were eased. Still, my heart was beating erratically and I admit I was shaking with fright. Determined not to show it, I said, "Robert, fetch me a napkin and some water. Sylvia, do you have your salts with you?"

The earl went to get the bottle she held out and Robert hurried to a tray set on a table near the door, to fetch the jug of water there, and a napkin.

As he gave them to me, he said, "Is she . . . is she dead?"

"No, she has only fainted," I reassured him as I began to bathe her forehead.

"I wonder why?" the earl mused, staring down at our cousin, so pale and still, the salts Sylvia had given him forgotten.

"This is the end," Alastair said in a trembling voice. "My health cannot support these almost constant jolts to the system. I shall probably have to retire to my bed for a week, I assure you, a week. Dear God, why did she give that ghoulish shriek?"

"I am afraid we'll have ter wait until she regains consciousness ter find out, sir," Douglas-Moore said from behind him as he folded his newspaper calmly.

Alastair gave a little squeak of alarm and I could tell he had forgotten the man was there. Then he looked angry; angry and disconcerted to be caught out so.

I abandoned the wet napkin in favor of the salts, and not much later, Cecilia moaned and moved her head, as if to escape the pungent smell. When she opened her eyes, I saw the horror in them, and I caught my breath as the earl said, "Come now, wake up, Cecilia. It is all right. Nothing will hurt you."

Robert knelt beside me to assist the girl to sit up as she began to moan and weep.

"What happened, Cecy?" I asked softly, patting her hand. "Why did you cry out that way?"

"Oh, I am so frightened," she whispered, her eyes going from one to the other of us. "It was dreadful, oh, just dreadful!" Her voice rose again and she began to wail in earnest. I felt the hair rise on the back of my neck. This was more than Cecilia's constant attempts to be the center of attention. This was real. Something had terrified her.

"What was dreadful?" Douglas-Moore asked. The question, asked in such a normal, prosaic way, effectively cut through the tension I am sure we all felt.

Cecilia stared at him before she cried out helplessly, "No, no, I cannot say!"

"Here, let me carry her to the sofa, Lila," the earl said, taking command, much as I am sure his grandmother would have done if Lady Cecily's assessment of her had been correct. "We must let Cecilia regain her composure before we question her further," he added, smiling at the girl as he lifted her in his arms. She was deposited gently on the sofa, a pillow placed behind her head, as we all watched anxiously.

"Here, give her this," Douglas-Moore said, holding out a glass of brandy.

"From you, sir?" Alastair drawled, his composure restored. "A Methodist advocating hard drink? The angels are weeping at your downfall, sir."

Douglas-Moore sent him a glance of pure hatred. "This here's medicinal," he said as he handed the glass to the earl.

Cecilia would have pushed it away, but Byford was having none of that. Finally she took a sip and the color returned to her face.

"Now then, Cecilia," Sylvia Danvers began in her piercing voice.

"Be quiet," the earl ordered, glaring at her. "Give the girl a chance to recover." Sylvia bridled, but she was forced to settle back in her chair and wait.   ·

"Lila! Oh, where is Lila?" Cecilia moaned, safe in Byford's arms, for he sat beside her holding her close. I saw he was patting her back and marveled he could be so gentle.

"I am right here, Cecy," I told her, kneeling before her to take her hands.

"Oh, Lila, how horrible it was, staring at me," she whispered. Then she shuddered and added, "I . . . I saw an eye."

"An eye?" I echoed, perplexed. "What can you mean? An eye? Where?"

"While I was looking for a book. I had just put one back in the case when—oh dear, shall I ever forget it?—there was an eye, right there in the wall behind the books, and it was glaring at me."

She began to sob again and I saw she was shaking all over. When the earl motioned to me, I rose to take his place so he could join my brother, who was already searching the bookshelves where Cecilia had been standing.

"There is nothing here," Robert said in disappointment. "Do you suppose she only thought she saw an eye? Perhaps it was a reflection of the candlelight that made her think so."

Sylvia Danvers sniffed. "Of course, it must have been," she said, fixing a baleful glance at our distraught cousin. "I do not consider Cecilia, although of course it pains me to say so, to be of more than moderate understanding. And then, of course, there is her unfortunate habit of dramatizing herself. I fear her parents have been much too indulgent. Furthermore . . ."

Cecilia was not attending to this litany of all her most grievous faults, for she was trembling still in my arms. I saw the earl taking down one book after another. He was obviously taking this seriously, although I wondered why. An *eye*? Glaring at her? How could such a thing be?

It was quite a while before Cecilia was calm enough for me

to take her to her room, and it was late before her maid and I had soothed and comforted her and put her to bed. I arranged for a trundle bed so Annie Deems could be there to help if her mistress woke and cried out. Only then did I make my way to my own room through the dark, empty hall. I had heard all the others come up to bed earlier, and for a moment, I paused at the top of the stairs, thinking I might go and make my own search of the shelves in the library.

It had occurred to me as I was helping to put Cecilia to bed, that Robert and the earl had looked on the wrong shelf. They had both forgotten that our cousin was only a slip of a girl, an inch or so over five feet. Instead, they had searched the shelf at their own level.

I had started down the stairs when I heard a noise below me and I stopped, my heart pounding. I told myself it was only a board creaking as they are apt to do in old buildings, but I could not make myself go any farther. It was so *black* down there! My candle cast such a tiny pool of light! I heard another noise, and terrified, I ran to my room.

It was then I remembered my promise to the earl, to be prudent, and I told myself tomorrow would surely be time enough. It is not that I am a coward, of course, but I admit the thought of venturing down those broad stairs and across that massive, echoing, dark hall to the library, and searching all by myself to find—and what might I discover?—was unnerving. Even more unnerving was the thought that something might discover *me*. Besides, I told myself stoutly, it was past midnight and I was really very tired.

But for the first time at Grimshead, I locked my bedroom door. Just in case that noise I had heard hadn't been just a creaking board. Just on the wild chance Cecy had seen something after all. And to be honest, I locked it because I knew I wouldn't get a wink of sleep if I did not.

Chapter Six

~~~

In spite of the locked door, my sleep was fitful, and I woke early the next morning. When I went to the window and pulled the draperies aside, I saw the snowstorm I had predicted had begun in earnest, the fat white flakes swirling past the glass. As so often happened, all sounds were muted for there was no wind. I could barely hear the breakers on the ledges below. Strangely, I missed them. Shivering, I hurried to dress in my blue woolsey gown so I could search the bookshelves before anyone else came down.

When I reached it, the library was empty and it had the disheveled look of a room untended by maids. There was no fire in the grate and Mr. Douglas-Moore's newspaper lay where he had dropped it. The chessboard patiently waited for the next move to be played, and Cecilia's glass of brandy was untouched.

I went at once to the bookcase where she had been standing. The old books were grimy and looked completely innocent, but I took several of them off the shelf to peer closely at the back of the case. Yes, there was something, I thought as I reached out to touch the wood. Although invisible to the naked eye, I could feel a circle that had been cut there, and I saw, below it on the shelf, a few grains of sawdust. I was thinking hard, trying to remember what lay beyond the library when Grant St. Williams came in.

"So, you found it, did you?" he asked as I returned the last volume to its place and wiped my fingers on my handkerchief. "Somehow I was sure you would solve this mystery."

"Yes, I did. There is a circle cut out, well below where you and my brother were looking last night. You forgot how much shorter Cecy is than you, m'lord," I told him, proud of my detecting.

He laughed. "I did forget it at the time, but I did not need to get my hands dirty to solve the mystery. I merely went and asked Crowell."

Before I could ask why, he held out his arm and said, "Let us retire to the dining room. There is nothing more to learn here, and I want my breakfast."

I allowed myself to be seated at the table before I spoke again.

"What did you ask Crowell? And why him?" I demanded as I buttered my oatmeal and reached for the cream.

"Well, from his age, it is obvious he has been here forever, and since so many of these old houses have priest holes, I was sure if Grimshead boasted one, he would be the one to know of it. You remember the religious persecutions, coz, when a man was hunted, killed, if he admitted his devotion to Rome? And the priests who came secretly to say Mass at the homes of the faithful?"

I nodded, impatient with his history lesson. He smiled as he poured us both a cup of coffee. "Well, there is a priest hole here, cleverly hidden between the drawing room and the library. It can be reached from Lady Cecily's room or from a closet in the hall. Crowell knew nothing of the spy hole though; that is a new development, for, according to him, the secret room has not been opened for years."

"How excited Robert will be when he learns of it," I said with a smile. "But how crushing for Cecilia to find out that far from the supernatural, it had to be only a human eye she saw."

The earl lowered his cup and frowned as I added, "But who could it have been? We were all of us in the library at the time, even Mr. Douglas-Moore."

"It had to be an inquisitive servant, but I cannot imagine why they would want to spy on us. In my experience, servants always know all about everything, although I have never understood where they get their information. My valet, for example, can often be found packing my portmanteau only minutes after I have decided to travel."

"It might not have been a servant. It might have been Lady Cecily," I said. "If there is an entrance to the secret room from her room, she might have used it last night. We don't know how ill she really is."

"I certainly wouldn't put it past her to have had the hole cut deliberately so she might listen to our conversations," the earl agreed. "After all, she was the one who decided we should use the library as our sitting room. And what we have had to say to each other, and about her, might very well help her to choose her heir."

Alastair entered the dining room just then and it was so unusual to see him up at this early hour that both of us stared at him in amazement.

"I know, I know," he said in a weary voice. "This stay in the country is ruining me. And this is such an uncivilized hour to be dressed. But I was barely able to sleep an hour last night so I decided I might as well rise. Just some tea, Cousin Lila. I may be up and dressed, but I shall certainly not eat at this ungodly hour."

After he sat down, the earl told him what we had discovered about the priest hole. I was surprised at his openness at first, until I realized he must not think last night's incident had any connection to the poisoned comfit. On reflection, I didn't think so either.

"Of course it was our *dear* great-aunt," Alastair said dryly. "I hope she was as startled by that piercing shriek as we were." He started to chuckle then, and I must have looked surprised, for he went on, "But it is truly amusing. Only think, coz, of all the comments she has heard these last two days. They say eavesdroppers never hear any good of themselves, and from what I can remember, there was nary a compliment that the lady might treasure. Instead we discussed her parsimonious ways, her eccentricity, and this crumbling old castle. I can hardly wait for Lady Danvers to make an appearance. She has been so very rude, she bears the palm. How she will gnash her teeth now all hope of calling the Douglas legacy her own has been quite vanquished."

His breakfast completed, Byford rose and excused himself. I was prepared to follow him till Alastair put out a lazy hand and detained me. You may be sure I was not a bit reluctant to settle back in my chair again, already feeling breathless at this chance to be alone with him.

"Thank you for bearing me company, coz," he said as the door closed behind the earl. "Do you think we will be summoned to the queen's chamber today? Or do you suppose what she has heard has given her such a disgust of the lot of us, we shall be asked to leave at once?"

"Even if she did, there is no way we could comply. There is a blizzard raging. How could we travel in such weather?"

He looked to the window and I drank in his perfect profile avidly. When he looked back at me, I hastily lowered my eyes to my empty coffee cup.

"I had not noticed. Let us hope it is not a storm of long duration."

He changed the subject then and began to quiz me about what I knew of London. I longed to remind him of our meeting there, chide him for forgetting me so completely, but I held my tongue. Alastair was a fascinating man when he forgot his affected manners, for he had a quick wit and turn of phrase. His comments on the latest fashions, as well as some of the more fabled of the *haut ton,* were interesting and amusing. Still, I could wish there was not always a little undercurrent of malice in his conversation, as if he delighted in pointing out the weaknesses and foibles of others. But perhaps his sharp tongue this morning was the result of a sleepless night.

I sat with him for almost an hour, but when the Danvers made an entrance, I excused myself on the pretext of having to see how Cecilia was doing. Alastair rose and bowed, and he took one of my hands and kissed it lightly before he whispered,

"It is too bad you do not stay to see for yourself the lady's reaction to the news. But never fear! I'll relay all the amusing details to you later."

His eyes held a wicked gleam and I could not help smiling in return, unkind as it was of me to find Sylvia's coming distress laughable. As I closed the dining room doors behind me, I heard her say in her strident voice, "But you cannot be serious, sir. How . . . how very unethical."

I found Cecilia languishing in bed, her face pale and her eyes heavy. She gave a start when I slipped into the room after only a perfunctory knock.

"Do not do that, Lila," she scolded, gripping the covers to her chin with both hands. "How you frightened me! And after I told Annie to lock the door behind her when she left, too. It is too bad of her."

"But there's nothing to be frightened of, Cecy," I said briskly as I came up to the bed. "Don't you want the draperies open? It is so dark in here."

"No, do not touch them. I am trying to rest after my horrible experience last evening. I declare, I am quite laid low still."

I told her then what the earl and I had discovered, and as I had expected, she was vastly disappointed that the eye had not belonged to a ghostly apparition.

"Of course, it *could* have been the ghost of a long-dead priest," she insisted, loath to give up her terrifying ordeal. "Suppose one had been shut up there centuries ago and forgotten, and now his spirit still cannot rest."

She shuddered in delight, and looking at the books on her nightstand, I understood completely. Besides *The Secret Ordeal of Rosalinda* or, *The Haunted Castle,* there was also a copy of Mrs. Blackburn's latest opus, which I had heard contained a villain who went about killing young beauties every chance he got, and who lived in a castle much like Grimshead complete with bats, creaking doors, and moaning ghosts.

"I hardly think such a thing likely," I said, trying not to sound too prosaic. "How difficult it would be to sit in your library while someone was banging on the wall, trying to get your attention. Besides, you saw an eye, remember? Trust me, Cecy, it had to have been a very human eye."

Cecilia sank back on her pillow and covered her own eyes with her forearm as she said she supposed I was fortunate not to have any imagination. She herself, she added in a fading voice, had always been extremely sensitive to nuance. Before she could develop that theme, I admit I beat a hasty retreat.

I found Robert in the library and when I told him the news, he was as delighted as I had known he would be. He went away at once to see if he could locate the entrance in the hall closet. I went to the window to watch the storm and shortly thereafter, Mr. Douglas-Moore came and told me the Earl of Byford had just been summoned to Lady Cecily's room.

"So it begins," I remarked, more for something to say than to begin a conversation. It had occurred to me as I stood at the window watching the snow, that I had very little time to myself here. And it had been pleasant, alone in the library, with Cecilia tucked away in bed a floor away and the Danvers closeted with Alastair in the dining room.

"Aye, it begins all right," Douglas-Moore agreed, recalling me from my musing. I looked at him. There had been something in his tone that reminded me of Alastair, something I could not place. Before I could think about it further, the Danvers arrived. I could see Sylvia was furious. Her husband hovered around her, all but wringing his hands in his distress.

"But, my love, we cannot be sure it was my great-aunt," he said. "It might have been a servant, you know."

"Will you be silent, Roger!" his wife hissed in a breathy whisper, pointing to the bookcase. She reaffirmed her command by making a grimace and shaking her head. Out of the corner of my eye, I saw Douglas-Moore put down his paper to stare at her in amazement, and it occurred to me no one had thought to tell him of the morning's discovery. Once I had brought him up to date, he broke into laughter, long, husky brays of sound that made Sylvia wave her hands and scowl at him.

"No need to fear the old girl's at her post, m'lady," he said when he was able to speak. He wiped his streaming eyes on a handkerchief and added, "She's called in the earl, so you are safe for a while at least."

"Well, I am glad to hear it," Sylvia said, casting a still nervous eye in the direction of the spy hole. "Not, of course, that anyone would say anything derogatory about such a sweet old lady, I am sure. I myself am much taken with her. She is such an original."

I couldn't help wondering if Sylvia was just practicing, or perhaps covering all her bets. But surely she hadn't forgotten her earlier comments, about the food, the frigid hall, her unfortunate room—all made right in this room, and clearly audible, her voice was so strident.

It seemed a very long morning. I wished I could go out for a walk, but the storm prevented that. Eventually I walked up and down the hall for some exercise and it was there Robert found me as he left the closet, brushing dust from his jacket.

"I see you were successful in your search," I remarked.

"Lord, yes. It was almost too easy. You have only to press one of the pegs at the back of the closet and turn it slightly to the left for a panel to open. I'm sure a child could find it, and I'm also sure any priest cooped up in there must not have had a moment's peace. But stay! Let me show you."

"No thank you. I'll take your word for it rather than soil my gown."

"I never thought you so hen-hearted, Lila. Besides, it's not dirty, merely . . ."

"Merely full of dust and festooned with cobwebs. You have a large one on your back right now."

"Well, brush it off for me, will you? What are sisters for?"

"I'll show the hidey-hole to Cecilia when she finally comes down. I know she'll want to see it, even if you don't."

"Can you hear what is said in the library, Bob—Robert?"

"Yes, as clear as anything. I could hear every word even though the spy hole has been shut. There must be air vents somewhere else for I could feel a definite draft. But there were no clues as to who has used it, or even who made the circle.

That is new, by the way. There was fresh sawdust and the edges of the cut were clean.

"I say, Lila, Sylvia Danvers is a flat, isn't she? I almost called out it was me in there, but I was afraid I would startle you."

At last Crowell summoned us to luncheon. Lord Byford joined us there, released from the interrogation of our hostess. He would answer no questions about it, to Sylvia's obvious disappointment. For myself, I thought him preoccupied throughout the meal, wrapped in his own thoughts. I wondered what they might be, not that I had any chance of finding out.

As we were leaving the table, Crowell came to tell Alastair that her ladyship would do herself the honor of receiving him now. He sent me a mischievous smile, which I can tell you elated me. It seemed to bond us together as conspirators or perhaps kindred spirits. As I selected a book in the library and excused myself from the company, I wondered how many pages I would even read for I suspected I would dream the afternoon away.

But I had little chance of that, for I had no sooner settled down in my room and opened my book when Cecilia knocked and came in. I was glad she had left her bed and dressed, but I wished she had chosen someone else to chatter and gossip with. I discovered immediately she knew all about the visits to Lady Cecily's room. Her maid's doing, no doubt.

"I am glad she has not asked for me; if she never does so I shall not repine, I can tell you," she said with a toss of her chestnut curls. "I was passing in the hall when Miss Spenser took in a tray of medicines—at least I think it was medicine— and I heard Lady Cecily and Alastair laughing in such a hearty way. I wonder what he said to tickle her fancy? I am sure I would never be able to do so."

She stayed with me until it was time to dress for dinner, and if I had thought the morning long, it was nothing compared to the tedious afternoon. After she left at last, I rang the bell for Polly, noticing the storm had worsened, for now the wind howled around the windows, and the snow seemed to have turned to sleet. I could hear it striking the panes with vicious little taps. I was glad to put on the warm cashmere shawl Polly insisted I needed before I went down to join the others.

After Crowell and the elderly footman had served the last meager course and left the dining room, Alastair began to tease Sylvia Danvers. He told her what a pleasant visit he had had with Lady Cecily. Sylvia had questioned him throughout dinner, but he had turned away all her queries with light answers and changed the subject again and again. I wondered she did not realize how obvious she was, how amusing to the rest of us. But now, as if tired of teasing, he gave her a detailed account.

Sylvia leaned forward in her chair, her little dark eyes intent with interest.

"You say she was pleasant?" she demanded. "That she actually laughed a number of times? How extraordinary. She did not seem the type to condone levity."

She fell silent for a moment and I wondered if she were thinking of several jokes that Roger might tell his great-aunt when they were summoned, or some pleasantry she herself might relate.

"Yes, she was most amused by my poor tales of London life and the *haut ton*," Alastair assured us all, one eye on Sylvia Danvers.

"I wish you would tell me what to say," Cecilia interrupted. "I am so afraid of her, I know I will look the perfect fool. How very strange that is; I am never at a loss for words with gentlemen."

Everyone laughed and conversation became general after Alastair had commiserated with her on her bad luck in finding a Great-Aunt Cecily instead of a Great-Uncle Cecil.

Our hostess was seen no more that day. Crowell told us she was in her room, attended by the faithful Spenser, for the visits had tired her and she planned to retire early. We adjourned to the library, even after Sylvia suggested we have the fire built up in the hall so we could spend the evening there. "I cannot be comfortable, Roger," she complained. "Knowing that she—that someone might be listening to us."

"I do not think the priest hole will be used again, m'lady,"

Grant St. Williams reassured her. "Not now that we all know about it."

I could see Robert, who had confided he intended to sit in the secret room to try and catch the eavesdropper, was delighted with this analysis, and he was quick to agree to make a fourth for whist with m'lords Byford and Danvers and Alastair Russell.

I had discovered an old journal on the library shelves that some long-gone Douglas had kept, and I was so fascinated that every so often I read a part of it aloud to the women. Cecilia had brought her needlework and Sylvia busied herself knotting a fringe, and if you had looked in on us that stormy night you would have thought us a pleasant family gathering, especially since Mr. Douglas-Moore had not joined us. There was something about that man that set everyone's nerves on edge. I had noticed that every time he was with us, the conversation grew more stilted, the silences longer. It was as if we were all aware he was not really one of us, that he was a class apart. I regretted it, for surely the man had done nothing to deserve it, but there it was.

We all went early to bed. Perhaps the howling of the wind made us restless, or our isolation, for we were lighting our bedroom candles in the hall shortly after ten o'clock. I found myself next to Grant St. Williams for a moment, and could not help asking him, in an aside, what he thought of Alastair's account of his visit. I wondered why he hesitated, why he looked down at me so intently, before he said, "Alastair may regret his moment of fun. I could wish he had not made so much of Lady Cecily's regard for him. Of course, he is used to being idolized, adored, even. But I wish in this instance, he had kept it to himself."

He paused, as if he had said too much—or too little? Then I wondered why that thought had come all unbidden as he bowed and wished me a good night. I found it hard to get to sleep however. Instead, I lay in bed and pondered what he might have meant by his remarks about Alastair. Surely he did not think he was in danger. Did he?

Only when I was dozing off at last did I remember my time alone with Alastair, the conversation we had shared, the way he had kissed my hand. Had his lips lingered for a moment longer than necessary? Had I imagined the growing intimacy we seemed to share?

And did it mean anything at all to him, those few moments that meant everything to me? Perhaps I was just another of the legion of admirers he attracted, and he considered my fascination only his due. Pray not.

Still, as I fell asleep, it was not Alastair's handsome face I saw in my mind, it was the Earl of Byford's—serious, concerned, intent as he stared down at me there at the bottom of the stairs. In my last moment of consciousness, I wondered why that should be so.

Chapter Seven

~~~~~~

The storm blew itself away sometime during the night, and a weak sun was trying to break through the clouds when I woke the following morning. I was trying to decide whether it would be possible to go for a short walk with my brother, or if the wind was too strong, when the Danvers joined me in the hall after breakfast.

"Good morning, Cousin Lila," Roger Danvers said, beaming at me. "I see the sun is shining, what? So much more pleasant, is it not? And what are you planning to do this morning?"

Sylvia only nodded to me and took a seat near the fire, for once content to let her husband do the talking. I mentioned a walk; Lord Danvers could not recommend such an undertaking.

"Drifts, you know, drifts," he said, waving a vague hand. "Dangerous things, drifts. Why, I recall a time when . . ."

"Roger," Sylvia interrupted, "summon that butler and have this fire attended to at once. It is smoking and there are not enough coals to warm even this end of the hall." She shivered as Roger obediently went to give the butler a shout.

Sylvia and I waited in silence until Crowell came at last, grumbling and complaining. After he had put a few more pieces of coal on the fire and poked it up a bit, he announced that his mistress wished to see Lord Danvers this morning, at his convenience.

Sylvia rose at once, smoothing her curls and straightening her gown. "Why did you not tell us so immediately, you old fool?" she demanded. "Come, Roger. We will go at once. It would not do to keep the dear old lady waiting."

"Beggin' yer pardon, m'lady," Crowell said. I thought his voice sounded triumphant somehow, and I did not have to wonder why when he added, "Her ladyship only asked for Lord Danvers."

Sylvia stared at him, her eyes narrowed. "You must be mistaken," she said in her positive way. "Of course Lady Cecily wishes to see me as well as Lord Danvers. Come along, Roger."

"Well, you can go in, m'lady, but you'll come right out again. Lady Cecily said to me, she said, 'And tell that wife of his there is no need for her to push her way in here for I don't want to see 'er.' Them was her exact words, m'lady."

Sylvia sank back in her chair, her face ominously red and her mouth working, although no words escaped. Lord Danvers patted her hand, his eyes popping as he looked around desperately for help. Seeing me, he beckoned and I swallowed the laughter I was having so much trouble containing.

"Do me the favor of staying here with Sylvia, cousin," he begged. "You can see she is upset. Perhaps it is all a misunderstanding. There, my love," he said, turning back to his wife, "I will attend to this. I am sure Lady Cecily did not mean it—er, in quite that way."

He bowed to both of us before he followed a triumphant Crowell to the drawing room doors. His wife watched him go, still speechless. I thought she looked as if she might have a fit of apoplexy, she was so very angry. After a few pregnant moments though, she said, "I have never been so insulted in my entire life. One would like to be able to make allowances for the elderly; their little whims and caprices, but this . . . this rudeness, this complete disregard for what is proper behavior, makes me seriously doubt Lady Cecily has all her wits. Surely she must be deranged." This thought seemed to afford her no end of satisfaction for her expression brightened and she appeared to be thinking. "Yes," she went on finally, "that must be the explanation. And if it is true, then of course any will she makes in her present state will not be valid. I shall require you to be a witness to this morning's unfortunate display, Delilah."

I suspected Sylvia did not trust her husband to make a good enough impression on his great-aunt without her assistance and I was revolted by her greed.

"I do not agree with you," I said, ignoring the lady's indignant gasp. "Lady Cecily appears to be completely in touch with reality. Why, the other evening when we all visited her, she was lucid and composed. Perhaps her request was simply a desire to deal only with the immediate members of the family." I could tell that was an unfortunate comment, for the lady positively spluttered as she said, "Immediate? *Immediate?* As the wife of Roger's bosom and the future mother of his children, who is more *immediate* than I? And I meant to point that out to her, for of all of you, Roger is the only one who has seen his duty plain and entered into holy wedlock."

And at such a cost, too, I thought wickedly, but I did not reply and kept my head bent meekly so Sylvia would not see the laughter I could feel bubbling up again.

Somehow I had lost all desire for a walk. I admit I could not bear to miss Sylvia's account of this morning's humiliation to the other members of the party as they straggled down to breakfast.

Alastair was the last, and by the time he appeared, Sylvia had perfected her performance. He heard her out without speaking, and without meeting my eye before he said, "How mortifying for you, to be sure, ma'am. I know you must feel the slight deeply. But Roger has not come out. Perhaps he is making an excellent presentation of his case? Even amusing Lady Cecily with a few *bon mots* and well chosen *on-dits* in his own inimitable style?"

Sylvia's face flushed dark red, for even she knew when she was being ridiculed so obviously. I rose in haste and excused myself, hoping she did not notice the quaver in my voice.

I found Grant St. Williams in the library, dressed to go out, and deep in conversation with Mr. Douglas-Moore. Both men stared at me as I shut the door, then collapsed against it, my hands over my mouth as I tried to contain my laughter. Alas, I had no such luck, and began to giggle uncontrollably.

The earl smiled in sympathy as Douglas-Moore said, "Well, I'm glad someone finds something funny in this place."

I moved aside as he made his way toward the door and managed to stop giggling as he left the room. When I explained what had amused me to Byford, he gave a great shout of laughter himself.

"Oh, do be still, cousin!" I said. "What if she hears you?"

He looked down at me and smiled and it occurred to me that we were standing much too close together for comfort. "Do you know, Lila, I find myself completely uninterested in the woman's feelings. I do, however, sincerely pity Roger."

"I almost forgot to tell you. Sylvia is very anxious to point out to our great-aunt that Roger is the only one of the heirs to have married. She seems to feel this shows a steadiness of character and observance of duty the rest of us, alas, lack."

Byford's brows rose and I wondered why I had thought to mention that, and wished I had not. It seemed a long moment before he said softly, never taking his eyes from my face, "Perhaps that might be rectified? What do you think?"

I did not answer. I couldn't, I was so confused. What had he meant? Did he intend to marry? And who was the lady? I shrugged instead and went to pick up the journal I had been reading. To my relief, the earl only chuckled before he excused himself.

"The grooms in Lady Cecily's stables seem as reluctant to feed the horses as her cook is to feed us. I must make sure they have been given enough oats," he said as he left.

Alone, I sat down by the fire, all thoughts of reading gone from my mind. I was glad no one came to join me, for I wished to think—think hard.

There had been something about Grant St. Williams that had made me uneasy. Some slight softness on his rugged face perhaps, a certain look in his eye, even a warmth in his voice I had never noticed before. I knew I was not the most experienced of young women, not where men and courtship were concerned anyway, but I was knowing enough to suspect there was more here than had met the eye. For why else had I felt so conscious of him as we stood so close together—his height, his strength, his *maleness*? Why had my breathing quickened, my heart begun to pound?

Half an hour later I was still alone, turning everything that had occurred since our arrival over and over in my mind, reliving our walk to the gatehouse and back, even recalling those occasions when our eyes had chanced to meet in company and we had both smiled at the same time. Suddenly the quiet of the morning was shattered by a loud explosion. Jumping to my feet, one hand to my rapidly beating heart, I hurried to the door of the library. The scene that met my eye caused me to gasp in shock, for there, in the center of the hall, lying very still on the flagstones, was Alastair Russell. Even as I watched, a red stain crept from under his body to darken the flags, and for a moment everything stood still except for that slow trickle. And then, as I told myself I must go and see what I could do to help him, the confusion began.

Sylvia Danvers appeared at the doors of the dining room and began to scream loudly. Robert and Cecilia came running down the stairs, both exclaiming, and Lord Danvers hurried to his wife's side from the back of the hall. Part of my mind registered all these things as I made myself move forward. Then the front door opened and Mr. Douglas-Moore stood there, a cigar in his hand. I do not think I was ever more glad to see anyone, for he went immediately to Alastair and began to examine him.

"You there, Danvers! Call Crowell and tell him ter bring some bandages at once. The man's been shot."

"Is he . . . is he dead?" Cecilia asked in a shaky voice.

Douglas-Moore did not answer as he turned Alastair over onto his back. He thrust a handkerchief beneath the blood-stained coat, and as I stared hard at the hole in that beautiful garment, I clenched my hands tightly together and told myself I would not, no, I would *not* disgrace myself by fainting. Still, I was glad when Robert came and put his arm around me in support. I saw Cecilia had sunk down on a lower step as if she dared come no closer, and she had covered her eyes. All the while, Sylvia kept up her keening.

"Shut that woman up, m'lord, if ye have ter throttle her," Douglas-Moore commanded. "No, he is nae dead—yet. I wish that doctor chappie was here. We could use him."

Crowell tottered into the hall bearing bandages. He was followed by one of the footmen and Miss Spencer, who was wringing her hands and looking distraught. Douglas-Moore looked at them all and shook his head.

"Come here, boy," he said to Robert. "It looks like it is up to us to get the gentleman to his room. You take his feet and I'll take his shoulders." Robert moved quickly to do his bidding. All I could do was stare at Alastair's still, white face. How pale he is, how still, I thought, wishing there was something I might do to help, too. I heard the front door open behind me, and turned to see Byford there. Immediately, I felt a lot better as he went to kneel beside Alastair and listen to Douglas-Moore's terse explanation. Byford will take care of Alastair, I told myself. He will take care of everything. The earl rose to take the bandages from the butler's hand and said, "Send someone for the doctor. Tell him to hurry!"

Crowell opened his mouth, I was sure to protest the state of the roads, and our isolation, but one look at Byford's dark, furious face, and he bowed without a word.

I wondered why Lady Cecily did not come out of her room, what with all the noise and confusion, for even though Sylvia had subsided into only a few moans, the servants were chattering, and Cecilia was still crying at the foot of the stairs. Miss Spenser went to the drawing room doors. "Dear, dear," she said to no one in particular, "how upsetting for her ladyship. I must go to her." As she left us, the little procession started for the stairs and Cecilia scurried out of the way. Robert and Douglas-Moore carefully supported Alastair while Byford followed them closely. He turned after he reached the fourth step to stare back down at everyone, his dark eyes angry and intense as he inspected the company. At last he said, "Bring the doctor up the minute he arrives, Lila. I will come and tell you everything as soon as I can. No one is to leave the castle except for that servant who is fetching the doctor. Do you understand? *No one.* Is that clear?"

I nodded, not trusting my voice, as the men moved around the bend in the stair and along the gallery at the top. Everyone stood frozen until we heard the door to Alastair's room close. I went to Cecilia then, for she was hanging on to the newel post, her face white with shock.

"Come, my dear, you need a cup of tea," I said as I helped her to the dining room. Over my shoulder, I added, "Bring Sylvia, too, cousin. She should have a restorative. And there is nothing any of us can do until the doctor comes."

Roger Danvers supported his shaken wife to a seat at the table. She continued to moan and cry and I wondered at it. I knew she disliked Alastair more each day. Why would his being shot upset her so? It was not many more minutes before we all discovered the answer. Faced with this mysterious shooting, it had dawned on Sylvia that perhaps the comfit had been poisoned, and meant for her as well.

"You must tell Lady Cecily that my nerves cannot support a longer stay here, and she must make up her mind about her heir as soon as possible," she commanded her husband. "Poisoned sweets, someone spying on us in the library, and now this! Why, we may all be murdered in our beds!"

I thought Roger Danvers looked uneasy, and I suspected he had not had a pleasant interview with our great-aunt and was not looking forward to approaching her again. Besides, it was obvious he was as upset as his wife at the turn of events. His eyes bulged and his hand shook, and it was not until he had downed a large glass of brandy that his complexion returned to its normal hue.

I sat holding Cecilia's hand. She still had not spoken a word, and I was worried about her. At last, after she had taken a sip of wine, she was able to say, "Please, may we not go home, Lila? Please?"

I had no answer for her, but I managed to smile a little and squeeze her hand and it seemed to comfort her.

Eventually, Crowell served a luncheon of sorts, but none of us did more than toy with the food. When Robert entered the dining room, even the pretense of eating ceased in our eagerness to question him.

Robert was white and nervous and I saw how glad he was of the wine Lord Danvers poured him. After a healthy swallow he told us that Douglas-Moore had managed to stop the bleeding and that Alastair had recovered consciousness briefly, but that the earl had said the bullet was still lodged in his side and must be removed. He thought Alastair would be all right as long as they were able to keep him from moving restlessly and opening the wound again.

I was glad Byford had sent him away. Robert was only twenty-one, and he had never been in a situation like this. Knowing he would do his utmost to stay the course, no matter what it cost him, I was sure he had matured a great deal in the last hour, and I was proud of him. He might be a careless young man, and constantly in debt, to our father's disgust, but there was good in him, and strength, and a steadiness I had not suspected.

His news cheered everyone considerably, for at least Alastair was still alive. They began to discuss who might have been responsible, and I excused myself by saying I must go to the library to await the doctor. I was glad Cecilia seemed perfectly content to remain at the table with Robert and the Danvers, for I wished to have a few moments alone.

Sitting down at the writing desk, I took up paper and quill and began to list the guests and where they had been right after Alastair had been shot. Robert and Cecilia were easy, for they had both come down the stairs from the upper floor together. Mr. Douglas-Moore had been on the front steps with his cigar, and Grant St. Williams in the stables. But Sylvia had appeared at the doors of the dining room, and surely her husband had come from the direction of the back hall. I wondered when Lady Cecily had dismissed him, and what he had been doing there. Alastair had been lying facing in that direction. It had to have been an intimate of the house, guest or servant, for no one could have entered the hall and shot him, not with Douglas-Moore right outside.

I studied my list and sighed. With the exception of myself, I could not be sure of any of the others; they all could have managed the thing. Even Cecilia or Robert, for they had not been together upstairs, I knew. And there were two sets of back stairs from the servants' quarters that could have been used.

And although I could not picture either one of them as a murderer, it would have been entirely possible to fire the shot and then run up the back stairs, appearing moments later in the upper hall, exclaiming in horrified accents over the incident.

Even Douglas-Moore or the earl could have done it, I supposed. I got up and went quickly into the hall. I was glad someone had wiped up the bloodstains, but I could not help but shudder as I passed the spot where Alastair had lain. Methodically, I went into every room on the ground floor, with the exception of Lady Cecily's, and inspected every window. My heart sank when I reached the back salon, near the door that led to the servants' quarters, and found the snow had been heavily trampled outside the French doors that opened on the terrace. So I had been right. Either Grant or Douglas-Moore could have shot Alastair, run out of these doors and down to the stables or around to the front door. As I stared at the confusing footprints, it began to snow again; in a short while this evidence, if that was what it was, would be gone.

Slowly I went back to the hall and feeling suddenly very tired and weak, leaned against a large table there. On the table were our bedtime candles, Crowell's tray, and an assortment of odds and ends. Putting my hands to my face, I closed my eyes. Surely it was terrible, to be suspecting any of the others. Then I remembered Roger had come from this direction, and over there, across the hall, Sylvia had been standing. I began to tap my fingers on the table as I thought. Surely either of them had been in the ideal position to shoot Alastair, or at least see who had done so. And I remembered as well how furious Sylvia had been when Alastair twitted her this same morning. Furious enough to do him harm? I wondered. She did have an explosive temper.

I was still standing there, deep in thought, when Miss Spenser came out of Lady Cecily's room carrying a tray. When she saw me, she gave a startled cry.

"How you frightened me, Miss Douglas, standing there so still," she exclaimed, her free hand going to the throat of her black gown.

I apologized and asked how Lady Cecily was doing.

"It is surprising she is so well," Miss Spenser said. "She heard the shot but she is taking it calmly, asking only that someone report to her as soon as Dr. Ward has seen Mr. Russell. I should be glad to wait for the doctor, Miss Douglas, for you. I feel I must remain close to Lady Cecily. It is no bother."

I told her I would not dream of imposing on her when she already had so much to do. I thought her gray eyes looked bewildered behind her thick glasses, but that might only have been a trick of the light, or her concern for her mistress. Idly I wondered if she loved the old woman, or if she merely put up with her because she needed the position. I would not have said my great-aunt was that lovable, but then I did not know her very well.

When I returned to the library, I put the lists I had made carefully in my pocket before I went to stand at the window that overlooked the drive, watching the snow fall and waiting for the doctor's gig to arrive. And I prayed. Prayed hard that Alastair would be all right.

Chapter Eight

Eventually, toward three in the afternoon, Dr. Ward arrived. The others had joined me in the library by then, and I began to think if I had to hear one more conjecture, one more comment, indeed, even one more word from any of them, I would explode, my nerves were so on edge with waiting. Even Robert annoyed me by constantly referring to the situation, and finally I ordered him to hold his tongue and let the matter rest. I could tell he was offended by this high-handed treatment, for from then on he ignored me to whisper to Cecilia. The Danvers, too, were whispering together, and I returned to my vigil by the window. I was beginning to wonder if the doctor had been unable to make it through the deepening snow when his gig struggled up to the front door and he leapt down with his black bag to hurry up the steps. As I went to take him upstairs, relieved that help was at hand at last, I saw Miss Spenser coming from the back of the hall, and I called to her to tell Lady Cecily that the doctor had come.

I was dismissed at Alastair's door by Grant St. Williams. He looked tired and distraught and had only a small nod for the doctor, and none at all for me. I went to my room to compose myself. In a short while we would know whether Alastair was going to recover, or if we would have to face the fact that Grimshead harbored a murderer. Then I shook my head. Even if Alastair was going to be all right, there was still a murderer here. He had just not succeeded. This time.

As I went to the comfortable old arm chair before the fire, I moved my shoulders, trying to dispel the icy little finger of fear that ran up my spine.

In spite of that fear, the warmth of the fire soon put me to sleep, and I did not wake until Polly came to see to my clothes for the evening. As I rubbed my eyes, I asked her how Alastair was doing, ashamed I had been so remiss. She told me the doctor had removed the bullet and was sure Alastair had a good chance of recovery, for the bullet had not struck any vital spot. I breathed a prayer of thanks, but when I would have hurried downstairs to hear the news firsthand, Polly announced that the second dressing bell had gone, and she would be obliged if I changed for dinner first, for I looked a perfect fright in my creased and crumpled gown. Polly has been my maid for a long time.

I didn't care this evening what gown or jewels I wore, but I contained my impatience until Polly declared she was satisfied. When I ran down the stairs to join the others, I found them standing before the huge fireplace in the hall, waiting for dinner to be announced.

Cecilia and Robert still had their heads together, with the Danvers standing somewhat apart, looking identically nervous. Grant St. Williams and Mr. Douglas-Moore were together before the fire. Feeling everyone's eyes on me, I went to them to ask how Alastair was doing. The earl frowned at me, although I didn't know why, and it was Douglas-Moore who assured me Alastair was better, that his valet was sitting with him and the doctor was in Lady Cecily's room. He was having dinner with her, for he intended to remain at Grimshead until the storm passed and Alastair was out of danger.

As I thanked him for the good news, I couldn't help but be aware of Byford standing so tall and straight beside me with that dark, thunderous look on his face. I hoped I was not the one who had incurred his wrath. Somehow that was important.

When Crowell announced dinner, we seven remaining guests filed into the dining room. Conversation was limited this evening, and often only the tinkling of silver or crystal could be heard, or the elderly footman's nasal breathing.

After dinner, when we ladies started to rise, Byford said, "I think it best we all remain together this evening. There is no point in putting it off; we must discuss what has happened and try if we can to find out who fired the shot at Alastair. Next time, whoever is guilty might not miss."

Sylvia Danvers squealed and sat down abruptly. I saw that Cecilia was very white and I smiled at her to give her courage.

The decanter of port went around and then Byford said, "If anyone has any suspicions, it would be wise to air them now when we are all together. We have a serious situation here. We can no longer pretend Lady Cecily's dog ate something he should not have on his walk, or an inquisitive servant carved the hole in the library to spy on us. No, it is more than that—much more—so speak up if you noticed something—anything—out of the ordinary."

There was only silence and he sighed as he looked around the table.

"I see. Can it be possible that there in the main hall, surrounded by all the guests and servants, Alastair could be shot and no one saw a thing? Come now, who was first on the scene?"

"I believe I was," I told him. His eyes never left my face as I continued. "I was in the library when I heard the shot and I ran immediately to the door. There was no one in the hall but Alastair, lying where we found him."

"No one else? Not even the glimpse of someone disappearing? No skirt whisking around a corner? No coattail?"

"Nothing," I said before I added, "of course I was so horrified I did not really look, for all my attention was on Alastair, bleeding there on the flagstones."

Cecilia whimpered and then fell silent as we all looked at her.

"Come, we must press on," Byford declared, impatiently running a hand through his dark hair. "Who arrived next, Lila?"

"I cannot be sure of the exact order, but I remember seeing Cecilia and Robert coming down the stairs together and then . . . then Sylvia appeared at the door to the dining room, and Lord Danvers from the back of the hall. And then it seems to me Mr. Douglas-Moore came in the front door. He went immediately to help Alastair." I paused, and then, looking directly at Byford, I said, "And of course you arrived a few minutes later."

"Yes, I had been to the stables. But you're sure there was no one else? No servant or perhaps someone whose face was not familiar?"

"No one," I said firmly. "Later, of course, Crowell and a footman arrived with bandages, and after them Miss Spenser. She went in to Lady Cecily almost immediately. There were some other servants milling about in the background, but I did not attend to them particularly. I am positive, however, there was no stranger there. Surely someone else would have noticed if there had been."

"Of course we would have," Robert said hotly.

"Very well," Byford said. "Let us go around the table and see what we can add to Lila's statement. Robert, where were you when you heard the shot?"

"Why, in my room. I was there to fetch my greatcoat, hoping I might interest Lila or Cecy in a walk. And when I left my room, I ran right into Cecy. Isn't that right, coz?"

She nodded. "And what had you been doing?" Byford asked her. I was glad his voice was so gentle for I suspected she was on the edge of hysteria.

"I . . . I had gone up there after breakfast to fetch my needlework. I intended to join Lila in the library," she whispered.

"And you and Robert came down the stairs together?"

"Yes. I thought to run ahead," Robert answered for her, "but I could see Cecy needed support, so I stayed beside her."

"Did either of you notice anything out of the ordinary?"

Cecilia shook her head and Robert admitted reluctantly that he had not.

"Now, then," Byford said, turning toward the Danvers. "Let us find out what the two of you were doing there at the back of the hall."

Sylvia bridled. "How dare you question us, m'lord? I should like to know who put you in charge of this, this investigation. I resent your tone and inference. Neither Roger nor I have anything to say to you. Why, one might suppose you suspect it was one of *us* who shot Mr. Russell."

"I not only suspect it, ma'am, I am sure it had to be someone in residence here."

Sylvia drew in her breath. "Roger, how can you sit there mumchance when this man has just insulted me? As for you, sir, how dare you?"

"Very easily, m'lady," Byford said, pointing a finger at her. "Don't you understand how dangerous this situation is? Here we all are, cooped up in this remote castle with a blizzard raging outside, and there is a murderer with us. Who can tell where he or she will strike next? Or do you feel safe, m'lady, because an attempt has already been made on your life? If, indeed, it was."

Sylvia stared at him. She was as white as her shawl now, but it was Cecilia who drew everyone's eyes. She gave a little cry and fainted, sliding off her chair to the floor beneath the table. I saw Byford rising as I hurried around the table to help her.

"Seems ter make a habit of it, don't she?" Douglas-Moore asked no one in particular. He did not seem very worried about Cecilia's health.

I shook her gently, even slapped her face while the rest sat in silence. "She has not really fainted this time," I told them. "I believe it is only a momentary weakness." As if to prove me right, Cecilia stirred.

Only a few minutes later, she was back in her seat, sipping the wine Robert handed her. All it had taken for her to return to normal was my whispered suggestion that she would be so much safer here with the rest than alone in her room.

"Shall we continue?" Byford asked, looking around the table. "Come, Roger. You are a reasonable man. You must see we have to get to the bottom of this. Of course we are all suspect, every one of us. Now, I ask you again. What were you doing in the back hall?"

"Why, why, I had gone to fetch Crowell to bring more coal for the dining room fire," Roger got out all in a rush. "Sylvia and I had come in here for a private conversation after my visit with Lady Cecily, and the fire was almost out. This house is run disgracefully! I seem to be constantly running back and forth to the servants' hall and the butler's pantry, for no one answers the bells promptly. Sometimes they don't even come at all."

"Very true," Byford murmured. "But forget that. Surely you must have seen something. The would-be murderer had to have fired from that direction, the way Alastair was lying."

Lord Danvers gasped, but before he could reply, Douglas-Moore said, "Beggin' yer pardon, m'lord, but that's not necessarily so. If the bullet struck him with enough force, he could easily have spun around as he fell. We canna be sure he was shot by someone standing back there in the shadows."

The earl nodded before he said, "But such a theory is to place you more firmly on the list of suspects, sir."

Douglas-Moore looked rueful as he replied, "That's so, all right. I could have fired the shot and then gone out the front door. You have only my word that I dinna."

"And of course, that means Lila could have done it as well," Byford mused. Robert sprang to his feet, his face flushed. "How dare you insult my sister, sir? As if Lila would shoot anyone! I've a mind to call you out for such an insult."

I was shocked, but still I managed to say, "Sit down, dear. I thank you for your support. But if what Mr. Douglas-Moore says is true, I could well have done it. We are none of us exempt." As calm and reasonable as I hoped I sounded, inside I was reeling. Why, on our walk, Byford had claimed he trusted me. So much for that trust, I told myself bitterly, wondering when it had been lost, and wondering as well, why I regretted it so deeply.

"But why _was_ he?" Cecilia asked in a plaintive little voice. Everyone turned toward her, for she had been so quiet we had almost forgotten she was there.

"What I mean is," she went on as she saw our confused faces, "why was Cousin Alastair shot at all? I don't understand. Can it be there is a madman loose here?"

I could see she was already picturing a dungeon deep beneath the castle, and a deranged monster who had escaped his chains to prowl at odd times of the day or night seeking victims. Fortunately Byford spoke before she could enlarge on this theme. "I think Alastair was shot because he was on such good terms with Lady Cecily after his visit to her yesterday. I am sure we all know how he amused her, had her laughing. He bragged about it enough, remember? Someone must have thought he stood too good a chance of being named sole heir."

"But that is to assume one of us did the foul deed," Roger Danvers protested. "It might not have had anything to do with the fortune."

"True. And Alastair delighted in insulting people; there is hardly a one of us he has not annoyed. But would that be enough to make someone attempt murder?" Byford said. "Does anyone have a better motive to suggest?"

We all shook our heads. Then Sylvia, who had been quiet for quite a time, remarked, "It seems to me, m'lord, that *you* are the only one among us who cannot be considered a suspect, for you were not even in the castle. How very convenient your concern for your horses was."

Without thinking, I said, "But he certainly is a suspect, Sylvia. While I was waiting for the doctor I went around the ground floor and inspected the snow beneath all the windows. In the back salon, near the servants' hall, someone had used the French doors that lead to the terrace. The snow there was disturbed by many footprints coming and going, so it is entirely possible Lord Byford came back in that way, shot his cousin, and then made his way around to the front door."

Dear Lord, I thought as I looked down the table to him, what have I done? There was a hushed moment while we stared at each other, and then he raised his glass to me.

"How very observant of you, cousin. If the footsteps were there, and I, for one, do not doubt that you saw them, then someone did use that exit. I could have done so, of course. I hope it makes you feel better, Lady Danvers, to have me join the list of suspects?" He spoke sarcastically, and I swallowed the lump I had in my throat.

"Unfortunately I cannot prove it," I said, determined even now to be truthful, "for when I found the prints they were being obliterated by the fresh snowfall." I looked down at my hands, trying to remember the last time I had been so unhappy.

"Well, so we're all in this together, eh?" Douglas-Moore observed. "Well, since I see no way this problem can be solved, ladies and gents, I suggest we try and stay together. And when we're alone in our rooms, we make use of the locks. Till this snow stops, there's small chance any justice can reach us."

"I don't know what he could do if he did," Byford said. "Remember, all of you, how serious this is. And until the culprit can be found, we are none of us safe."

"I heard something from Crowell today," Roger said in the heavy silence that followed these remarks. "That is one good thing, I suppose, about all this running back and forth to the servants' quarters—you do hear things. It seems the boot boy reported he had found an open can of rat poison in the gardener's shed. Seems he was meeting one of the maids there—frightful morals, the lower classes, what?—and he said it had not been there last week."

His wife glared at him. "Why did you not mention this before? How very upsetting."

"Went right out of my mind, my love, what with all the excitement we have been having."

I stared down at where I had clenched my hands in my lap. The knuckles were white. In my mind's eye I saw a picture of Grant St. Williams hurrying along the path from the shed the day I met him in the garden. I also remembered how angry he had been when Robert had mentioned the old dog might have been poisoned. Mentally, I shook my head. No, it couldn't be him. I was sure it couldn't be him. Because if he had shot Alastair, Alastair would be dead now. He would not miss an easy shot like that.

"Lila, I have spoken to you twice," Robert's voice interrupted my thoughts. I looked up to see the others regarding me, and I flushed. "Come, we are going to adjourn to the library."

As we strolled to the library, Byford excused himself, saying he intended to sit with his cousin so Alastair's valet might get a few hours' sleep.

"Perhaps tomorrow we had better take turns sitting with the patient," Robert volunteered. Sylvia frowned, and he added, "Perhaps we should do it in pairs . . . I mean . . ."

He turned bright red as Byford bowed to us all, his stormy gaze going right through me as if I were not even there.

It was a very long evening. Dr. Ward did not join us and no one was summoned to Lady Cecily's room. I tried to read, but Byford's rugged face kept getting between me and the page. Cecilia and Robert played cards in a desultory way, and Sylvia Danvers sat staring into the fire in injured silence. No one, including her husband, cared to ask what the trouble was. I saw that only Douglas-Moore was at ease. His eyes darted from one to the other of us, a little half smile on his lips as if he found us, and the situation, vastly amusing. I'm sure everyone was as glad as I was when the clock struck ten and once again we were able to go to our rooms.

I did not call Polly. Instead I undressed myself and put on a warm dressing gown of navy velvet before I began to brush my hair. As I brushed, I reviewed everything I had heard this evening. Something bothered me, something more than the identity of the person who had tried to kill Alastair. Something no one had thought about. Suddenly I put down my brush and stared at my reflection in the glass. Of course! No one had mentioned the gun. But where was it? Surely the murderer must have disposed of it quickly, for keeping it in a pocket would have been too dangerous. No, as soon as the shot had been fired, the gun must have been hidden in a safe place.

I rose to pace my bedroom. I did not believe Douglas-Moore's theory that the shot might have been fired from the front of the hall, for one of us would have seen anyone who tried to make an escape that way. And then it came to me that I would have heard the door as well. Whenever it was opened or closed, there was a distinct, loud creak. I had noticed it first the evening we arrived. There had been no creak today.

Obviously the shot had to have been fired from the back of the hall by someone who had escaped through the salon or the servants' quarters. I closed my eyes, trying to picture that particular room. It had been dark and cluttered, the furniture covered by cloths. Surely it would have been simplicity itself to push the gun under a cushion until it was safe to retrieve it. I knew I should go down right now and search for it before that happened, but I could not make myself do it.

Finally I climbed into bed. It would be foolhardy to go down there alone, in the dark, I told myself as I pulled up the covers. But just as I closed my eyes, a picture of the hall table where I had stood this afternoon came to mind, as clear as if an artist had painted it. There were all the candles to light the guests to bed, and over there, Crowell's tray. And right in the center, there was a large Chinese vase.

I knew if I stopped to think about it, I would convince myself to remain in bed, so I got up and threw on my robe and slippers, and softly unlocked my door. I did not light my candle right away. Instead I listened, but I could hear nothing but the thudding of my heart. I had no idea of the time, but thought it must be late. Surely everyone was asleep and I would be perfectly safe, I told myself stoutly. Taking my candle, I crept down the dark stairs, obscurely pleased that the hand holding it did not shake and so did not cast weird moving shadows on the wall. Once in the hall, I ran to the table and put my candle down to lift the vase. I forgot the black, threatening void behind me when I heard something metallic knock against the side, and I reached inside to draw out the gun I knew now was there.

And then, while I held it gingerly and tried to replace the vase, the dining doors were flung open and light streamed out from a high-held candelabrum.

I whirled, my heart beating wildly with fright, to see Lord Byford pointing a very dangerous-looking pistol at my head. Unnerved, I dropped the gun I was holding and it clattered on the floor.

"You!" he said harshly. "It was you all along."

"No, m'lord!" I exclaimed. "No, you are mistaken."

He strode toward me. As he reached the gun on the floor, he kicked it away, never taking his eyes from my face or relaxing his aim.

"Pick up your candle and walk before me into the dining room, Miss Douglas," he commanded.

I did as I was bade, my candle shaking violently now. When I turned, he had shut the doors and was motioning me to a seat. I saw he had been sitting there alone, drinking a glass of port, and perhaps trying to resolve the puzzle. I must have made enough noise to attract his attention. I looked at him briefly then quickly lowered my eyes. There was anger in his face, and disgust, but there was something else as well; something very like regret.

"Before we begin, a glass of wine?" he asked. "I am sure you are distraught to be discovered." Without waiting for my answer, he poured me a glass and pushed it toward me before he took his seat, carefully putting his pistol within easy reach of his right hand.

"No doubt you have invented a perfectly good explanation. Come, what have you decided to tell me?" he asked, his eyes never leaving my face.

"I will tell you the truth, m'lord," I said. "I suddenly remembered the weapon and in thinking it over was sure the person who had used it must have disposed of it as soon as possible. But where had he put it?"

"He?" Byford inquired in a deceptively soft voice.

I am sure I paled. "I am aware how this must look, but if you keep interrupting me I won't be able to tell you what happened," I said, and he nodded.

"Remembering the footsteps in the snow, it seemed to me the murderer must have hidden the gun in the back salon before he—or she—went out the French doors. But then something else occurred to me and I recalled the large vase on the hall table. Surely that was the easiest hiding place. I did not want to come downstairs, but I was afraid if I waited until morning, the gun would be gone. And I could not sleep knowing the murderer would have it back, perhaps to use more successfully next time."

I paused, confused by his frown. "A very plausible, pat explanation, coz. My congratulations. But how foolhardy—although brave—of you. Weren't you the least bit afraid of meeting the murderer on the same errand?" He paused then added, "But of course, as the guilty one, you knew there would be no danger of that. No doubt you thought I was with Alastair, as I said I would be. That was just a ruse to try and flush out the culprit. And it worked, for you did not expect to find me waiting for you here, did you?"

"I can only give you my word that I am not the murderer, sir," I said. "What I have told you is the truth."

"And yet, by your own admission, you were the first on the scene with plenty of time to drop the gun in the vase and hurry back to the library door and pretend you had just left that room," he said.

I bowed my head in defeat. He did not believe me; there was nothing more I could say to convince him. Suddenly I heard him groan and I looked up in astonishment to find him staring at me, then rising to come and pull me to my feet, his hands tight on my arms as he looked down at me. The planes of his face looked chiseled in the candlelight; half light, half dark, both halves anguished.

"I want so much to believe you, Lila, so very much." He groaned again and then pushed me away so I staggered a little and had to reach out to grasp the back of a chair to keep my balance, while I watched him pace up and down the room. I saw he had picked up his pistol again, but at least he was not pointing it at me. I was confused at what he had said, how he had looked, and afraid I might cry, I said, "I know how this looks, m'lord. And of course I have no proof that what I told you is the truth. But it is. My word as a Douglas, it is!"

He stopped pacing and went to lean on the mantel to look down at the dying coals.

"How dangerous women are," he said as if speaking to himself. "I have known it for a long time, but until now I was not aware of the extent of their perfidy. What a mistake it is for a man to think he understands women, that it is safe to care for them, even love them."

He looked at me then, his eyes bleak. There was nothing more I could say. I could tell he had made his decision. Finally he sighed and came toward me again.

"I will escort you to your room. Forgive me if I take the precaution of locking you in. I am sure everyone will sleep more soundly for it. I know I shall." His voice sounded sad and resigned, yet determined as well.

I picked up my candle and went past him to the door, trying to keep my head up and my tears in check. There would be plenty of time to cry, all night in fact. As I stepped into the hall, Byford close behind me, I stopped suddenly. He jumped back, as if I had been planning a trick.

"Grant," I whispered, staring at the flagstones, "where is the pistol?"

With a startled oath, he held the candelabrum high, but the gun that he had kicked to one side was nowhere in sight. He turned to look at me again, despair on his face for the accusations he had made. It was then we both heard, very clearly, the sound of a door closing somewhere above us.

Chapter Nine

"Lila, dear Lila, forgive me," the earl whispered in the silence that followed the shutting of that door.

"I would be glad of your escort upstairs, m'lord," I replied, my voice tight. "Especially now that the pistol has been reclaimed by the person who made use of it in the first place. I trust you will not need to lock me in now, although of course I intend to do so from the other side of the door." As I spoke I moved toward the stairs, Byford following in my wake.

"Lila, you must listen to me . . ." he began, reaching out for me. I raised my free hand to stop him after I picked up the skirt of my dressing gown to climb the stairs. I was furious, as furious as I had ever been in my life, and I wanted none of his facile apologies now. Or ever, for that matter, I thought grimly.

"Do me the favor of not speaking to me further, m'lord," I said, my voice icy. "We have nothing more to say to each other."

He nodded and stepped back in defeat. Do you know, women are the strangest creatures? For a moment I was disappointed he had given up so easily. Instead I had wanted him to argue, even take me in his arms as he had done in the dining room. No doubt that was because I wanted to continue to give him a setdown he would not forget, I told myself as we reached my room and I swept inside and closed the door in his face. I made a point of locking that door as loudly as possible, and I hoped he was still standing there, and that he heard it.

I did not sleep very well, for after my initial anger at the earl had faded, I felt a deep sense of loss and regret. I had liked my cousin Grant, liked him very well indeed. In fact I had been delighted at our growing rapport, the glances we were wont to exchange when one or the other of the party made some ridiculous, fatuous remark. The little smile he sometimes had for me, the warmth I was beginning to feel deep inside whenever he was near me—oh, how upsetting it was to know he had not trusted me! And that is all it is, this malaise I feel, I told myself as I punched my pillow into shape and turned over once again to try and go to sleep.

I was still in bed dozing the next morning when Cecilia knocked. After I unlocked the door, I saw she was accompanied by a wide-eyed Annie Deems. The maid was clutching a poker, but I did not feel like smiling as Cecilia dismissed her. Knowing there would be no peace for me now that my cousin was with me, chattering away, I rang for Polly. She was still chattering after Polly had helped me into my gown and done up my hair, but I could tell it was only nervousness that made her so loquacious. I did not tell her what had happened in the night, for I knew that announcing the murderer had recovered the gun would only upset her further. Besides, I did not want to speak of Byford.

At last we went downstairs together to breakfast. Crowell was waiting to give Cecilia the message that Lady Cecily would be pleased to see her that morning. As he tottered away Cecilia sat down quickly to stare at me in horror. "No, oh no," she exclaimed. "I will not go."

"Come now, Cecy, she is not a dragon or a witch," I said as I took some porridge from a dish on the sideboard. It occurred to me I was growing very tired of porridge. "You must make some push to get to know her after your long journey here," I added in a bracing away. "Your mother will ask, you know."

"I will not see her alone," Cecilia said, her voice rising and her pretty face set. "Not if she is as rich as Golden Ball, I won't. But wait! We are all supposed to stay together, are we not? That was the plan that was made last night. Well, then, in that case you must come with me."

She brightened up and poured herself a cup of tea as I took my place at the table. "But, Cecy, she did not ask to see me. I hardly think it the thing to . . ."

"We go together or I don't go at all," Cecilia said. I wondered I had never noticed what a firm little jaw she had. "Please, Lila. What difference will it make? I certainly don't care if you hear what she asks me, or my replies."

She continued to plead and beg till at last I agreed, more because I could feel a headache coming on than from any desire to help. When Roger and Sylvia entered the dining room, Cecilia announced her arrangement. Sylvia studied me with horror. I could tell she thought me dim-witted to help another aspirant to the fortune. How fortunate it was I didn't care a ha'penny what Sylvia Danvers thought.

When we left them, the Danvers were busy drawing up a list of people to sit with Alastair that day, in pairs of course. The last I heard, they were arguing about Douglas-Moore's partner.

I knocked on the drawing room door and was told to enter. Grasping Cecilia firmly by the hand, I forced her to accompany me to where our great-aunt was sitting by the fire. The lady's bushy brows rose when she saw the two of us.

"And what is this, miss?" she asked me in a haughty tone. "I did not ask to see you."

I explained the guests had decided to go everywhere in pairs in the interest of safety. Lady Cecily snorted and shook a bony finger at a cringing Cecilia.

"This is all your doing, I'll wager. Scared to death to face me alone. Well, never mind, never mind. Sit down, both of you."

I took the armchair across from her and Cecilia settled nervously between us, smoothing her gown with a shaking hand.

"Tell me what is happening," our hostess demanded. "I never leave this room, you know, and so I have to depend on Spenser to give me the news. I know that Alastair Russell was shot at yesterday, but since Dr. Ward arrived, Spenser is not nearly as attentive to me as she ought to be."

She chuckled, as if to herself, and I said, "I believe she is assisting the doctor, ma'am, when he attends to Alastair. I heard from my maid this morning that although he spent a restless night, he has no fever and, now that the bullet has been extracted, is expected to recover completely."

"I am glad to hear it, very glad. I like him. I imagine most women do."

I nodded, and she chuckled again before she turned to Cecilia and said, "Come, Miss Worthington, have you nothing to say for yourself? How is your mother, girl? Tell me something about your home, your life, the things you like . . ."

Cecilia said in a little voice that Mama was very well, thank you, and had sent her love. I was glad Lady Cecily refrained from one of her acid comments at that, for it most assuredly would have brought Cecilia's conversation to a complete standstill before it even began. When the old lady did not interrupt her, Cecilia was bold enough to go on and describe her home and her friends, and to tell her how much she was looking forward to her come-out.

"Yes, you'll be fired off with no trouble at all, you are so very pretty," Lady Cecily remarked. "How fortunate there are always gentlemen who do not care if the wife they choose has a brain in her head, just as long as she is attractive. But then, some gentlemen are easy to please." She turned to me then. "And you, miss? Not married yet? I hear you are all of four-and-twenty. Take care lest you end an elderly spinster like me."

I looked at her closely, but there was no disappointment or bitterness in her face, and I remarked, "I would prefer it so, ma'am, rather than marry a man I cannot love and respect. So far, at least, I've not found anyone to suit me."

Lady Cecily cackled with amusement. "Neither could I. You may not believe it, looking at me now, but I was a great beauty in my day; had any number of beaux dangling after me. But not a one compared with my father, and I vowed I would never settle for second best. I have not been unhappy, but it takes a special sort of woman to live alone without regrets. I wonder if you are such a one?" She peered keenly at me for a moment, then added, "You have honest, clear eyes, gel, and a determined look about you. But of course you are much too young to put yourself on the shelf just yet."

The conversation moved to other things. Cecilia thought to ask about Miss Spenser.

"Spenser? I cannot remember when she has not been with me. She came to me as a young woman over twenty years ago, and she was lucky I took her in. There are too many people who remember her mother was a Douglas bastard, so there was small chance she could ever contract a marriage. Well, she tells me she has been happy here. But come, Spenser is of small interest to anyone, for although she means well, she is a very dull person, with no charm, and little conversation. Tell me, instead, who is suspected as the murderer?"

I looked at Cecilia, willing her to speak, and she said, "We have no idea, m'lady. It is so frightening to think there is such a person here among us. And truly, it was decided that none of us should ever be alone except in our own rooms with the doors locked. For anyone could have done it, anyone."

"Except for Alastair Russell," Lady Cecily said. "I was shocked to hear he had been wounded, and I have thought perhaps I was wrong to invite you all here for an old woman's whim. However, I never thought it would bring trouble to you all."

She looked sad and upset, and I hurried to say, "So far, at least, we have escaped serious harm, even Alastair. I suppose we must hope our good luck continues for the remainder of our visit."

"I have always enjoyed my wealth. I am aware that the thought of gaining possession of a fortune can sometimes make even a normal person do things that are not in character," Lady Cecily said, looking at both of us impartially. "But I only wanted to be sure that my father's money should go to the best one of you. I shall see your brother this afternoon, Miss Douglas, and then perhaps I will be able to make up my mind. Hopefully, that will stop all this nonsense." She nodded and added, "It is sooner than I would have liked, but no doubt it will be for the best."

We spent the rest of the morning with our great-aunt. I felt a certain admiration for the old lady in her outmoded wig and old-fashioned gown, for I could tell from the way she twisted sometimes in her chair that she was in pain. When I asked if I could fetch anything for her to relieve her discomfort, she pointed to a bottle on her nightstand. After she had taken a spoonful and made a face, she said, "Horrid stuff! I much prefer spirits, but the doctor has forbidden me to touch them. Silly old woman, Dr. Ward. As if it made any difference now."

Eventually Miss Spenser came in with a tray, and we were dismissed. I thought our great-aunt looked tired and worn as I nodded to Miss Spenser, who was standing by the door to see us out. She was dressed in her customary black gown, her hair pulled back in the tight bun, but I thought her face looked softer somehow. Could it be she fancied herself in love with the doctor, I wondered, then had to smile at such a thing. Miss Spenser must be many years older than he.

"Whew!" Cecilia whispered as soon as the doors to the drawing room were safely shut behind us. "Thank heavens that is over, and with any luck, she will not ask to see me again. And I can tell Mama that I did everything she told me to, and smiled and was charming, and it still did not answer." She skipped a little as we made our way to the library, she was so relieved.

"But perhaps she will choose you, Cecy," I teased. "It is true you were charming, and she did say how pretty you are."

My companion stopped short. "I do not depend on it, for she also as good as called me a pea-brain. But I don't care. I intend to marry a very wealthy man, and that's an easier way to get a fortune, so there!"

We found the Danvers in the library. Sylvia began at once to question us. What had Lady Cecily asked us, and how had we replied? Had she mentioned Roger, and had she thought to point out to her great-nieces they should emulate his example and marry? I said absently that no one had given Roger a thought, much less spoken of him, and his wife frowned.

"And as for marrying, she practically said Lila did not have to if she didn't want to. After all, she is a spinster, too," Cecilia said pertly, so happy to have the ordeal of a visit she had been dreading over with, she became quite bold.

"I must say, Cecilia, these snippety ways you have fallen into do nothing to add to your consequence. Mind your tongue!"

"Well, I like that! I guess I can say what I want to, can't I? Besides, Sylvia, you are only four years older than I; your behaving as if you were a dowager duchess does not become you either. Pooh!"

Roger bustled over from the window, where he had been watching the snow that had begun to fall again. "Now, ladies," he said, rubbing his hands together and peeking at his wife's rigid, disapproving face. "Let us strive to be happy and serene. No words, mind! And no quarrels or disagreements, for we wouldn't want them to get back to Lady Cecily, now would we? We must be all one big happy family together."

I stood up and excused myself in the silence that followed. "I have the headache," I told Cecilia when she begged to come to my room with me. "I have to be alone for a while. You will be fine here with Roger and Sylvia. No, no, don't bother, Roger. I am sure I can manage by myself."

But this I was not allowed to do. Roger insisted on escorting me to the stairs. He clutched my arm tightly, his fat face turning this way and that as we traversed the hall. Crowell, who happened to be in the hall at the time, stared at him in amazement. But Roger did not relax his vigilance, in fact he remained at the bottom of the stairs until I reached the safety of my bedroom door.

"I think I shall go quietly mad," I told myself as I went in and shut that door firmly behind me. "No, I shall surely go mad if I have to remain here much longer. A fortune is not everything."

My brother Robert was summoned to Lady Cecily's room after luncheon, and Crowell announced that Mr. Russell had asked particularly for me to visit him as well. Both of these pronouncements were made before the whole company at table, and I flushed as all eyes turned my way, careful not to look in

Byford's direction. He had appeared for the first time at luncheon. He was quiet and seemed oblivious to the general conversation. I thought he looked tired as well, as if he had not slept and a part of me I deplored hoped it was because he had so much remorse for misjudging me, sleep had been impossible.

"Well, this is beyond anything great," Sylvia declared, her eyes wide. "Go alone to a man's bedroom, Delilah? Your mother would not believe you could be so bold!"

"Do not be so silly, nor so busy about my affairs, Sylvia," I was stung to reply. "Alastair is my cousin, and he has been sorely wounded. The tone of your mind is disgusting."

Sylvia bridled and turned pink. I ignored her and rose from the table. "I shall go to him at once. Excuse me, all."

As I turned to go, Sylvia said, "I shall certainly have a spell if I am subjected to any more rudeness, and from spinsters, too. No one seems to have the least idea of my consequence! Furthermore, as the only married lady present, I feel it is my duty to set the moral standard here. Besides, he is only her *second* cousin."

I was delighted when Crowell shut the double doors behind me and I was free of not only Sylvia, but the lot of them. Mr. King, Cousin Alastair's valet opened his door when I knocked. I was glad to see that Alastair, wrapped in a dressing gown, was propped up on several pillows and looked much better than the last time I had seen him. His handsome face had regained some color, and his eyes were bright. He had even had Mr. King shave him, so I knew he was feeling more the thing.

"Thank you for coming, coz," he said, indicating a chair placed beside the bed. "It is such a bore to be confined to bed; I depend on you to tell me everything that has been going on below stairs. That will be all, King. I'll ring when I need you.

"There, now we may have a comfortable coze. How kind of you to keep me *au courant.*"

"You must tell me when you become tired, sir," I said with a smile. I admit I felt a little edge of excitement. I was alone with Alastair. We were going to be alone for some time. My heart seemed to be beating erratically at the base of my throat and I felt short of breath. Recalling what I had just said, I added, "I will go away immediately if you do."

"Do not worry. I slept most of the morning after Dr. Ward changed the dressings," he replied. "He seems a competent surgeon; one must give thanks for that. I wouldn't have been surprised to have had some ancient Scottish crone called in with her herbs and cobwebs and potions. Miss Spenser was very efficient as well although I'd wager she is seldom summoned to the bedsides of men who have been shot."

"Did you see who fired that shot, Alastair?" I asked.

He frowned, as if trying to remember. "I am afraid I did not. I was crossing the hall, going towards the fire, when suddenly, without warning, the shot came from the back of the hall. It was dark there; I certainly didn't see anyone. And yet . . . I have the strangest feeling that at the time I *did* know who it was, but now I do not remember."

"You had better keep that to yourself," I cautioned him.

"I have every intention of doing so. I wouldn't even have mentioned it, dear Lila, if Grant hadn't told me all about last night, how you figured out where the pistol must have been hidden and went down alone in the dark to get it. You are certainly a gallant, plucky girl! Women constantly amaze me.

"And now that pistol has been recovered, by my would-be murderer, of course. You may be sure I shall exercise caution."

He reached under the covers then and brought out what appeared to be a dueling pistol. "I am ready if he or she should make another attempt. And we three must stick together, you and I, and Grant, for we are the only three who could not have been doing any of these things."

I thought he looked at me intently and I wondered if I had paled. Then he went on, "I admit I am puzzled by Grant. I really don't believe he is so fond of me that he has fallen into a depression because I was shot. Yet this morning he looked so angry and black! Has anything happened that you know of, to cause that?"

When I shook my head, he went on, a wicked gleam in his

eye. "I think it all began when I asked you to remain with me at breakfast. Remember? Can it be that he is jealous? Every time he saw us together, he frowned. And perhaps he thought you braved the dark hall last night because you were in love with me, and feared for my life. What do you think?"

"I think you have been dreaming," I said, trying to sound amused. I could not like the way he continued to study me, the little twist of his handsome mouth, that knowing look he sported. "Byford and I barely know each other. Besides, last night he was convinced I was the murderer, until the pistol disappeared. Nothing I could say would change his mind. So you see, your theory will not work, for surely a man who was attracted to me would not behave in such a way."

I was glad he did not pursue the subject further. When he had said Grant must have thought I was in love with him, it had been all I could do to preserve my countenance. So when he asked who had been in to see Lady Cecily, I told him how Cecilia had insisted on my accompanying her that morning, and what had happened in the library later with the Danvers. He laughed at that, and then grimaced as the movement caused him pain.

"You are hurting! I am so sorry," I exclaimed. "I promise I will not say another amusing thing."

Alastair waved this away. "But that is why I asked you to come, and not any of the others." he said when he had caught his breath. "There is no one here, with the exception of you and Grant, who is the least amusing. And he has turned sour. Just consider; Roger Danvers is a tedious fool, his wife a tiresome, greedy shrew. Cecilia, for all her beauty has more hair than wit and no conversation. Your brother—do forgive me if I speak plain—is green and untidy and he does nothing but stare at my clothes. Do you know, I even considered sending King to him, to try and get him into some sort of shape fit for the dining room, before I decided I really could not spare him. King, that is. Your brother I could certainly spare. As for the bastard in our midst, he is not worthy of a moment's thought."

He sighed and looked out the window for a moment. I had no comment to make. His remarks about the others might be true, but they were unkind. I especially deplored his scorn of Robert. My brother was only a young man with a young man's admiration for an older, celebrated man. It occurred to me that while Robert might hero-worship Alastair, to me his halo had slipped a trifle.

"Come now, Lila, no woolgathering," he said. "Tell me what you think will happen next. I assume you, like I, do not believe our trials are over."

"No, I agree we are not out of the woods yet. I have thought and thought, but I cannot imagine who might be doing these things and why. It remains a mystery. The earl did say you might have been shot because Lady Cecily liked you so well. It is enough to make me hope she has formed a fervid dislike for me.

"Robert is with her now, but he is so young and careless with money I am sure she would never choose him as her heir, even if he is the only male with the Douglas name. I think, you see, she must have had us all investigated, so she knows everything there is to know about us. Don't you agree?"

He did not answer, and I wondered why he looked so thoughtful.

"I am beginning to believe it would have been better if none of us had come to Grimshead," I added, getting up to wander over to the window. I saw it was still snowing, more lightly now. "I am sure I will never have a fortune to dispose of, but if I should, I will remember this time and quietly name my heir as soon as possible."

"Money is always a problem," Alastair agreed. "If you don't have any, you are in trouble. If you have a great deal, like Lady Cecily, you are in another kind of predicament. But I can certainly understand why she could not resist pitting us all against each other and then sitting back to watch the fun. I should most assuredly do the same."

I turned back to him. "Even after all that has happened?" I asked, not really believing him.

"Of course. I am not very nice, Lila," he said, looking at me frankly. "Did you think I was? How sad to have to disillusion you. I imagine our great-aunt is as deplorable as I am. After all, no one is going to do *her* any harm. You remember how carefully she told us that if anything happened to her, none of us would get a penny?"

"Yes, of course. But I refuse to believe what you say about yourself, Alastair. I shall certainly go on thinking of you as a gentleman."

"Well, I should hope so. I did not say I was not a gentleman," he replied, looking so indignant I had to laugh as I returned to his bedside and took my seat again.

And it so happened that the Earl of Byford came into the room just then and found us laughing together. His expression was not only black, it was thunderous.

"I am sorry to have to interrupt your amusing tête-à-tête, cousins, but Mr. King tells me it is time for your medicine, Alastair," he said, his voice cold. I rose at once and Alastair reached for my hand, to kiss it. "Come back soon, Lila," he said with a grin. "I feel so attuned to you, so close."

I withdrew my hand from his, disappointed. From the gleam in his eye, I could tell he had behaved the way he had from a sense of mischief. He seemed determined to make trouble, just because it amused him. I hoped none of my thoughts showed on my face and I made a special effort to smile warmly at him as I took my leave. The earl had to make do with a distant bow.

That evening at dinner, my brother was the center of attention. He had remained with Lady Cecily for most of the afternoon, and Sylvia seemed determined to ferret out every little bit of information about the meeting that she could. I tried to catch his eye so I could hold a finger to my lips to suggest he remain silent, but I was not successful.

"Why, she's a great gun," he enthused as he beckoned Crowell to pour him more wine. It would be his fourth glass, too, I noted, ever the big sister.

"I tell you, I never thought to like her so well. Some of the stories she told me of things that happened to her when she was

young, you would not believe. Did you know her father took
her to France and Italy for the Grand Tour when she was fifteen,
disguised as a boy? He wanted her to travel and see the world,
something she could not do as a girl. She had fencing lessons,
learned all about pistols and marksmanship, and several other
things besides, and she said no one ever suspected she was not
young Lord Douglas."

"Really? No wonder she is so eccentric in her old age,"
Sylvia said.

"Did she like you as well?" Cecilia asked. I wished I might
throttle them both, as he replied, "Well, she seemed to. She
smiled at me and said I was a proper Douglas. And when I told
her tales about some of my special cronies and our escapades,
she laughed till she cried."

He sounded so proud of himself, I could barely conceal a
startled exclamation. I looked around the table carefully, to see
how everyone was taking his boasting. Mr. Douglas-Moore
looked disapproving and a little bored. Cecilia was smiling and
nodding. Sylvia looked indignant, and Roger didn't seem aware
of anything but the possibility of his wife making a scene.
When I looked at Byford, his face was stern and set. Catching
my eye, he shook his head at Robert's impetuosity. For a moment, I felt a wave of regret. How sad it was that Byford and I
should think so much alike about most everything, yet be so
firmly estranged.

I was relieved when Sylvia gave the signal for the ladies to
withdraw, and I did not look the earl's way again.

Chapter Ten

I slept late the following morning, and when Polly came in to open the draperies, I saw it was still snowing. For a moment I snuggled down under the blankets, then with a sigh I got up and wrapped myself in the warm dressing gown my maid held out for me, content to sip my morning chocolate while she made up the fire and laid out my clothes for the day.

I had known Polly since I was a little girl, and I was glad she was here with me in Scotland. Unlike Cecilia's maid Annie, Polly never got flustered or excited, and even the events that had occurred here, she took calmly. I wondered if she wished we might go home, but I knew she would never say. Instead, as she did my hair, she told me of an altercation that morning between the cook and one of the maids. I listened with half an ear. It was obvious that Polly felt vastly superior to any of Lady Cecily's servants. In my mind's eye, I could see just how she would make her exalted position plain.

When I went downstairs, I greeted Crowell as he came out of Lady Cecily's room with a tray, and nodded to an elderly footman crossing the hall slowly with a hod of coal for the library fire.

There was only one occupant in the dining room. Grant St. Williams rose and bowed to me, although he did not speak. Now why did he have to be here, I wondered as I said good morning and went to the sideboard for my breakfast. I wished Robert or Cecily, even the Danvers might come in, for I had no desire to sit here alone with the man, involved in a travesty of casual conversation.

I hoped none of these thoughts showed on my face and I nodded when Byford asked me if I cared for coffee.

I ate my porridge with my eyes lowered, and after he had handed me my cup, Byford returned to his own seat and the remains of his breakfast. I could not help noticing he was eating a plate of eggs and ham and scones, and wondered how he had wrested them from Crowell and the cook. There had been nothing as appetizing on the sideboard.

For a moment there was silence in the room, then I was startled when he said, "Lila! Miss Douglas, I mean . . ."

I looked up to see him leaning toward me, his dark face serious and one hand stretched out. In supplication? I wondered. "Yes, m'lord?" I asked, proud my voice was steady, even if my heart was pounding in my breast.

"My dear Lila, I must ask you again to forgive me. I am very sorry I suspected you, but what would you have thought if you had caught me with the pistol that shot Alastair? And if I had told the same tale you did, wouldn't you suspect me still, even if I gave you my word I was telling the truth? Come now, admit you would have come to the same conclusion I did. This situation has become intolerable, with you avoiding me and never speaking if you can help it, and now Alastair . . ."

He stopped, as if he wished he had not said that.

"What has Alastair to say to anything, sir?"

He had the grace to flush a little. "I should not have mentioned him, of course. But, Lila, dear Lila, can't you forgive me and call me 'Grant' again?"

I looked into his dark eyes set in that rugged face. They pleaded with me, and I almost relented until I remembered how hurt I had been at his suspicions, how he had not believed me, how he had been going to lock me into my room until the law could arrive, and how he had been fully prepared to give me up to the local justice as a potential murderer, and I could not.

"No, I can't," I said, putting my coffee cup down quickly so he would not see how my hand had begun to shake.

He sighed and ran one hand through his dark hair in that now-familiar gesture. "Very well," he said grimly. I knew he would not ask for forgiveness again, and I felt a stirring of regret. "However," he added in an impersonal tone, "I would remind you that of everyone in this house, I am the only one, besides yourself and Alastair, who could not be the culprit. I must ask you to come to me if you discover anything, or have any suspicions at all, even if you would rather not speak to me. This person is still dangerous. I am afraid that whoever is guilty has not given up his or her mad plan. In fact, the failures that have occurred may well drive him or her to desperate measures."

I nodded. "Of course. I . . . I was very upset last evening when Robert insisted on bragging on and on of his conquest of Lady Cecily. I saw you agreed with me. I tried to get him alone later to tell him so, but he was adroit in avoiding me, and I could hardly make a scene."

"It is true we must keep an eye on him. I've a mind to part his hair myself when he comes down this morning," he told me, and then Cecilia and the Danvers came in together and there was no chance for further private conversation. In fact, the only thing that was discussed was how Byford had acquired his breakfast, and how Sylvia might do the same.

As soon as I could, I rose and excused myself. I did not feel comfortable in the same room as Byford, not after what had just transpired between us. I went into the hall, wondering what to do with myself all morning. Of course, I could write some letters in the hope the post might go soon, or I could work on my tapestry, or search the library for another book to read. After deciding on this final course, I wondered where Robert was. He was generally an early riser in the country, but it had been apparent from all the clean place settings at the table that the earl and I had been the first ones down.

I frowned and would have gone on to the library except I recalled Byford saying we should keep an eye on Robert, and turning, I went to the stairs. I knocked on his door, called his name, but there was no answer. Even though I knew the door was locked, I tried it anyway. You can imagine my anger when

it opened easily. Furious, I stepped inside to give him a piece of
my mind for being so careless. I saw the fire had gone out and
I went to the windows to fling back the draperies. As light filled
the room, I saw Robert's bed had not been slept in. I put both
hands to my mouth lest I cry out. Where was he? What had happened?

Without pausing to think, I flew back down the stairs and
across the hall to the dining room.

Sylvia Danvers was holding forth at great length, lecturing
the company, but I did not hesitate. "Lord Byford, I must speak
to you at once, if you please," I demanded. Sylvia's jaw had
dropped; now she took a deep breath and said, "How dare you
interrupt me, Delilah? Such rudeness, why, I have never . . ."

But I did not hear any more. Byford had taken one look at my
face and risen to take my arm to lead me swiftly from the room.
He paused only to shut the doors behind us, and whatever
Sylvia had been about to say was lost forever.

"Come in here," he said, quickly crossing the hall and taking
me into the back salon with its dust-sheeted furniture. "Now,
what is it?"

"I am so frightened," I whispered. "I went up to see why
Robert had not come down to breakfast, and he is not in his
room. Furthermore, his bed has not been slept in. Where can he
be, oh, where can he be?"

I began to cry and I felt a faintness come over me. Before I
could give in to it, he said harshly, "Control yourself! Hysterics
will not help your brother. Come, take me to his room. He may
have left some clue to his whereabouts."

Now that I had told him, and with a course of action to follow, I felt better. When we reached Robert's room, the earl
stared at the smooth counterpane of the bed and frowned, one
hand rubbing his chin before he said, "He came up to bed with
the rest of us, at eleven. I remember because he said something
to me about hoping the snow would stop so we might get outside today. He was obviously restless at being confined by the
storm."

"Yes, that's true," I said. "He has always hated inactivity, and to be pent up here, in this company . . ." I paused for a moment before I went on, "I told him to lock his door, for I was afraid for him. He promised to do so, and that was the last time I saw him, as he went into his room laughing at my concern."

I had to swallow hard then, swallow the tears that were threatening to disgrace me. Fortunately Byford did not notice. He seemed deep in thought as he prowled the room. "His bedroom candle is missing. I remember Robert always took the candle in the pewter holder. It is strange, is it not, how we all take the same one every night? Lady Danvers prefers the silver one, and you the china with the blue flowers . . ."

Breaking off, he went to the wardrobe and threw open the door. "Look through his clothes, Lila. See if anything is missing while I go down and organize a search of the house."

He was gone in an instant, and I ran my hands through Robert's coats and waistcoats and breeches. When Byford came back a few minutes later, I was able to tell him Robert's greatcoat was missing, as well as the clothes he had been wearing last night.

"So he did not undress for bed. And the greatcoat implies he meant to go outside."

I sank down on the side of the bed for I was afraid my legs would not hold me up. "Outside? In this weather, in the middle of the night?"

"He took his candle," Byford reminded me. "I checked the table downstairs where the bedroom candles are kept, and it is not there. Crowell says he has not seen it either. But the front door was bolted, and so were the French doors in the back salon, as well as the kitchen. That implies he never left the house. The servants are searching it now, room by room."

I could hear for myself the bustle and excited chatter that wafted up the stairs from the hall below, the slamming of doors, and the calls from one servant to another. "Not here!" "The green sitting room is empty!" "Not in the servants' rooms!"

I got up to pace the room, my hands clasped tightly before me. At last Byford said gently, "Come downstairs, Lila. There is nothing more we can do until every part of the house has been investigated."

Obediently, I went with him back to the dining room and did not protest when he poured me another cup of coffee after pushing me down in a chair.

I could hear Cecilia and Sylvia exclaiming and questioning me, and I was delighted when Byford ordered them both to be quiet. Such was the force of his personality, they obeyed at once. Mr. Douglas-Moore came in moments later. When appraised of the situation, his frown warmed me a little.

Bobby, I thought, where are you? As children we had been so close we had often been able to know what the other was thinking, and now I concentrated on him, as if in doing so, I might divine his whereabouts. It seemed an endless time before Crowell came to tell us the house had been searched from attics to cellars and Bobby was not to be found anywhere. But then, Grimshead was such a huge old pile of stone, with so many nooks and crannies and cupboards, it was no wonder. As he stood there awaiting further orders, I suddenly remembered the priest hole and asked him about it. It took Byford only a few minutes to ascertain Bobby was not there.

"Nothing," he said bitterly when he came back. "He is not in the house, so we were right, Lila. He took his greatcoat because he meant to go outside."

"But . . . but the locked doors," I protested.

Suddenly I knew who had locked the doors, after Bobby had left the house, and I had to grip the edge of the table hard to keep myself from fainting. I saw Byford starting to come to me, and I said, "I am all right, m'lord. We've no time for spells, as you pointed out. We must search the grounds and the stables at once." I rose, trying not to dwell on a picture of those huge black ledges below the low stone wall—the height of the cliff Grimshead was perched on—the breakers roaring in . . .

"But Robert could not be outside, Lila," Cecilia's high voice protested. "It is still snowing, and it is so cold."

I saw her shrink back in her chair and caught a glimpse of the murderous look Grant St. Williams gave her.

"Mr. Douglas-Moore, I would appreciate your help organizing the servants. Crowell, have all the male servants gather in the hall. Send a message to the stables, too."

Dr. Ward appeared at the dining room door, drawn there no doubt by all the bustle and excitement. Byford went and took his arm, bending his head to speak to him. I could not hear everything they said, but I did catch a few words—"... get his room warm ... extra blankets ... if, that is ..." The doctor frowned and shook his head and I turned away, unable to look or listen further.

After the men disappeared, I began to pace again, and I was amazed to hear Sylvia Danvers say, in quite the kindest voice I had ever heard her use, "Do sit down, Delilah. You are wearing yourself out to no purpose, and when Robert is found, you will have no strength left to help him."

"When he is found ..." I repeated. "But I cannot remain here, tamely waiting!"

I ran to fetch my fur-lined cloak and mittens, and changed my house slippers for a pair of sturdy boots. No one tried to stop me. I suppose they realized it wouldn't do a bit of good.

When I stepped out the front door, the cold air hit me like a blow, the snowflakes striking my face as they swirled in the wind. I fought a feeling of panic as I set off to find Byford.

There were fresh tracks everywhere. Some led to the stable area, some down the drive where huge drifts had formed, some around the castle in both directions. I realized then the fresh snow had covered any tracks that might have been made last night, tracks that surely would have made the search a simple matter. No, I told myself fiercely. No, he is not dead. I would know if he were, I'm positive I would.

I went around the castle in the direction of the neglected gardens and it was there I found Byford and my own John Coachman coming from the direction of the ledges. The despair on the older man's plain red face made me cry out, the cry ripped away by the wind. The earl put his arm around me as he said, "No, he was not there. There was nothing to see, no sign of any struggle."

For a moment we stood silent, buffeted by the wind. Bobby, I thought again. Where are you? Tell me! Nothing answered, of course, except for a low moaning in the fir break. And the ever-present pounding of the breakers. I decided I hated that sound. Hated the power of it, the omnipotent, never-ending, merciless . . .

"The shed!" Byford exclaimed. I started, remembering the small stone structure at the back of the gardens. I had seen the earl coming from that direction once. It was isolated and not used anymore, especially in the winter. If someone had not wanted Bobby found, then . . .

"Quickly, now," Byford ordered as we set off in that direction. John Coachman soon fell behind. He was old and the drifts and the wind slowed him. I tried to walk in Byford's steps but they were too long and I sank into the deep snow. I could not feel my toes, or my fingers in their wool mittens. And if I were cold after only a few minutes outside, how must it be for my brother?

When we reached the shed we could see it was securely bolted and innocently quiet. "Robert, are you there?" Byford called, wading through a drift. I followed close behind, clutching his sleeve. "Bobby, it's Lila!" I called, as loudly as I could.

There was no answer. Byford reached the door and heaved the iron bar that held it fast up and away. I could hear John Coachman behind me now, panting with his exertion, but all my attention was on the open door of the shed, and the dark space beyond it. It was difficult to see in the gloom after the snow's glare, but after a moment I saw that the shed was empty. There was only a rude bench and some tools inside, and over against one wall, a pile of gunnysacks. My hopes died.

"Robert," the earl breathed, moving forward toward those sacks and I peered at them more closely.

"God have mercy on his soul," John Coachman said in a broken voice.

I stood frozen, unable to move as Byford knelt beside my brother to take one of his hands. He had not worn gloves, and it was blue with cold.

"He is not dead," the earl said quickly. "John, get back to the house as fast as you can and tell the doctor we have found Mr. Douglas. Then send someone here with blankets. I do not want him exposed to the air until he is more warmly wrapped." As he spoke, he rose and stripped off his own greatcoat, to put it snugly around Bobby.

As I rushed forward and knelt beside him, too, the earl said, "Help me chafe his hands, and speak to him. Speak loudly. We must bring him around before it's too late."

I did as ordered, scolding Bobby much as I had when he was a little boy, three years younger and under my care. Those years had been fleeting. All too soon he had grown taller, gone away to Eton, taken the lead, teaching me to shoot and swim and hunt.

"Cold . . . so cold . . . dark," he muttered, and I looked up from his face to see Grant smiling at me, echoing the relief I felt. I put my mittens on Bobby's hands then, and I would have given him my fur-lined cloak as well, except the footmen came with the blankets and it was not necessary.

When we reached it, the hall seemed full of people, but the earl did not pause as he directed the men to carry Bobby up to his room, where the doctor was waiting. At that door, he barred my entrance.

"Go and take off your cloak, Lila," he said in a gentle voice. I was startled when he reached out and cradled my face between his big hands. They were oddly gentle. "There's a good girl. This is men's work now," he added, releasing me. "We have to undress him and put him to bed, and until the doctor has examined him, you will only be in the way. Trust me to come the instant I can tell you how he does."

I wanted to argue but I held my tongue. I did not go downstairs to join the others. Instead, I went to my room a little way along the corridor to wait with my door open so I might hear what was going on. Miss Spenser ordered a maid to bring more hot water, and I heard the doctor's soft voice answering the earl's questions. As I watched, more coal was brought for the fire, and additional stone water bottles. I wished there was something—anything!—I could do to help, and I said a fervent, garbled prayer of thanks for Bobby's safe delivery, along with a plea for his survival.

When Grant came to my room I had retreated to the fireplace so no one would see the tears that streamed down my face. I don't think I could have stopped those tears, or the deep sobs that wrenched my body in my relief, if I had tried. "Is he . . . will he be all right?" I asked as I held out my hands to him in supplication.

He did not answer right away. Instead he came and put his arms around me and held me close, resting his chin on the top of my head. I could hear his heart thudding in his chest, right beneath my ear, hear as well the deep rumble of his voice as he said, "The doctor assures me of his complete recovery, although there is some danger of frostbite which must be watched."

His voice sounded strange, and much as I hated to leave the security and warmth of his arms, I leaned back to study his face. I was released at once. He went back to the door as he said, "Robert was able to tell me very little before he fell asleep. You may sit with him. I am sure you are longing to do so. He will want to see you when he wakes. I'll arrange for some hot food to be sent up for you. Miss Spenser has already ordered some broth for Robert. It can be kept simmering on the hob until he needs it."

"I do not know how we are to thank you, m'lord," I said as I went to the door to hurry to my brother's side. The earl stepped back to give me passage. "Surely Bobby would have died if you had not thought of the shed . . ."

I thanked Dr. Ward and Miss Spenser, too, before they left me alone with Bobby. I bent over him where he lay in bed and kissed him, smoothing back the chestnut curls that tumbled on his forehead. He mumbled but slept on as I sat down beside him.

Byford came in the late afternoon to see how we did. Bobby had not wakened, but he slept more lightly now, moving often and making sounds I could not understand. While I was telling

Grant this, Bobby opened his eyes and looked around, as if he were confused. He smiled when he saw me, then gave a start when he noticed the earl close behind me.

"What . . . what is going on?" he asked. Before I could answer, he went on, "I remember now! The shed—last night—but how did I get up here in bed? Not that it's not grand to be warm again, you understand. I never thought to be warm again."

Grant went to the fireplace to fetch the broth. "Here, have some of this before you tell us what happened," he ordered. Meekly, Bobby obeyed, but he grimaced at the taste. "I think I'd rather have wine, sir, or a tot of brandy perhaps?"

"Dr. Ward says you are not to have spirits," the earl said. "Drink the broth."

I barely waited until he had done so before I said, "Why on earth were you out there in the shed, Bobby? Whatever could have possessed you to go out there, at night, alone?"

He flushed, and I do not think it was my inadvertent use of his childhood name that made him do so. "I know," he said sheepishly. "It was stupid of me, wasn't it? I—I had too much to drink last night, I was so happy at the way my interview with our great-aunt had gone. In fact I was pot-valiant and I couldn't resist the bait. I know now it was bait."

His voice was grim and I bit my lower lip.

"Why don't you tell us what happened, Robert?" the earl asked. "Start at the beginning."

He struggled to sit up and the earl piled some pillows behind his back before he pulled up a chair for himself. "You know, of course, I went to bed at the same time you all did," he began. "I even locked my door as you ordered me to do, Lila. But then I found a note on my pillow." He looked around, as if confused. "I foolishly took the note with me when I went out. It is in the pocket of the coat I was wearing."

"What did it say?" Byford asked.

"It said that if I wanted to find out who was bent on doing away with Lady Cecily's guests, I should go to the shed in the garden at midnight. It claimed I would find evidence there to uncover the culprit."

There was silence for a moment, then I said, "And you *believed* that?"

"I . . . why, yes I did, because I wasn't thinking clearly."

And because you wanted to cut a dash before the others and solve the mystery, I thought, but I did not say so.

"I put my greatcoat on, took my candle, and crept out of the castle just before midnight. When I reached the shed, the door was ajar. I called out, but no one answered. It was then I wished I had my pistol with me, but I had left it in London. I was sure someone was in that shed, and I stood well to one side to throw the door wider. But nothing happened, and I went in, determined to light my candle and see if there was any evidence to be found. I had no sooner put the candle down on the bench there when the door slammed shut behind me and I heard the bar that secures the door come crashing down. I called out, beat on the door, but of course nothing happened."

"What did you do next," Byford asked in the silence that followed.

"Oh, various things, sir. First I lit the candle with my pocket luminary. At least I had thought to bring *that*. Then I tried to burn the door down. The kindling I devised caught easily enough, but that door was oak, and thick. Besides, smoke filled the shed. So I dug a small hole beneath the door with a rusty nail I found. Some of the smoke escaped, but I did not try fire again."

I took his hand in mine and squeezed it. My throat was tight as I lived the story with him. How frightened he must have been! How lonely there, knowing it would be hours and hours before he was missed. I remembered how cold the shed had been, and I did not know how he had been able to survive it. As if he read my mind, he went on, "The candle burned down and went out a little later. I spent the night telling stories to myself, singing every hymn and ditty I could remember, and doing exercises—throwing my arms about, jumping up and down, that sort of thing."

He grinned a little. "I even made up some dandy couplets to

amuse my friends, not that I can remember a one of them now. Just as well, I guess. They were very rude."

I did not feel like smiling. Instead I shivered. What if I had had to go home and tell my mother and father Bobby had died in Scotland? Especially my mother. Bobby was her favorite. In her eyes he could do no wrong. I had never resented this for I knew my father loved me best.

"I was worried, and I admit it," he said next. "I thought the murderer might come back with a gun to make sure I died. As the night went on, and it got colder and colder, I realized he probably didn't think there was any need for it for I was going to freeze to death, just as he planned.

"That made me angry, I can tell you! I made up my mind I wouldn't die, and I fought harder and harder to stay awake, to keep moving. But I admit it got to be almost impossible. I was so sleepy, all I wanted to do was curl up in those gunny sacks and give in to my fatigue. I don't think I would have lasted much longer if you hadn't found me, sir, you and Lila. I must thank you for it, although mere thanks could never be enough when you saved my life."

Byford waved a careless hand and rose to search the pockets of Bobby's coats that had been thrown over a chair earlier. He found the note and read it, his mouth set tight.

"I do not know the handwriting of course. I suspect it is disguised," he said, tossing it to me. I took it reluctantly but after I read it, I could see how it had lured an impressionable twenty-one-year-old outside, especially one whose judgment had been impaired not only by the drink he had consumed, but by all the attention he had been receiving. It was then I felt a hatred I had never suspected myself to be capable of, begin to grow. Whoever had done this—this thing, would pay, I vowed silently. Oh yes, I would do everything I had to, to make sure of that.

Chapter Eleven

I did not go downstairs again that day. Instead, I remained with my brother and ate from trays brought up to us, and, I assume to Alastair. I wondered if anyone had told him about my brother's close call. During dinner, I mentioned him, and Bobby said, "He's the top of the trees, isn't he, Lila? I heard a story about him in town that I questioned at the time, but I don't anymore now I've met him, spent some time with him."

"What story?" I asked idly.

"It seems he and a crony were set upon one night when they were returning to Mayfair after a night spent drinking in a tavern near Seven Dials. There were two footpads, sure they had easy pickings with the gentlemen. Mr. Russell's companion fought with his fists, but not Russell! Oh, no, not he! He pulled a small pistol from an inner pocket and shot one of the men. The other broke off the engagement and ran away."

"Any man would have fired in those circumstances," I remarked.

"Yes, but would just any man have left the body there, not even calling for a night watchman? I heard Russell told his friend when he remonstrated with him, that he thought they had been put to enough trouble as it was, for surely it was not their responsibility to clean up the filth in the streets. Whew! Can't you just picture him saying it?"

Unfortunately I could, and it made me feel uneasy for some reason.

"I've been watching him a lot," Bobby went on. "And not just how he wears his clothes, either. Which is not to say I don't think him bang up to the nines . . ."

"Best you don't speak cant when you're home, er, Robert. Father won't like it," I reminded him.

He grinned at me before he continued, "Wish I could tie a cravat like he does. Wish I could be like him in other ways, too."

"I don't," I found myself saying, much to my astonishment. "If there is anyone here you should emulate, it's Lord Byford. In spite of his faults, he's a good man."

"Never said he wasn't," Robert said cheekily. I reminded him it had been Byford who had organized the search for him, found him, knew what to do to help him survive.

"Oh, Lord, I know all that, and mighty grateful I am, too. But Byford's no leader in society. No one studies his style, talks about him, oh, you know what I mean."

I changed the subject. I had no idea why I was singing the earl's praises, when the man had believed me a murderer. But it bothered me to hear my dear brother idolizing a man who only yesterday had mocked him so severely.

It was sometime after dinner when someone knocked on the door. I went close to it before I asked who was there, so as not to disturb my brother. When I heard the earl's deep voice, I unlocked it and let him in.

"He is sleeping again," I whispered, smiling at him. "He ate a good dinner."

We moved toward the window, where we could converse in normal tones. Bobby had been sleeping for some time, and during that time I had been thinking—hard. I had come to a decision as well, and now I took a deep breath and said, "I do not know how we may ever adequately thank you, m'lord, Robert and I. If you had not remembered the shed, he most certainly would have died." I was horrified to hear my voice shake as I spoke, and I could feel the tears gathering in my eyes. Not looking at him as I fought for composure, I continued, "Dr. Ward stopped by to see how Robert was doing, and he said it was a very near thing; another hour at the most . . . and if it had not been for you . . ."

"There is no need to thank me anymore," he interrupted. I wondered why he sounded almost angry as he went on, "Anyone would have done the same. I only remembered the shed because that was where I had the servants put Lady Cecily's dog after he was poisoned. I wanted the doctor to look at him."

He stopped and I could feel the tension between us and hurried to say, "I am so ashamed of myself! I began by suspecting *you,* and then, after you caught me in the most compromising position and behaved as anyone would, I was unable to forgive your actions. What must you think of me, m'lord?"

I turned to him, my hands outstretched in supplication. It had become important to me that I be returned to the earl's good graces. Very important.

To my surprise, he did not respond, nor did he take my hand. Instead he pulled me close in his arms and kissed me. I was startled at first by this unprecedented move and by the kiss itself. How can I describe it? It was unlike any kiss I had ever received. For Grant did not merely *kiss* me. Rather he showed me a man's hunger. His hands, too, caressed my back as if to learn every inch of it by touch. Oh, I am not making any of this clear! Let me say then that his kiss was passionate and urgent and at the same time warm and pleading, and it opened a world I had had no idea existed.

You may imagine then what a shock it was to me when he lifted his head to stare down at me and I discovered he was scowling. Not only scowling, but drawing away from me quickly.

"Grant?" I whispered. "What . . . what is it? Why do you look at me like that?"

He buried his face in his hands for a moment, then looked straight at me as he said, "No, Lila. It will not do. Not this way."

I saw he had clenched his hands into fists by his side, and I could hear his hurried breathing. I was speechless. For a moment there was only silence between us, then he added, "I must ask you to forgive me once again. What I just did was hardly the act of a gentleman, to take advantage of you while you were so distraught. No," he added, holding up his hand as if to keep me from interrupting. He need not have bothered. I was incapable of speech. "No, it was inexcusable. I pray you will be able to find it in your heart not only to forgive me, but to forget what has just occurred. On my honor, it will not happen again."

He bowed and went swiftly to the door while I stared after him. At that door he turned back, and I felt a surge of hope that he might return, tell me he hadn't meant a word of it. Instead, he only looked at me and added, "Be sure to lock the door after me. Good night."

It was a long time before I was able to do that, for I felt frozen in place. At last I returned to my post by Robert's bed and waited for my maid to relieve me. Polly had insisted on taking over the vigil at midnight so I could get some sleep. As if I will ever be able to sleep after what has happened, I thought, observing my brother's peaceful expression, his deep, even breathing. I envied him his oblivion.

But I still did not understand. Why had Grant said what he had after that wonderful embrace? Surely he had wanted to kiss me. I couldn't have been mistaken about the passion he showed me. Of course, I admitted, I knew very little about it for I had never been kissed that way before. Maybe it had meant nothing at all to him. Maybe he had been taking advantage of me. How could I know? I groaned when I remembered how I had put my arms around his neck, clung to him, returned his kiss so eagerly. Putting my hands to suddenly hot cheeks I wondered what he thought of me to be so wanton, so—so immodest.

That must be why he had stepped back and left me so quickly. I had given him a disgust of me. And no gentleman, I was sure, wanted a wife lacking in both self-control and decorum. Why, such an unfortunate could never be sure his wife might not take to tying her garter in public! I did not know how I was ever to face him again, and I wished I had never come to Grimshead, never met Lord Byford, all six feet four inches of

him, with his crisp dark hair and intent disturbing eyes, and the
wry way he had of smiling, and his strong hands, and . . .

I got up abruptly and took several turns around the room,
forcing myself to think of other things. The weather. The Season to come. How to make a poultice for a sore throat.

I was not successful.

When Polly finally scratched on the door, I was more composed, however, for I had decided the only thing I could do was
to take the earl's advice. If he asked me, I would say that of
course I had forgiven him, forgotten the incident as well, and I
would say it lightly, in an indifferent voice, as if the whole subject bored me immensely, so he would be instantly relieved.
And then I would avoid him as much as possible until I was
able to go home.

After a whispered consultation with Polly I marched off to
bed, my head high and my chin firm with resolve. It was a long
time before I slept, though, and I was horrified at the lateness
of the hour when Polly finally came to wake me the next morning.

"How is Robert?" I asked as she knelt to put on my slippers.

"Just fine, Miss Lila, just fine. Lord Byford sent his own
valet to tend to him, and Bobb—er, Mr. Douglas, told me to go
away so he could be shaved."

I heard her sniff, and I hid a smile. Polly had known Robert
since he was a small boy, and she still did not consider him very
grown-up. She would not take kindly to being ousted in favor
of a strange manservant.

"He *says*," she added, "that he will not stay in bed, and in-
sists on getting dressed. I told him he was to do no such thing
till the doctor had seen him and given his permission."

"Did he agree?" I asked idly as I sipped my chocolate.

"Of course he did," Polly said as she poked the fire. "I had
only to tell him I would not leave the room until I had his
promise. Men!"

By the time I had dressed and gone to my brother, Dr. Ward
had seen him. Robert was dressed and sitting in a chair by the

window, tucking into a large breakfast. He waved to me as Byford's valet bowed himself out.

"Come and join me, sister. There's plenty for both of us and
an extra place setting as well. And I wonder who saw to it that
we are served more than porridge and cold toast this morning?
Byford, I imagine, don't you? He is the most forceful fellow."

I kissed the top of his chestnut curls before I took the seat opposite. "I see I will have to make haste before you eat it all," I
said, ignoring his comment as I helped myself to eggs, some
fish, and a scone.

"I admit I'm ravenous. Perhaps there is something about almost freezing to death that increases the appetite. Some coffee?
Or do you prefer tea?"

"Coffee," I said absentmindedly, for I had suddenly remembered something. "Bobb—Robert, do you have any idea who
locked you in the shed? Did you see anything that might give
us a clue to the person's identity?"

He frowned. "Not a thing, worst luck. I had my back turned
to the door, for I was trying to light my candle, when it was
slammed shut. And the bar was dropped into place before I
could force the door open."

"Would it have been possible for a woman to do that?"

"Somehow I assumed it was a man, although I don't know
why. The bar is not heavy, though. Anyone could lift it, even
you or Cecilia or Sylvia."

"Thank you," I said dryly. "And of course we were all sepa-
rated, alone in our rooms and supposedly in bed. Once again, it
could have been anyone at Grimshead."

"Well, not the stablehands," he protested. "Can't see one of
them getting into the house and up the stairs to deliver a note.
Come to think of it, I'll wager not a one of them can even write
their names."

"Very well. We'll discard the stablehands," I agreed, before I
put down my fork, my breakfast forgotten. "I am so frightened,
Robert! This person, whoever it is, is very, very clever. And we
have no idea if he or she will try again, now that the first
scheme did not work."

"But no one has tried to shoot Alastair again," he reminded me, the freckles he loathed standing out against his suddenly pale face. I saw he had not considered he might still be in danger.

"No, but that is because he is kept in bed, locked in his room. He does not see anyone but the doctor, Miss Spenser, and his valet. Oh, and Byford, of course. And once he asked to see me. "Please, please, Bobby, don't go downstairs today. It is not safe! Oh, how I wish we had never come to Grimshead; no fortune is worth what we have been through."

"Very well, at least until luncheon," he told me before he sighed deeply. "Although what I am to do with myself till then, cooped up here, I've no idea."

I suggested a game of cards to pass the time. I knew it was useless to suggest a good book, or a morning spent writing letters, not where my brother was concerned.

I had lost an immense pile of fictional shillings when Polly knocked to tell us luncheon was being served and offering to see us safe to the dining room.

"I say, of course you won't," Robert announced. "The very idea!"

He was revolted and it showed in his voice, and it was left to me to soothe my maid and thank her for her help.

All the way down the stairs and across the mammoth hall, I worried. Not about the murderer, but about seeing Grant St. Williams again. I need not have worried. He ignored me completely.

Robert found himself in the pleasurable position of being the center of attention, lionized by everyone throughout the meal. He was begged to tell the story of his adventure himself, to Cecilia's exclamations of horror. When Robert paused for breath, Douglas-Moore remarked, "Stupid thing ter do, lad. Especially after everything that has happened here."

I saw Robert blushing as he agreed, and then he was forced to listen to Sylvia as she read him a lecture on prudence, patience, and perspicacity. He did not look as if he were taking her strictures to heart. Instead, he looked ready to explode, especially when she accused him of trying to steal a march on the rest of us so as to get into Lady Cecily's good graces by his daring and success, if he should solve the puzzle.

I almost spoke up then, in his defense, except Byford said in his deep, commanding voice, "That will be enough, ma'am. I think we all know it was nothing more than boyish bravado. Now, may I suggest we forget the whole thing? I begin to find these constant references to the incident not only repetitive, but boring. Surely we can talk of something else."

He sounded so blasé about Robert's near death he angered me, but my brother sent him a grateful smile.

As we were rising from the table, Crowell announced Lady Cecily wished us to come to her room. He added Alastair Russell was already there, for he had insisted on being present. One of the younger footmen and his valet had carried him down.

I saw Sylvia's face was thoughtful as she smoothed her gown and straightened her cap. I could tell she was thinking this a golden opportunity to undo any harm Roger might have committed when he had had his interview with his great-aunt, and I almost looked to Grant St. Williams to share a smile. Fortunately, Cecilia came to my side then and whispered, "Now what do you suppose she wants? I had so hoped I would not have to see her again until I went to bid her good-bye and thank her for her *gracious* hospitality."

Once again, we all followed Crowell's slow, measured footsteps along the hall to the drawing room. When we had been announced, and had stepped into that overly warm, crowded room, we saw that in addition to Alastair, reclining on a chaise, Dr. Ward and Miss Spenser were also present. The latter was in her usual position, close to her mistress. Lady Cecily stood before the fireplace, leaning on her silver-headed cane and watching us all carefully as we filed in. Her expression was unreadable, but Dr. Ward was frowning and Miss Spenser was all but wringing her hands in her distress. As for Alastair, he wore a cynical little smile. I wondered what about the situation he found amusing?

Lady Cecily did not speak to welcome us. Instead, she pointed a bejeweled hand to the chairs we had used before, and we took our seats.

"Dear Lila," Alastair called to me, his beautiful green eyes sparkling with mischief, "do come and sit beside me. It seems an age since our last delightful visit together."

I had no choice but to obey. As I took my seat, I asked how he did, all the time very much aware of Byford, leaning against the table nearby as he had done the first evening we had assembled here.

"Come, sit down," Lady Cecily commanded. "I am gratified by your prompt attendance, dear relatives. I would not have seen you all together again, except there is something we must discuss. Dr. Ward thinks I should summon the law to join our little party, after what happened to young Douglas there."

She paused, and then with an expression of grave concern on her face, she asked how Robert did. I flinched, wishing she did not show her partiality so plainly. Just look what had happened the last time she had favored him!

Robert told her he was in top form and none the worse for his adventure, and she nodded.

"But next time . . . who can say what might happen?" she said, turning her attention to the rest of us again. "This person, who has so far shown himself to be inept, is gaining experience and might easily have improved his or her skills to the point there will be a successful conclusion on the next attempt."

Cecilia whimpered, and Lady Cecily nodded to her as she made her way to her large wing chair, as if she were suddenly too tired to stand any longer. Miss Spenser hovered over her until she was told, in no uncertain terms, to make herself scarce. I saw the poor woman flush and steal a glance at the doctor before she retreated behind Lady Cecily's chair.

"Yes, you are right to be afraid in this instance, Cecilia," our hostess continued. "All of you should be frightened."

"I rather think I must beg to be excused from such paltry behavior, m'lady," Alastair drawled. As everyone's eyes turned to him, he drew his right hand from beneath the light blanket that covered him to show the company the dueling pistol he was holding. "It is loaded, of course," he went on in an ordinary, chatty way. "It never leaves my hand except when I am safely locked in my room." As he spoke, he waved the pistol to and fro gently.

"Put that away before there's an accident, man," Douglas-Moore said harshly.

"If I fire my weapon, it won't be by accident, and I am an excellent shot." Alastair's voice was cold as ice and full of menace and I shivered. "I find I take exception to being shot at; why, the whole experience has made me quite cross. And when I think of the irreparable damage done to my new coat, fresh from Stulz's hands, I can only say that that alone would be enough for me not to hesitate if I felt I was being threatened again."

Chapter Twelve

"That will be quite enough, Alastair," Lady Cecily said loudly in the silence that followed the gentleman's speech. "I quite agree with your preventive measures, but enough.

"Now, as I see it, there are only four people in this room who could not be the one so intent on doing away with the others: Alastair Russell, Robert Douglas, Dr. Ward, and myself. Everyone else is suspect, yes, each and every one of you."

Her keen eyes under their bushy brows swept over us. "Is it Grant St. Williams? Cecilia Worthington or Lila Douglas? Mr. Douglas-Moore? Or could it be Tweedledum or Tweedledee?"

I almost spoke up, but I chanced to glance at Byford to see him shaking his head almost imperceptibly. For some reason he did not want me to mention how the gun I had found had disappeared when we were together, thereby exonerating us both. I settled back in my chair, bending my head meekly, although I wondered why I was so quick to agree to his wishes, every time he expressed one.

"I must point out to you, m'lady, that neither Roger nor I can be considered a suspect," Sylvia said pleasantly but firmly, as if she were going along with some irrational fancy of the old lady. "You forget, dear ma'am, that I was supposed to be the first victim."

She sat back smiling in triumph, but that triumph was short-lived. "Not necessarily so," Lady Cecily retorted. "You could have poisoned the comfit yourself, to draw off suspicion. You did not taste it, after all, but let it drop where Exacalibur could find it. As for Lord Danvers, there have been many husbands who did away with their wives, some of them with even less provocation than he has had to bear, poor man."

Sylvia turned an angry purple, and she gasped. Roger leaned toward her, whispering in a perfectly audible voice that Sylvia was not to listen to such awful talk; why, he adored his dearest, sweetest wife, 'pon his word he did, and to say otherwise was to lie. Sylvia waved away his expressions of devotion, to take out her salts and a handkerchief. I saw Robert and Cecilia exchanging glances, and remembered how they had made Roger Danvers their first choice. How long ago that seemed!

I wondered why Sylvia had suddenly recovered her good spirits until she caught my eye and tapped her brow. Then I realized she was not at all vanquished by this setback, for such remarks from an elderly, sick woman only reinforced her notions that Lady Cecily was senile, and therefore incapable of writing a valid will.

Beside me, I heard Alastair say in an undertone meant for my ears alone, "Do you know, if this were not so terribly dangerous, I would have to admit I have not been so diverted in years. Sylvia Danvers is quite the stupidest, and the most transparent woman, is she not? Besides being so repulsive and grasping."

I did not nod. I couldn't. It had suddenly occurred to me that I not only didn't love Alastair Russell anymore, I barely liked him. He had insulted everyone in the house party at one time or another. I wondered what he had had to say about me, for I was not so naive as to imagine I had escaped his vitriol. It was too bad. He was quite the most handsome man I had ever seen, and the most beautifully dressed, and he was witty and intelligent. But he had no heart, no empathy. I myself disliked Sylvia Danvers, but I would never have scalded her to another.

"My lady, if I might speak?" Dr. Ward said as he came forward a little from where he had been standing apart from the family. "I must repeat what I said to you this morning. You would be wise to summon the justice to Grimshead. The roads are open to riders; he could be here tomorrow afternoon. And as you yourself said earlier, this person has only to succeed once for there to be a tragedy."

"No," Lady Cecily said, banging her cane on the floor for emphasis. "There will be no minions of the law at Grimshead, prowling around and cutting up all my peace. Why, the scandal of it . . . here! My father would be furious. The Douglas family has never had anything to do with the law. We've always settled problems ourselves, and I'll not be the first one to do otherwise."

"But what if there is murder done?" the doctor pressed her. "Then you would have no choice. And surely you cannot wish any of your relatives to die?"

Lady Cecily opened her mouth to reply and then closed it as her eyes darted around the assembled company.

"I quite agree, ma'am," Alastair said. "So much better *not* to say what you had in mind, eh?"

She laughed, that belly-deep chuckle of hers. "I like you, Alastair," she said. "You are no better than you should be, and probably a great deal worse, but at least you are honest. Very well, for the sake of peace, I will hold my tongue. But to return to the subject we were discussing, let us put our heads together and think hard. Perhaps we may discover the identity of this mysterious would-be murderer.

"Oh, do keep that pistol handy, Alastair," she added.

Grant St. Williams spoke for the first time. "Can we assume it is not one of the servants, at least for now, and leave them out of our deliberations?"

"Indeed," Lady Cecily agreed. "There's not a one of them who would have any good reason. They've been with me for years. I can vouch for them.

"Spenser, sit down at my desk and write what I tell you. Hurry up, woman," she ordered as her companion went to do her bidding. "You're as slow as an old horse on the way to the knackers. Don't know why I put up with you.

"Make two columns. In the first put the following names: Alastair Russell, Robert Douglas, and my own. In the other column, list Grant St. Williams, Cecilia Worthington, Delilah

Douglas, Roger and Sylvia Danvers, and Mr. Douglas-Moore."
She waited impatiently until the scratching of the pen stilled.

"Now, write this down: poisoned comfit and Lady Danvers,
Alastair Russell's shooting, and the locking of Robert Douglas
in the garden shed."

She turned to us then and said, "I want you all to think! Who
had the opportunity, the wits, and the nerve to commit all these
things?"

"Perhaps it would be wise if we could decide first *why* they
were done," Byford suggested. When Lady Cecily nodded and
motioned him to continue, he said, "I have no idea who poisoned the comfit. Somehow it does not seem to be a part of the
whole. You will remember, ma'am, that both Alastair and
Robert were attacked shortly after their visits to you. They both
of them made a great deal about how much you seemed to like
them; Robert from innocence and Alastair from a love of malice. You will pardon my analysis of your character, coz," he
added, bowing to a completely unconcerned and amused Mr.
Russell. "It has occurred to me that the murderer wanted to do
away with them because they were clearly your favorites as
heirs to your fortune. But as Lila pointed out to me, why kill
Sylvia Danvers? She only inherits through her husband, not directly. Why not, therefore, kill him instead?"

"I think you're right and that mishap has nothing to do with
the others," Alastair remarked in the silence that followed his
cousin's commentary. "Or it might have been as Lady Danvers
has maintained. The dog got into some poison on his walk that
Miss Spenser did not notice, and there was no poison in the
comfit at all."

"How could that be?" Douglas-Moore asked. "No one puts
down rat poison on frozen ground. And it's a sure bet the dog
dinna get into the shed by itself."

Alastair raised one white hand. "Stay! There is another solu-
tion. Did *you* poison the dog, Miss Spenser?

The woman gasped and dropped her quill. Her face turned
ashen, and the doctor went to her aid as her mouth worked helplessly and she began to cry.

"I . . . I . . . of course not," she finally got out. "What . . . what a terrible thing to suggest."

"But, Miss Spenser," Dr. Ward said as he patted her hand, "you must be calm. It is entirely reasonable that out of the kindness of your heart, you felt the animal had suffered long enough. You have heard me so many times suggesting to Lady Cecily she have the dog put down. It was obvious it was in almost constant pain."

"Oh, no, I couldn't . . . Lady Cecily has always been most adamant about it, Doctor," she whispered. "You know she would never permit it."

"And you, of course, always did everything she wanted, is that right?" Alastair persisted.

"She had better," Lady Cecily snapped. "If she knows what's good for her!"

"You are all forgetting the poison could have been put out by a former servant, or a small boy bent on mischief," the doctor said. "Lady Cecily does have her enemies—er, I mean . . ."

"No need to soften your words for me, sir," the lady retorted. "I've never courted popularity, any more than my father did in his day. I am a Douglas. Take me or leave me, I care not."

"Shall we move on?" the earl suggested mildly. "Perhaps we should forget the poisoned comfit for now, since it clearly does not fit with what happened to Robert and Alastair."

"But what about the eye in the library?" Cecilia spoke up, overcoming her fear of her great-aunt at last. "You are all forgetting that, not that I ever will. It was so horrible!" She shuddered, and Lady Cecily leaned forward, grasping her cane.

"What is this foolishness, miss? An eye? In the library? Whatever are you talking about?"

I was stunned. I could tell by Grant's expression, he was as well. Was it possible the lady had not been told about someone using the priest hole to spy on the guests? Somehow I had thought that Grant, or Miss Spenser, or someone, would have mentioned it. Now as Cecilia, aided by Robert, related the incident, Lady Cecily stared at them in amazement.

"I do not understand," she said finally. "If you were all, each and every one of you, in the library at the time, who could it have been?"

"Naturally we assumed it was you yourself, ma'am," Alastair told her. "And what would be more natural, after all, when you were trying to make up your mind about your heir. We have it from Crowell himself there is an entrance to the priest hole right here in your room. How revealing it would be for you to hear us talking when we did not know you would be listening. Sort of thing I would do myself and perfectly understandable, I assure you. You must not think we mind."

"How very kind of you, sir," Lady Cecily said. "Perhaps I might have spied on you if it had occurred to me, but I did not."

"You did not?" Sylvia asked, her tone incredulous. Quickly Roger said, "There now, of course she did not. The lady's notions of propriety are much too nice. She is just teasing us. Told you all along it had to be a servant; sort of thing they get up to y'know, spying on their betters."

"But why?" the earl asked.

"I should rather think they see too much of their betters, in their opinion anyway," Alastair drawled. "You know how we are always ringing for them."

"Perhaps it was someone who does not have all his wits," Roger persisted, pleased to be able to show his great-aunt he had an intelligent grasp of the situation. "Sort of thing someone who doesn't have much in his cockloft might find amusin'."

"I do not employ idiots," Lady Cecily said icily.

Roger quickly retreated, saying he had not meant, of course he understood, he knew she would never, and other sentiments of like nature, until his wife pulled on his sleeve and in a fierce aside, told him to be quiet for he was just making things worse.

"Never mind that," their hostess said. "Does it really matter who it was? I see no thread between a spy hole and the attempted murders, but I say to you, all this must stop. I never meant such things to happen when I summoned you all here, indeed, I would not have done so if I had known that one of you wanted my fortune so badly that you would kill to get it."

"If only it were that easy," Grant St. Williams remarked.

"But let us admit it is unlikely to happen, just because you give an order, m'lady. After all, one does not order a murderer to reform and expect obedience. No, ma'am, not even for you."

Lady Cecily nodded, looking thoughtful.

"What I suggest," the earl went on, "is that we all be constantly on our guard. That no one goes anywhere alone, that we all meet at specified times and remain together either in the library or the dining room or the hall. That there be no wandering off alone to investigate"—and here I swear his eyes briefly met mine before he continued—"and that as soon as the roads are passable, we leave Grimshead. I know you planned for us to wriggle on the end of your pin awhile longer, ma'am, but you must see it will not do, not now. In this situation."

"Of course you are right, sir," she said. "I beg you, Doctor, to remain with us. I have a regard for your wisdom. Perhaps you and I can solve this mystery."

Matthew Ward nodded his graying head, but he did not seem at all pleased with the prospect of an extended stay, or the lady's compliment.

"And there is also the fact you will be on hand if there should be any further, ah, mishaps," Alastair added. "Allow me to beg the pleasure of your company as well, sir. You may believe I have seldom been more sincere."

I looked around. Everyone was busy with their own thoughts and it was obvious Lady Cecily was tired. She had slumped a little in her chair, and one hand shaded her eyes. I looked to the doctor and nodded in her direction, and he rose at once.

"Come, m'lady," he said. "As your doctor, I insist you rest now, and that the others withdraw. This has been upsetting for you, and it has tired you."

For once the old lady did not protest. "Yes, I am tired," she muttered, and then said, in a stronger voice, "Spenser! Bring me the paper you have been writing. I would study it later."

As we left the drawing room, I heard her criticizing Miss Spenser's handwriting, and I did pity that poor lady. I wondered how she was able to remain Lady Cecily's companion when she was so constantly abused and belittled. Surely it must be a miserable life she led. But I was not allowed the pleasure of my own thoughts for long, for Cecilia began to whisper to me as we moved to the library, and I had to put the unfortunate Miss Spenser from my mind. To think that even her misfortunes were preferable to Cecilia's confidences showed the problem I now had to face. How on earth was I going to be able to stand being confined with everyone for most of the days and evenings, I wondered as I went to the window seat and the book I had left there, hoping Cecilia would take the hint. But even as I thought these things, I knew neither Cecilia's idiotic chatter nor Sylvia's instructive sermonizing was the real reason I felt slightly ill. No, it was because I was going to be confined with Grant St. Williams. And how was I to bear being in the same room with him, after what had happened between us?

Chapter Thirteen

~~~~~

As it happened, I was able to escape that fate, for after only a few minutes it occurred to me there was no reason I could not go for a ride. And even if the horse had to walk through the snow, at least I would be outside, free of all these tiresome relatives. Only a moment's reflection told me I could not ask Robert to join me. He should not be exposed to the cold weather so soon, not after his recent ordeal. But I could certainly take my groom, and no one, not even Grant St. Williams, could argue with that. Henry would be armed as well, for I knew my father had insisted on it for the journey north. And no doubt he would welcome the activity for he had been as confined here as I had been. I did not bother to wonder if Lady Cecily had a horse suitable for a lady, and a sidesaddle. I left the window seat and went to ring the bell. Everyone stared at me, including the earl as I announced I intended to go to my room. I saw Robert begin to rise, Cecilia, too, and I said quickly, "There is no need to bestir yourselves, my dears. Surely there is nothing to fear since everyone is in this room. If Lady Cecily is right, that is."

"And if she is not?" the earl asked, frowning.

"Crowell's escort will suffice, m'lord," I said politely, not quite meeting his eye. "I am only going upstairs."

He could say no more, and feeling triumphant, I made my escape. As we went upstairs, I asked Crowell to send my maid to me, then ask my groom to saddle horses and meet me at the front door as soon as possible. By the time Polly arrived, I had laid out the habit I had brought with me but had not had an opportunity to wear as yet, and was down on my knees dragging out my riding boots from the back of the cupboard.

"Now then, Miss Lila, and what do you think you're doing?" Polly demanded, arms akimbo. I had not suspected the servants would already know of the decision that had been made to stay together.

"It will be all right. Trust me," I said as I stood up to present my back so she could unbutton my gown. She complied out of habit as I went on, "I simply cannot stay in that library with everyone all afternoon or I shall go mad. I must get away, have some fresh air. I'll be all right with Henry. He'll be armed, of course."

"You're supposed to stay with the others. Never mind how annoying they are. That's the safest way."

"Is it? I don't think so. And just consider sitting with a would-be murderer all afternoon. Would you like that?

"Come, Polly, surely I'd be safer away from Grimshead. There's nothing to fear outside but the cold, and we did bring my winter habit. I'll even wear the heavy woolen stockings and the quilted shift."

"You'll not go without the warm chemisette as well," Polly decreed as my gown puddled at my feet.

I smiled to myself then, knowing I had won her over.

As soon as I was dressed, right down to my plumed riding hat and crop and gloves, I told Polly my plan. "You will come downstairs with me," I said. "After I've left, you are to wait at least fifteen minutes before you go to the library and tell everyone I have gone riding. That way there will be no concern about my whereabouts as there was the last time I went out. Since I don't know which way we will be riding, you won't be able to tell them the route. It will be perfect."

I saw her eyes were troubled and I bent and kissed her cheek.

It was very quiet when we left my room together. The corridor was dark and empty. I held my fingers to my lips so Polly would not talk when I recalled Alastair was back in his room. I prayed he would not send his valet on an errand. As we went down the stairs I could see there was no one below in the hall. Even Crowell had deserted his post. Still I held my breath until the hall had been safely negotiated. I eased the door open as carefully as I could, frowning at the noise it made, and I shooed Polly back upstairs before I ran down the shallow steps to where Henry waited for me, a huge grin on his homely face.

"At least you're not trying to stop me," I told him as he cupped his hands so I could mount. As he tossed me up, he said, "Wouldn't do a bit o' good if I tried, Miss Lila. I know that."

"You have your pistols?" I asked as I settled myself in the ancient sidesaddle provided and arranged the skirt of my habit.

He nodded, and I inspected my mount. It was not a horse my father would have kept in his stables, but it looked sturdy, and with all the snow, a sturdy horse did not seem amiss. Henry had not fared so well. His horse was swaybacked and elderly.

"Were these the best horses Lady Cecily's stable boasted?" I asked as we set off at a walk down the drive. I was very conscious of a certain library window as we did so, for that window had a clear view of the drive. Pray no one was peering from it, as bored as I had been!

"No one here's been ridin' for years, miss," he said as we avoided a drift. "This old hunter now, well, he was a fine chap at one time, weren't you, sir? But he's past it now, and tired. I hope you weren't planning no long ride, Miss Lila."

I reassured him. "And my horse?" I asked, concentrating as the animal stumbled.

"That there's the horse Mr. Robert hired when he left the stage. There's nothing else in the stables but a couple of workhorses and Lord Byford's team and his mount. You should see them, Miss Lila! Prime goers they be, and matched as well. As for his mount, well . . ."

I stopped listening. I could tell from the admiration in Henry's voice it would be some time before he finished extolling the earl's cattle. Instead, I took a deep breath. The sun was shining and for once there was no bitter wind. As we reached the gatehouse, I pulled up. "Do you know what lies in that direction?" I asked as I pointed to the road that went north.

"I hear there's a fishin' village not too far away. It even has a small inn. Mebbe not good enough for a lady though."

"I don't care for an inn," I said as we set off again. "I just want to enjoy the scenery."

The main road we traveled was still impassable for coaches, but several riders had come this way before us, and there was a passage of sorts. Certainly we could not gallop or even canter, but we were able to trot and only occasionally did we have to walk the horses through deep drifts. We passed a few stone crofts, crouched near the road. I knew they were inhabited from the trampled snow around them and the dark stain of manure and wood ash near the sheds, as well as the smoke that issued from their chimneys. We were not completely alone here in this frozen white world we rode through, although there was no denying Scotland was a lonely place.

At last we came to a small village at the bottom of a low hill. The road had led downward for some distance and now I saw why. The village was set right beside the shore. There were none of the cliffs and ledges of which Grimshead boasted, only a broad beach of sand and stones.

"Help me dismount, Henry," I ordered as we pulled up before the largest building in the village. A faded sign before it proclaimed it the inn he had mentioned, but I decided I would rather explore the beach. There were a few fishing boats there, pulled well up on the shore, and quite an expanse of sand, bare of snow below the tideline.

"See to the horses, then get yourself a hot drink," I said, handing him some coins. "I'm going for a walk."

I didn't wait for him to argue with me. Instead I set off for the beach. It was hard going, and I was awkward in my heavy boots until I reached firm sand. As I strolled along, I admired the waves, so gentle today in the sunlight. The breakers were almost mute as they fell over and ran up the beach. I smiled. It was so good to be alone, and the air was so fresh and tangy.

Above me a few gulls hovered before they gave up hoping I would throw them a tidbit and flew off down the beach.

As I walked, I wondered at how relaxed I felt, how easy. I had not realized how stressful being confined to Grimshead with the others had been, especially since there was no denying one of them was a would-be murderer. To be always on guard—to be constantly watching and listening closely on the off chance that person might give him or herself away, to be eternally assessing, gauging, *questioning* every word, every gesture, every look. No wonder all of our nerves were on edge, our tempers stretched thin.

But *who* could it be? Not I, of course; nor Robert, Alastair, or Byford. And I did not think any of the servants were involved. They would have no reason to kill strangers in the house. It was hard to think it could be any of the others either. Surely Cecilia was not just pretending to be a shrinking, fearful girl. I did not consider her capable of playing such a part so expertly. The Danvers wanted the inheritance enough, at least Sylvia did, but they would have had to be acting in concert, and Roger, as my brother would say, didn't have enough in his brainbox to be convincing. That left Mr. Douglas-Moore. I sighed. He had motive enough I supposed, and I could understand how he must dislike us all, poor bastard that he was. I felt a pang of regret. It had to be him, I supposed, but I could wish it otherwise. I found I rather liked Mr. Douglas-Moore. At least he was honest. As far as I knew.

Finally I began to feel an edge of cold and I turned reluctantly to head back. You may imagine my astonishment when I saw, still some distance away, the Earl of Byford galloping toward me. He did not look at all pleased and I braced myself.

"Just what do you think you're doing, miss?" he asked as soon as he had reached me and dismounted. He towered over me, and uneasy, I eyed the crop he carried.

"I was riding. Now I am walking," I explained in my kindest, most reasonable voice. "Not that what I do is any of your affair, sir," I added.

"If you remember, it was decided we should all stay together," he snapped. "But what must you do but ignore that agreement. Take it upon yourself to go off alone and . . ."

"I was not alone. I was accompanied by my groom. My armed groom."

"I see no groom, armed or otherwise. Besides, you lied to me. You said you were only going upstairs."

"Well, and so I did. First."

Suddenly I was angry. Angry at this confrontation, his persistence. No, not angry, *furious*. What gave this man the right to question me? This man who had held me and kissed me and then walked away from me? All the pain of being discarded, all the worry, all the aggravations and fear I had been subjected to since arriving at Grimshead came into thundering focus.

"Now see here, m'lord," I began, and that was the last nice thing I had to say. I then proceeded to give him a piece of my mind I was quite sure he would never forget. I poured out my distaste for Grimshead in particular and Scotland in general, the loathing I felt for the situation I found myself in and the company of the cousins who surrounded me, up to and including him. I told him he was meddling in something that was none of his concern, making him a busybody of the lowest sort, and I informed him I would do exactly what I pleased, when I pleased, and how I pleased. I then discussed at some length the failings of men in general. Their arrogance, their omnipotence, their habit of ordering one about—I even mentioned their untidiness, their liking for drink and snuff and cigars, their loud voices and disgusting language, and their unfortunate habit of spitting whenever they felt like it.

At that moment I am sure I could have instructed Wellington on the disposal of his troops and artillery and how best to set up a battle line, or advised King George on the selection of the next prime minister. Certainly I would have had no trouble pointing out to the Regent the error of his profligate ways and sybaritic existence, and if any of those gentlemen had been present, I would have done so in a minute.

To my surprise, the earl did not interrupt me. Instead, he stood holding his horse's bridle, facing out to sea. He had such a rugged face it was impossible for me to see how he was taking my lecture since I had only his profile to go on. But just as I began to wind down, I noticed a slight quiver at the corner of his mouth and it inflamed me once again. Was he *laughing* at me? Did he *dare*?

I marched up to him and planted myself firmly before him, to stare at him.

"You *are* laughing at me. You *are*!" I accused him.

"I beg your pardon," he managed to get out before he gave up the struggle and began to howl. Great bursts of deep laughter rang out, frightening some sandpipers scavenging the seaweed nearby, and they took flight. I wanted to hit him. No, I *longed* to hit him but I managed to control myself by telling myself that even if he could not be considered a gentleman, I, at least, was a lady.

"I am so glad you find me amusing, m'lord, even if that was not my intent," I snapped as I set off for the village, moving as quickly as I could. Alas, it is impossible to hurry in sand, even firm sand. Besides, he caught up with me easily, he had such a long stride.

"No, I am sorry, truly I am," he said. He sounded contrite and I stole a glance at him. He wasn't laughing anymore. Why did I feel he still wanted to?

"It does not matter to me how you feel," I told him, staring straight ahead now. The village seemed miles away. What on earth were we to discuss all the time it would take us to reach it?

"It matters to me how *you* feel, however," he said. I had no idea what he meant by that statement and decided to ignore it.

"Cousin . . . no, Lila . . . can't we . . . no, I guess we can't," he ended ruefully, answering himself. "Still, perhaps we could pretend civility, at least until we reach Grimshead again. What do you say?"

I hesitated. I wanted to walk on, refuse to talk to him, even acknowledge him, but I saw that for the futile move it would be. Besides, it would make me look ridiculous and somehow it was important I not look ridiculous before the Earl of Byford.

When I nodded, he said, "You are warm enough?"

"Quite warm, thank you," I replied.

"It is a fine day, is it not? I wonder what this part of the world would look like under a summer sun."

"I have been enjoying the briny air. We are nowhere near the sea at home."

"And where is your home? Ah, I remember, in Oxfordshire, is it not . . ."

The conversation continued in the same stilted way and I was almost in despair until he said, "Tell me, did you ever have the chance to find out what Roger and Sylvia did that first afternoon they arrived?"

"Why, yes, I did ask my maid. It seems they did exactly what we did; walk around the ground floor inspecting all the rooms."

"That doesn't tell us anything, does it? Perhaps Roger poisoned that comfit after all."

"I have been wondering about everyone," I said. "I cannot imagine killing someone for a fortune, but obviously there is one among us who can. Have you any idea how everyone is fixed? I should tell you my brother is constantly in debt, outrunning his allowance to my father's despair. I, of course, live at home."

"Roger is well-to-do. I suspect his wife is one of those people who can never have enough. As for Alastair, I have no idea. He lives luxuriously in London and appears to have a horn of plenty somewhere. He was an only child."

"At first, I thought you two did not get along. Sometimes you looked at him as if you were wondering what kind of man he was—oh, I am not saying it right."

"No, I understand. It is true the only thing we have in common is that we are related. We never seek each other out. I do not approve of the life he lives. It seems so silly to think the cut of your coat is a matter of prime importance. Of course, that is only my opinion." He sounded stiff and cold, and I wondered at it. "Perhaps Douglas-Moore is in need of money," I contributed when the silence between us stretched too long.

"He has been very reticent every time I've tried to question

him about his family, his life in Edinburgh. As for Cecilia Worthington, her mother has let it slip to some of London's prime
gossips, that her dowry is substantial. I do wonder about that,
and suspect it to be no more than adequate. There's no need for
concern, however. The girl's so pretty she'll make a famous
match, just you wait and see."

I felt suddenly like a sack of old potatoes, lumpy and ugly
and utilitarian and it was a moment before I could change the
subject and say, "Oh, how I wish we were gone from here. I
have been so frightened, so apprehensive. I am apprehensive
still about my brother. Did you notice him last evening when he
joined us for dinner? He enjoyed being the center of attention,
but he still stared at everyone in turn. There was something in
his face that was not there before, a stillness, as if he had
erected a wall between him and the rest of us . . ."

"He is becoming a man. What happened to him is forcing
him to grow up sooner than he would normally."

"I *hate* Grimshead. It is well named. *Grim*—brrr!"

"Some great-great-great-grandfather Douglas would not approve of those sentiments. He built the castle after he returned
from exile in England, and he was proud of it."

"Why exile?"

"It was self-imposed. Douglas is a fine old Scottish name,
and many a one of them has fought for the bonnie Prince and
all the others before him who not only wanted Scotland for
their own, but the English throne as well. But that James or
Robert—I am not sure which name came first for him—saw the
writing on the wall early last century and moved his family to
London to make his fortune, the same fortune we dispute today.
The old man did not return until Scotland was firmly under England's foot. It was a good thing he lived in the borders. Farther
north he would have died a traitor's death."

"He does not sound at all honorable," I remarked, suddenly
wishing the village was still a distance away. Behind us,
Grant's horse neighed as if he agreed with me.

"He was unprincipled. A pirate, if you like."

"Does Lady Cecily know this? She is so proud of her name."

"I am sure she does. But she has twisted the facts to make them glorify the past, rather than denounce it. And you must admit, she has a touch of pirate herself. You have seen how much she enjoys making us all squirm."

We had reached the village again. Surely we had behaved well, both of us. Quite like ordinary people in fact. But even so, I had always been conscious of him beside me, tall and dark and strong, and always, always there had been a thin silver thread of memory woven through the conversation, the memory of an embrace and a man's hunger. And my own.

Without asking, he lifted me to sit sideways on his horse so I would not have to struggle through the snow to reach the road. The horse behaved like a perfect gentleman, and, a little breathlessly, I told the earl so. He looked up at me then and grimaced before he said, "Would you agree I have been one as well, Lila? But perhaps it's just as well you can have no idea what it has cost me."

As soon as we reached the inn, a young man came running with my horse and I looked around for Henry.

"I sent him back," the earl said. "I told him I would see to your safe return."

I swallowed my retort. The man was high-handed. Nothing I could say would change that.

"I wish I could offer you Hal for the ride home," he went on. "Unfortunately he has no sidesaddle and I am unable to use yours." He studied it for a moment before he said, "It must have been Lady Sylvia's, it's so ancient."

I smiled as he transferred me to my own mount, trying to ignore the feel of his hands on my waist, hands I was aware of right through my heavy habit and even my woolen chemisette. "I am sure your Hal would object," I said when I saw the horse nudge his shoulder affectionately. "I wish I had some sugar for him. He is so beautiful."

"Yes, and good and true and full of heart, which is a great deal more important. In people, as well as in horses, don't you agree?"

There was something in that statement that unsettled me, and I only nodded.

The ride back to Grimshead was uneventful. We said little more, I, because I was depressed my afternoon of freedom was coming to an end, and he, because he seemed to be thinking hard about something.

At the castle door, he offered to take my horse to the stable if I could dismount by myself. I slid down and handed him the reins, then hesitated for I did not know what to say in farewell.

"Take care, Lila," he told me. "Don't let down your guard for a moment."

Crowell let me in and once again escorted me to my room. As he did so, he told me he was sure there was going to be a thaw on the morrow. When I smiled and said I sincerely hoped that would be the case, he added, "Nae more than I will, lass, I can tell ye that," and it was all I could do not to laugh. I could just imagine how eagerly he was looking forward to seeing us all gone so he could return to the quiet, uneventful somnolence he had enjoyed before. We had caused the old man no end of trouble.

I was about to enter my room when I saw Alastair's valet standing a few feet away, and I paused.

"My master wonders if you would have a moment for him, Miss Douglas," the man said in a monotone. He was such a retiring man, so slight and deferential, and so intent on Alastair's well-being, it was easy to forget he was even around.

I nodded, and followed him along the corridor. I wished I might have denied him, for I wanted to bathe and change, perhaps even wash my hair if Polly could wrest enough hot water from the kitchen. Still, as little liking as I had for Alastair now, I remembered he had been wounded, and it must be terribly boring, cooped up alone all day. The least I could do was look in on him.

"I understand you ran away this afternoon, coz," he said after we had exchanged greetings. "And our perfect knight went charging after you. How glad I am he has brought you back."

"I hesitate to say how wonderful it was to be out in the fresh air, not when you are still tied to your bed, coz," I said as I took a seat beside him. "Tell me, are you any better? Out of pain?"

He waved an impatient hand. "Thank you, but I prefer not to discuss it. It's tedious, even to me. Instead, tell me of your ride, what you saw, and what you and the ethical earl talked about. Hold nothing back! You owe me some amusement."

"I set off with my groom—armed, of course—fifteen minutes before my maid was to tell the rest of my departure. I wanted some margin of safety. We went north. The countryside was empty, with only a few stone crofts to show it was inhabited. Eventually we arrived at a small fishing village, and I took a walk on the beach. There was no wind. It was not too cold."

"And it was there Grant found you?" he asked. "I'm sure he rang a peal over your head, did he not?"

I felt uncomfortable under his clear green eyes, but I nodded. "You might well say that. He was *not* pleased with me. I'm afraid I rather lost my temper and returned the favor. However, we did manage some degree of civility on our return walk." Since I knew he was about to press me again for our conversation, I added, "We discussed the family, the first Douglas who made the fortune that built Grimshead, and of course our stay here, and the unfortunate things that have been happening."

"Did he make love to you?"

"I beg your pardon?" I asked, astounded by his question.

"He's in love with you, any fool can see that," Alastair retorted, twisting on his pillows as if he were uncomfortable.

His valet materialized from somewhere behind me, to help him sit up and rearrange his pillows more comfortably. I felt flustered knowing the man had heard Alastair's last remark, and I must have shown it, for Alastair said as he settled back with a sigh, "Pay no attention to King. He never repeats things he should not. He is devoted to me. Aren't you, King?"

Before I could wonder at the edge in his voice, he went on, "Oh, yes, I've known Grant loves you for some time now, and I am rarely mistaken in such matters."

"But you are mistaken now," I managed to say. "And if you don't change the subject, I warn you I will go away."

My throat was tight and I had trouble swallowing. I knew far better than Alastair that the earl was not in love with me. I was, after all, only ordinary-looking, and I was much too tall for a woman. And although I knew my figure was excellent and there was that perfect skin my mother kept extolling, those things were not enough to make an experienced man of the world fall in love. Besides, if he had been, he would not have been able to walk away from me as he had, beg my pardon so calmly, assure me he would never kiss me, hold me, again. Nor would he have been able to discuss the Douglas family and all those other innocuous things he had today, as if I were a mere acquaintance.

Alastair questioned me about the household then. He wanted to know how everyone was behaving, what had been said, and what inferred. "It is so unfortunate I must remain in bed like this," he said at last, looking petulant. A lock of his golden hair fell over his forehead and with his lower lip thrust out, he looked like a small boy. I marveled I felt nothing for him except an amused regard, I who had thought once I could die happy, if he would only notice me.

I remained with him for a few minutes longer. Then, claiming I needed to change, I excused myself. As the door closed behind me, I heard Alastair begin berating his valet, and as I picked up my skirts and scurried to the safety of my own room, I did not envy little Mr. King one bit. I forgot him, however, for I was intent on reaching the safety of my room, with a locked door between me and the other guests. I leaned back against that door and tried to still my hurried breathing, closing my eyes as I realized that once again I was an unwilling captive here at Grimshead, with a resident murderer who might well turn his attention to me next. I shivered.

Chapter Fourteen

The evening seemed endless. I did not go down and join the others until the bell for dinner rang, for I knew what I was in for. Sylvia barely waited for the first course to be served before she began to lecture me on my inappropriate disappearance. She seemed especially incensed by my deceit; my pretending I was only going to my room when I had been planning my escape the entire time. I did not know who was worse; Sylvia with her scolding, or Roger with his prosy lectures whenever she paused for breath. And then there was Cecilia, who sighed so piteously whenever she looked my way, and who toyed with her dinner as if my desertion had completely broken her. Even Robert fired off a salvo or two, but I knew he was angry only because I had gone without him. At the end of the table, the earl sat eating his dinner, his sole contribution signaling Crowell to refill everyone's wineglass. Finally, Mr. Douglas-Moore put down his knife and fork with a clatter, and said, "Oh, gie over, all o' ye! If you could hear yourselves, you wouldn't wonder why the lass was sae eager to get away from yer nattering. Worse than a flock o' jackdaws, ye be."

Sylvia gasped that the bastard Douglas-Moore would dare to take her to task. She was so indignant with him, and with her husband as well for neglecting to take the man to task, she remained dumb for the rest of the evening. I could only applaud.

Later, in the library, holding a book I was not troubling to read, I thought again of the situation here. All the threads that made up the fabric of pleasant relationships were wearing very thin indeed. Grimshead itself added to the problem. Cold, in-hospitable, confining, *unwelcoming,* it seemed to enclose us like a pall. I looked around the room. Was everyone wondering, as I was, what would happen next? Was everyone bracing themselves for another disaster? Did Cecy there, drooping over her needlework on the sofa, fear she would be the next victim? I am sure she had come to the conclusion that the things she read in books that made her shudder with delicious terror, were nowhere near as tantalizing when they were real. And the Dan-vers, seated close together intent on an old account book they were studying, were even they considering an early departure before Lady Cecily named her heir? Were they afraid? Had they decided that even gold was not worth putting yourself in peril for?

My brother caught my eye. He was sitting at the card table with Byford, and he had been looking around the company just as I had been doing, while the earl shuffled the deck. Robert's face seemed harder to me, thinner. There was no trace of his devil-may-care attitude now. I remembered Grant had told me he was growing up, becoming a man. Only the earl, sitting there with the pack of cards, was unchanged, but then he had always been enigmatic. And Mr. Douglas-Moore, returned from the front steps smelling of cold salty air and cigar smoke, seemed at ease, too. He told us it was much warmer and I remembered Crowell had predicted a thaw, and prayed it would be so. It was time to leave Grimshead, more than time. And yet . . . and yet . . . I wondered why I could not seem to forget what Alas-tair had said this afternoon, no matter how I tried.

I was early to breakfast the next morning. When Polly left me at the door of the dining room, Crowell was just setting the usual crock of porridge on the sideboard. There was no one be-fore me. It was a beautiful day, and warmer, just as the butler had predicted. The sun streamed through the windows and I could hear the dripping of melting snow even this early. I ate quickly and did not linger over coffee, for I hoped to avoid meeting anyone, especially the earl. As I was leaving, Crowell appeared to tell me Lady Cecily would be glad to have a word with me.

Intrigued, I followed him to her room, where he handed me over to Miss Spenser. I wondered if anyone else visiting was beginning to feel, as I was, like a parcel being delivered here and there.

I found my great-aunt and Dr. Ward having breakfast and I envied them the shirred eggs and sirloin and poached fish, the muffins still hot from the oven, and the strawberry jam. I could not help resenting it as well. It was shameless of Lady Cecily to treat us so shabbily while she ate so well. After all, we were her guests. Where were her manners?

"So, it is to be Miss Douglas. Come in and join us," my delinquent hostess said as she took another muffin. "Spenser, another cup."

As her companion went to a cupboard, I said, "But surely you asked to see me, didn't you, ma'am?"

She chuckled. She seemed in excellent spirits this morning and I wondered why. "I had no idea who would come in. I merely asked Crowell to bring me the first person down to breakfast. I wanted someone, anyone, to listen to my conversation with the doctor, even if that person was the culprit. But I will require you to voice your opinions, miss, correct any misapprehensions, put forward your own views—that sort of thing. And you must promise me, on your sacred honor, that you will not repeat what we say, or the conclusions we may reach, to anyone else. Are we agreed on that?"

She did not wait for me to speak. Instead, she turned to her companion and said, "Pour Miss Douglas some coffee and then take yourself off. I shall not require you this morning."

I saw Miss Spenser look quickly at Matthew Ward, as if begging him to intervene. The doctor did not notice for he was busy finishing his breakfast. I thought again how unfortunate the poor woman was, dressed in her drab black gown with her hair pulled back in the awful bun. It was so tight, it made my scalp ache in sympathy. And those thick glasses that enlarged her pale eyes so much. She hesitated for a moment, all but wringing her hands in her distress, before she sighed and left the room. Neither her mistress nor the doctor noticed she had gone.

Lady Cecily put her plate to one side and smoothed out the paper where Miss Spenser had written down what she had dictated. She stared at it for a minute before she said, "I wanted to ask you in particular, sir, if you have any suspicions as to who might be the culprit here. If it is Miss Douglas, you may tell me later, of course. I ask you because you came late on the scene, and as a stranger, might have seen something the rest of the family has missed."

"I wish I could help, ma'am, but no obvious name leaps to mind. And yet I cannot help but suspect Mr. Douglas-Moore. He never says very much, but I have noticed how carefully he watches the others, smirking as he does so, as if he knew something they did not."

Lady Cecily waved a dismissing hand. "Probably he is just uncomfortable to be here amongst the legitimate Douglases. I am sure he has been treated badly by some of them during his stay as well. I know Alastair Russell has not been able to resist twitting him, and no doubt Sylvia Danvers has put him in his place times without number, horrible woman that she is."

"It cannot be easy for him, knowing he is a bastard through no fault of his own. But if he is discarded as a culprit, who else could it be?" the doctor asked. "Surely not Cecilia Worthington. She is so shy and young and she is so frightened of you, ma'am, from what you have told me. That leaves only m'lord Byford and Miss Douglas. I do beg your pardon, miss," he added, turning toward me and smiling a little. "I must consider all the guests, to be fair. Please do not be offended."

I smiled in return, thinking what a nice man Matthew Ward was. He had such a pleasant personality, such a warm regard for others, you almost forgot his rumpled jacket and darned cravat.

"How could she be offended?" Lady Cecilia demanded. "She knows she is suspect here. She is an intelligent gel." She turned to me then and said, "And I must say, miss, I think you would be capable of harming others, if you set your mind to it. Oh, yes, you could do it as easily as I could myself. Neither of us are weaklings."

I was startled, but she went on, "I do not think you did so, however, any more than your brother could have. Only the threat of harm to one you loved could turn you to murder. Certainly gold would not do the trick. Besides, I like you and surely I could not misjudge your character so completely."

"That leaves only the earl," the doctor reminded her. "No, I am wrong. There is Lord and Lady Danvers."

"It is not Roger Danvers we have to fear. He hasn't the wits for it, nor the stomach. But wouldn't it be satisfying if his gentle wife were the one?" Lady Cecily smiled in delight. Still she shook her head at last. "Unfortunately I cannot picture her firing at Alastair or luring Robert to the garden shed. She is greedy enough for the inheritance to try anything, but unless she and her husband are in it jointly, it is just not possible. They have adjoining rooms, how could he not know of any heinous activity she might be up to? Besides, Roger Danvers is the most boring, idiotic man I have ever met. He is so stupid that even if his wife were the culprit, and with his connivance, he would not be able to keep the secret. No, not the Danvers, either one of them, more's the pity.

"I will tell you both, my favorite suspect as villain is Alastair Russell. At least it was until he was shot. I consider him quite capable of destroying his fellow men—and women—if he stood to gain by it. Now, however, he is off the list."

She sounded so regretful the doctor and I were careful not to look at each other, lest we laugh.

"That leaves only the earl," the doctor reminded her.

"Yes, another one who has the will and heart to kill, if necessary. But why would he do such a thing? He doesn't need the money, he is rich. In fact, I had my man in London look into his finances. Of course, he may have fallen on hard times, as I suspect Russell has. I'm not worried about either of them—they'll come about. These young rakes are all alike, wasting their substance on women and gambling and living high."

I wanted to protest it was *not* Byford, that he was not the sort of man she described, but I held my tongue. What did I know of him, when all was said and done? He might be only a heartbeat away from debtors' prison in Newgate for all I could tell.

"You have been very quiet, Delilah. Have you no opinions?"

"I am afraid I am as much in the dark as everyone else. Like Dr. Ward, I think Mr. Douglas-Moore the most likely. But even that is hard for me to accept. I have begun to like him. He is a good, steady sort, the kind of man you turn to instinctively when you need help."

"He would be happy to hear you say so." Lady Cecily smiled at me before she turned to the window beside her and appeared to forget us as she lifted her face to the sun. Her eyes closed as she relished the warmth. I am sure I don't know why she needed it. As usual, her room was overheated by a huge blaze in the fireplace.

"If you will excuse me, m'lady. I must dress Mr. Russell's wound," the doctor said as he rose from the table.

"I'll leave you to rest as well," I told her.

"Ring that bell for Spenser, will you, sir?" she said. Turning to me, she added, "I hear you left the castle yesterday. Rode off to Grimshead village with no one but your groom for company."

She chuckled again. "But someone came after you, isn't that so, miss? Well, it's true Byford is a great catch, but I advise you to wait until the culprit is identified before you go setting your cap for him. Ah, you blush. No need for that. Here, come and give me a kiss, there's a good girl."

Miss Spenser had run in and I was embarrassed before her and the doctor as I bent to kiss my great-aunt. She kissed me in return and I was glad to make my escape.

I found my brother and Cecilia dressed for the outdoors when I entered the hall. Robert bade me fetch my cloak and come with them for a walk. I was only too glad to do so, and avoid not only the Danvers, but more importantly, Grant St. Williams.

The air was much warmer, and the snow was melting rapidly

when we stepped outside. All the stablehands, guests as well as residents, were out. Some were busy tackling the drifts and the paths, while one drove a heavy sledge pulled by Lady Cecily's old workhorses back and forth to flatten the snow and make the drive passable. It looked as if we would be able to leave soon after all.

We went first around the castle to the front, for Robert insisted Cecilia must see the ledges and breakers. I could tell she was frightened by them, and the height, but she pretended she was not. So as not to incur Robert's dislike, I wondered idly? I almost enjoyed the sight today. The day was so fine the view was stunning for we could see for miles. Far off I spotted a sail and wondered where the ship was headed. Below us, the waves moved in leisurely and broke over the ledges, the foam tossed up sparkling with brilliant lights. In contrast to the dark, almost navy color in the distance, those breakers were the tender green of spring leaves.

As we turned to go back, Robert looked up to where Grimshead loomed over us. "You know, it's not a bad old place," he mused. "If it were mine, I'd see to restoring it. It would make a fine retreat, when London grew tiresome. And the hunting and trout fishing are superb in Scotland."

"What?" I asked, pretending horror. "You would live here? Heaven forbid!"

"No, Lila, just imagine, if you please," he began, in his enthusiasm grasping my arm and pointing to the bedroom floor. "It would be an easy matter to put balconies up there, so guests could admire the view in the summer. And the ground floor could be improved with larger windows and some doors opening to a terrace running the length of the front. And if the gardens were brought back, it would be a showplace. There is no need for it to stay a castle for defense. The Vikings are no more, and Napoleon is not going to try and take it. What for? And you know, you could sail north from London, leaving the ship in Newcastle. That's no more than two days' journey from here."

He grinned. "Of course I'd have to be named heir to do all this, and I don't depend on that."

Cecilia brightened. "Who do you think Great-Aunt will choose, coz?" she asked. She looked so tempting in her sky blue cloak and the fur hood that framed her pretty face, those big blue eyes and soft lips, I felt alarmed. Robert deserved better than a pretty widgeon.

"No doubt in my mind it will be Byford," he said. "He's older, and a lot more sensible than I am, and that's sure to influence her choice."

"But she liked you so well, remember?" Cecilia protested. "And you are so much handsomer than the earl."

Robert looked over her head and grinned at me as I raised my eyes heavenward. "I really don't think she'll choose her heir for his—or her—looks, Cecy," he said.

"Well, she won't choose Roger Danvers, I know that," she said pertly. "And surely she wouldn't pick Mr. Douglas-Moore."

"No, because he's a bastard," Robert agreed, using the word she could not bring herself to say. "She's too proud of her name and her father."

"What about Alastair Russell," I said. "He's handsome, too, Cecy."

"Yes, but there's something about him, isn't there?" she said, a frown wrinkling her perfect forehead. "I don't know. He makes me feel uneasy somehow, and it's not just that I know he despises me and makes fun of me whenever he can."

I was startled by her intuition. Robert had lost interest in the conversation and was busy making a snowball.

"Shall we walk down the drive?" I suggested as we reached the gardens again. I did not want my brother reminded of his ordeal in the shed. But I credited him with a sensibility he did not possess, for before we did so, he insisted on taking Cecilia there so she might see where he had endured a long, cold night. She was suitably horrified, and made so much of his fortitude and courage, I wished I might go off by myself. I am sure Cecy wished I would, too, but I resigned myself to acting as chaperon, adjusting my steps to Cecy's dawdling ones as we made our way to the drive.

We saw the men had made great strides. We could hear them ahead of us although they were out of sight of the castle.

"We'll be able to leave in a day or so at the rate the snow is melting," Robert said. "If it doesn't come on to storm again, that is."

"I wish we could leave this ghastly place tomorrow," Cecy said. Then she looked over her shoulder as if Grimshead itself might be listening. "I would rather stay in a hedge tavern than here, I swear I would."

"Do you know, I tend to agree with you, still, it would be unfortunate to leave before we knew who had been doing all these things," I remarked. "If we did, that person would get away with it, and that would be too bad."

Cecilia stared at me as if I had gone mad and even Robert looked a question as he made another snowball and threw it at a nearby tree. As it hit squarely and splattered, I continued, "I do not think I will ever be able to forget. Alastair's shooting, of course, but especially the way you were left to die, bro. No, I want to know who was responsible for that, and make sure they pay for it."

"How fierce you are, Lila," he said.

I smiled at him as I made a snowball myself. "I happen to love you, you silly thing, that's why," I told him, sending my own snowball after his. I missed the tree and he crowed. Before long we were all engaged in a wild contest. To my surprise, Cecilia was as good as my brother, and since it made her forget the cold we were able to go all the way to the gatehouse. We found the men there, finishing the snow removal, the two old workhorses snorting and stamping their feet, the breath from their nostrils white plumes in the cold air.

Robert went off to have a word with John Coachman and Cecilia sighed. "He is so nice, your brother," she said softly. "I do like him."

I smiled but I had no reply. When Robert came back and announced he had decided to travel south with us, I felt a stab of alarm. Robert was only turned twenty-one. It was too soon for him to choose his life's partner. And when he did, I hoped it would not be a silly little girl like Cecilia Worthington, sweet and docile as she was.

After a luncheon that was even more ill-conceived than those we had become used to, I decided to spend the afternoon reading and writing letters in my room. As I went to the stairs, Grant caught up with me and offered to escort me there. I could hardly refuse, not with the rest of the family staring at us, but still I seemed to hear Alastair's voice telling me Grant loved me and I was not at all comfortable. Which, of course, was why he had told me, I reminded myself.

"I understand you were closeted with the grande dame this morning," he said as we started up the stairs.

"How does everyone know everything that goes on in this place?" I said. "How is it possible?"

"I asked. Where you were. When I came down to breakfast. Why did she call you in? What did you talk about?"

"I can't say. She swore me to secrecy," I replied, trying not to feel too elated that he had sought me out. "The doctor was there, too. And let me tell you, they were both finishing a breakfast the likes of which I have not seen since I left Oxfordshire. Shirred eggs, and the beef looked marvelous. And those warm muffins. Mmmmm."

"We are served bad meals, aren't we? They are well cooked, but there is so little selection, such small portions."

"I am so sick of porridge, I never intend to eat it again," I declared. He chuckled as we reached the top of the flight and turned left toward my room.

"Have you had any further thoughts about the mystery, Lila?"

"No, not a one. But I do hope I do not have to leave Grimshead before we discover the culprit. I said as much to my brother and Cecilia this morning and they both looked as if I were mad. But I must find out who locked Robert in that shed and left him there to freeze to death. Whoever did that is going to pay."

"You sound quite fierce. Remind me never to annoy you."

"You have annoyed me more than once, but you don't seem to have suffered for it," I was horrified to hear myself saying.

He stopped and turned me to face him in the dim corridor. For a moment, he stared down into my face, as if he were searching for something. I stared back, wondering why I found his rugged face so appealing. His hands tightened on my arms and I am sure I did not imagine he bent closer. I wondered if he were going to kiss me again and waited in avid anticipation. But I never found out what he had been going to do, for just then Alastair's valet came along the corridor followed by two maids carrying copper cans of hot water. We moved aside.

"Alastair must be feeling better if he has called for a bath," Grant remarked in the silence that fell between us. "I suppose I had better go and help King. He is too small to lift our cousin by himself."

"How is Alastair's wound?" I thought to ask as we reached my door. "I forgot to ask the doctor this morning."

"Healing nicely, from what I can tell. He must be careful of any strenuous exercise lest he open it, but with Alastair there is little to worry about on that account. He is famous for not exerting himself. Not that I mean to criticize him to you, of course," he added, frowning now.

"You should not frown," I told him, reaching up to smooth it away. "It makes you look quite ferocious."

He grasped that hand and turned his head so he could kiss the palm. One of the maids scurried by us, eyes averted, and I stepped away and opened my door. I wished everyone in Grimshead were elsewhere, that we were alone, that I dared to ask him . . .

Ask him what? Ah, that was the problem, I thought bleakly as he bowed to me, his face masked now. "Be careful, Lila," he said in a husky voice. "I have the feeling things may be coming to a head very shortly. You might be in danger. Be very careful."

Chapter Fifteen

I found I could not concentrate on a book that afternoon, and the letters I tried to write were so far from my usual garrulous style I discarded them all after reading them over.

Every so often I turned the hand the earl had kissed over so I could stare at the palm, as if hoping it could give me the answer I sought. Sometimes I swear I could still feel his lips there, warm and somehow possessive, almost as if he were setting his seal on me. And then I wondered why, if he were in love with me as Alastair had claimed, and now in the light of his words and actions I must consider at least a possibility, he did not tell me so. He had had plenty of opportunities—why, yesterday we had been alone together for almost two hours. But he had only spoken of Grimshead's history then. Why?

Because you attacked him like a Billingsgate fishwife, I reminded myself with a grimace. I could still hear myself going on and on. And had I really mentioned the way men *spit*? I asked myself as I squirmed in my chair. It creaked alarmingly as if to agree I had been ungenteel, unladylike, and downright gauche. Grant St. Williams could not love me, his two kisses notwithstanding. He was a man of the world, well traveled, educated, suave. No doubt he had his choice of beautiful sophisticated women to marry. Why would he choose me, so plain and undistinguished, so ordinary? So *tall*? Why, to just consider the children we might have together was ludicrous. They would be giants. Not that height in a man was a bad thing, of course, but girls of that size would be miserable. To say nothing of impossible to fire off.

It was then I began to laugh at myself. Here I was, not only visualizing a marriage to Byford, but one endowed with several children as well, each taller than the last. Was anything so ridiculous, I wondered, and a mental picture of all those gigantic maidens leaning pensively from a castle's windows in search of a husband had me laughing out loud.

I felt better then. Not happy, you understand, but at least more at ease with myself and the situation, and when the dinner bell rang I was able to go downstairs with a serene mind. My maid did not have to escort me, for Cecilia scratched on the door so we could go down together. I told Polly not to wait up for me, as was my habit. It had always seemed so silly to me to keep her up merely to undress me. Polly worked hard enough.

"I have been thinking," Cecilia announced as we went off down the corridor arm in arm. Nobly, I did not comment. "Do tell me if you agree with me, coz. What good does it do for us all to remain in pairs or be trailed by our maids? If this mad person decided to harm us, that would not stop him, isn't that so?"

I thought for a moment as we reached the stairs. "No, I suppose not," I said. "But the list of suspects grows smaller and smaller. If we take Alastair and Robert away, as we must, there are only five of us left. And to shoot at a pair of us would mean it had to be one of the three remaining unaccounted for. Oh, this is a complicated way to put it, but do you see what I mean? He—or she, don't forget—might just as well confess."

We both hesitated at the foot of the stairs, searching the shadows in the corners of the huge hall for any sign that things were not as they should be. It was depressing to realize how this had become a habit without any conscious thought of doing it.

"Yes, I suppose so," Cecy said slowly. "How tiresome as well as scary this whole business is."

I was amazed, not only at her ease in discussing such a thing but at how petulant she sounded. Then I realized because it had not touched her directly, it did not seem real to her. The eye she had seen in the library, yes, that had been horrible for her. Alastair's wounding, even Robert's narrow escape were less so.

Robert held her chair for her in the dining room. Beside his, I noted. I found myself next to Douglas-Moore at the end of the table where the earl sat at the head.

Conversation was general, and with the change in the weather, a good deal more cheerful. Roger Danvers especially seemed buoyed by it as he discussed possible routes south, the unpredictability of job horses, and the continuing thaw.

"There's a heavy fog rolling in," Douglas-Moore announced when Roger paused for breath at last. "Ye'll nae be traveling in that, sir."

"It may disperse at dawn," he said to us all, for he never addressed Douglas-Moore directly.

"I wonder when Lady Cecily will finally name her heir," Sylvia remarked as she scraped her plate to get the last bit of sauce. The noise her fork made grated and I looked up to see Byford smiling at me. It was as if he knew what I was thinking and agreed with me, that yes, she was a maddening woman. Quickly I said a fervent, silent prayer he could not generally read my mind.

After we left the gentlemen, Sylvia led Cecilia and me to chairs near the inadequate fire in the hall. She took the one that allowed her a clear view of Lady Cecily's doors and proceeded to stare at them, frowning. The only time she roused herself was to intercept one of the footmen passing by and order him to bring us more coal.

As he went off, she said, "Fool! I had heard the Scots were miserly, but I see no reason we should have to suffer for it. It's not as if any of us will remain here much longer."

"Are you planning to leave tomorrow?" Cecilia asked.

"No, not until we know who inherits, no matter what Roger says. But if nothing has been announced by noon tomorrow, I have told him he must beg an interview with the old lady and insist she do so."

I could not see Roger Danvers insisting on anything where Lady Cecily was concerned, but I did not say so. Since Sylvia turned her attention to the doors again, and Cecilia dreamily watched the fire, I was thoroughly bored by the time the gentlemen joined us.

Cecilia became quite animated then and I felt that little stab of alarm. I was almost sure she was setting her cap for Robert, although she did flirt with Byford as well. I told myself she could not help it. Flirting had obviously been part of her education.

Once again we all took up our candles at ten, with the exception of Douglas-Moore, who headed for the front door, cigar in hand. As he opened that door the fog poured in, damp and briny, a thick, impenetrable gray curtain. I was glad to say good night and hurry up to my room.

To my surprise, after I had lit other candles, I discovered a cup and saucer set on my dressing table. The cup was covered with one of my handkerchiefs, and when I removed it, I saw it held eggnog, fragrant with cinnamon and nutmeg. I have a weakness for eggnog. I have adored it since I was a little girl, something Polly was well aware of. At home she would often bring me a cup if I were ill, or even feeling low. I decided to save the treat until I was ready for bed, and hurried to undress and get into my nightrail. Washed, and with my hair brushed, I took the cup to my nightstand and climbed into bed. I was glad to get under the covers. The fire was already dying down and the room was growing cold. There was no wind tonight. The draperies hung perfectly straight and still, and the breakers were barely audible.

I settled back on my pillows and picked up the cup to take a sip. It was creamy and delicious and I smiled. How kind of Polly, I thought. I must be sure to thank her for—

Be very careful, Lila. Careful . . . careful . . . I seemed to hear those words echoing in my head. Horrified, I stared down at the cup. I did not know for sure that Polly had made it for me, I realized as I set it down. It might have been anyone in the castle, even the one intent on harming us all. After all, poison had been used before. Rat poison. I felt the bile rising in my throat and threw back the covers to race to the dressing room. After I had vomited, I rinsed my mouth over and over to be sure there was no trace of poison left. Only then did I make my way back to bed, holding an aching, but hopefully empty stomach.

My feet felt like ice and cold all over, I curled up into the smallest ball I could manage. I was almost afraid to go to sleep, afraid I might never wake again. Then I told myself I was in no danger. I had had only a small sip of the eggnog. Most of it remained in the cup. Surely that little sip could not hurt me, especially since it was gone now, along with my dinner.

I wondered if I should ring for Polly, question her. But I hated to wake her and perhaps cause a stir. Some time had passed now and I still felt normal. Surely it could wait till morning.

I did not sleep at all.

Polly came promptly with a steaming cup of hot chocolate when I rang the next morning. I was so glad to be alive to see her smiling, homely face I could not have stopped the tears that ran down my cheeks if I tried.

"Here now, Miss Lila, whatever is the matter?" she asked, sitting down on the bed beside me to take me in her arms and rock me as if I were still a baby.

Wiping my eyes, I explained the drink, and what had happened.

"No, I didn't make you an eggnog, dearie," she whispered wide-eyed when I had finished.

Horrified, we stared at each other. Then Polly got up, saying, "I'm going down and tell that Lady Cecily what's happened and then we are going to pack and leave here. I'll tell Bobby, too. Insist he come with us. This is too dangerous to . . ."

She was almost at the door when I called for her to stop. "No, Polly, don't tell a soul what's happened," I ordered, thinking fast. "Instead, go and fetch Lord Byford. Make sure his valet does not hear you when you explain. The fewer people who know of this, the better. Then maybe, just maybe, we can use what has happened to find out the villain at last."

I saw she was about to protest, but I shooed her away. "Go quickly," I said. "There is no time to waste."

While she was gone I got up and washed my face. When I looked in the glass I saw I was pale and heavy-eyed from lack of sleep. Plainer, too. And then I scolded myself for worrying about my appearance at a time like this.

I had barely climbed back into bed before Byford strode in, followed by a worried Polly. I could see it had just dawned on her that she had brought a man to my bedchamber, and she was regretting it. But when I looked at him, I forgot her. He was clad only in a pair of breeches and an open-necked shirt, and he had not been shaved. I saw he had a heavy beard, and if I had not known him, that and his dark frown would have frightened me.

"How much did you drink?" he demanded, looming over me, hands on hips.

"Only a small sip. Then I realized how dangerous it might be."

He snorted. "If you had any sense, you wouldn't have drunk it at all," he retorted. "And why didn't you call your maid then? Get me? Fool! Don't you understand you might have died last night?"

I was indignant and not far from tears again. I had expected sympathy, not a scolding. I wondered why Polly was smiling now. Smiling broadly, too.

"I didn't wake her because there was no need for it. I vomited it right up, along with my dinner," I said with as much dignity as I could muster. Really, how much more unattractive could I make myself, I wondered, describing all the horrid details.

"But to be alone all night, worrying about it," he persisted. "You should not have had to bear that by yourself."

He turned then and ordered Polly to build up the fire and as she did so, he paced the room, deep in thought. Covers pulled to my chin, I watched him. At last he came back to the bed and sat down beside me to take my hand. "If your maid had nothing to do with this eggnog, we can assume it was made by someone else for the express purpose of disposing of you. But why? Why would you suddenly attract their attention?"

I thought back over recent events. "Because Lady Cecily called me in to see her yesterday morning?" I suggested. "No other relative has been summoned twice. Of course, Dr. Ward was with us. We were not alone."

"Let us consider this eggnog," he said, staring at the thin china cup that sat on my nightstand still. An unattractive skim had formed on the surface of the drink. It did not look appetizing now.

"It puzzles me that someone could make it in a busy kitchen where they could be seen by any of the maids, or the cook—even a footman or the butler. In my experience, the kitchens are the busiest part of any house, the place where the servants congregate for a cup of tea, or a gossip. Isn't that so, er, Polly?"

"Yes, m'lord, generally, but not in this place," she said as she rose from the grate dusting off her hands. Small orange flames began to lick the coals. I looked forward to the warmth that was coming.

"See, there's a servants' parlor just beyond the kitchen. It's where we eat and all. Mrs. MacKay, she's the cook, sir, doesn't encourage people in her kitchen except for her helpers. And after dinner is over, she goes to her room. We sit around the fire in the parlor. There's even a separate corridor to get to the front rooms and the back stairs, so there's no need for anyone to traipse through the kitchen. Anyone could have been there making the eggnog and no one would have known it."

"Even a guest, I suppose, if they knew the routine," Byford mused.

I remembered Roger Danvers remarking how disgraceful it was how he had to keep running back to the servants' quarters to get anyone's attention. But Roger? Why would he poison me? I felt my stomach lurch and I groaned.

That got the earl's attention. "I shall fetch the doctor at once," he said. As he began to rise, I grabbed his sleeve. "No, don't do that. I'm all right, truly I am. But isn't there some way we can use what has happened to catch the culprit? Someone must be waiting to hear some very bad news this morning. Perhaps we should not disappoint them?"

Byford stared at me as he sat back down. "Now what are you thinking, Lila? What is going on in that devious head of yours?" he asked. We looked at each other for a moment, then he said, "Let's see. How would it be if we give out that you are very ill? That no one is to see you but your brother and the doctor? I'll see to it Robert holds his tongue, and I have found Ward to be discreet. We might even let it be known you might not recover."

"How will that help find the poisoner, sir?" Polly asked, coming to the other side of the bed to put her hand on my shoulder. It felt good there. I was comforted by her support.

"Someone might let something slip—a word, a facial expression. At the least, it will keep everyone out of here while we investigate further, and it will give Lila the chance to rest. Tell me, at what time did the cook leave the kitchen last night?"

"A little past nine it would have been. She always stays to be sure the washing up is done proper. A holy terror, that Mrs. MacKay. Likes things her way, she does."

"And we all went up to bed shortly after ten," he mused. "Whoever did this must have nipped into the kitchen smartly if Lila found the eggnog waiting for her. I think we can assume this was not done by a servant. Dislike us they may, they wouldn't kill any of us, certainly not Lila."

Polly nodded, and feeling neglected, I spoke up. "What I find confusing is how someone could have known how fond I am of eggnog. It is my favorite drink. Polly often makes it for me at home. That's why I tasted it. I was sure she had brought it for me."

"There's no mystery about that, Miss Lila," she said, looking upset now. "Yesterday, or was it the day before, we were all sitting in the parlor talking and the subject of particular things our mistresses or masters like came up. I . . ."

"Who started that discussion? Do you remember?"

"Why no, no, I don't."

"Go on, then."

"I happened to mention eggnogs. Oh, I wish I had not said anything!" she cried.

"How could you know it would be used for evil?" the earl asked. His matter-of-fact voice had Polly wiping her eyes. "Who was there at the time?"

"Let me see. Annie Deems, your man Mr. Buttles, and Mr. King. Was Miss Harley there? I can't remember. She's maid to Lady Danvers, poor thing. Then there was Gladys, the parlor maid, and Mrs. McKay. She was having a sitdown waiting for her pies to be done."

"Oh, I am so hungry," I said. "Even a bowl of porridge would taste good to me now."

"Sorry. You'll have to wait until we can smuggle some food up to you," Byford told me. "We can't have anyone wondering why you are eating when you are supposedly so ill. Polly, when you take down the slop jar, announce that Miss Lila has been vomiting, and she is feverish. Say I've summoned the doctor, but no one else will be permitted in the room, in case what she has is contagious. The poisoner will know that's not true, but it is something we might worry about. Oh, and empty this cup before you take it down to be washed. Let whoever it is think she drank it all and they must have misjudged the dose."

On her way to the dressing room, Polly turned. Her cheeks sported two red spots as she said, "You don't intend to stay here, do you, sir? Mrs. Douglas would be horrified, and so am I."

To my surprise, Byford grinned, his smile white in the dark stubble on his face. "Don't worry, Polly," he said. "I'm off to fetch the doctor. I won't come back until later, when I'm more presentable, and you are here, on guard. You have my word on it."

Chapter Sixteen

I spent a long day. The doctor arrived shortly after the earl left me. He had few questions. Byford must have told him of the situation. After a brief examination with Polly beside me, he told me I had had a lucky escape.

"There's no need to fear further sickness," he said as he closed his bag. "Since you have not been ill again, you must have purged it from your system. Stay in bed today, rest, and eat lightly"—here I almost groaned for I was still without so much as a cup of tea—"and drink a lot of water."

I thanked him for his good advice even as I wondered why Miss Spenser was not with him. But perhaps she considered my maid sufficient assistance?

After the doctor left, Polly regaled me with everything that was happening below stairs. "That Mrs. MacKay was that upset you got sick after eating her dinner," she said. "Slammed her pots and pans around something fierce, she did. It wasn't until Buttles spoke up and said you probably caught something from your trip to Grimshead village that she got over it."

She smoothed my covers before she continued, "Miss Cecilia is that cast down, she's had to take to her bed herself." She sniffed in derision. "Like that Annie of hers, she does like to be the center of attention, and now you've stolen a march on her."

"She could have had this one with my blessing," I said, listening to my stomach rumble. "Did anyone else say anything? Look peculiar?"

"No, can't say they did. Everyone was talking about it, except Mr. King. 'Course he never does, much. Very high in the instep is Mr. King. Can't say I blame him, valet to one of London's highest. The work that man does, now that Mr. Russell is tied to his bed after the shooting—whew! Running, running, running, I swear."

Robert arrived then, full of anger and wild plans. It heartened me to see he was quite as fierce for me as I had been for him. And almost as importantly, he had brought me some shortbread from the breakfast table.

"I'll tell you this, Lila, when we find out who did this to you, I'll make them pay!" he threatened. Since my mouth was full of shortbread, I could only nod. "Byford has spoken to Lady Cecily. She promises to name the heir by tomorrow. Oh, and she sends her love to you," he added, getting up to walk about restlessly.

He did not stay much longer. Sickrooms made him nervous, even imaginary ones, and I knew how eager he was to be gone. The fog still lingered, as dense as ever, so I knew he would not be going out. Instead, he told me he intended to watch the other guests carefully, hoping to discover something that would tell him who the poisoner was. I did not think he would have much luck, but I kept that to myself.

I slept for the rest of the morning. At noon, Polly brought me a pot of tea and some toast. Nothing had ever tasted better to me. Much refreshed, I sat up in bed and asked for the book I had been reading. Polly stayed with me, seated by the window with her sewing and only occasionally getting up to tend the fire or speak to people who came to the door.

Sylvia Danvers was one of the first. Polly talked to her through the door, saying, "Miss Lila can see no one, ma'am. Doctor's orders."

"I am not 'no one,' " came the frigid reply, and both Polly and I grinned.

"Well, you can't anyway," Polly said. There was a long silence and then we heard her say, "Such insolence! I don't know what . . ." We never did learn what she had been about to say, for she had gone away in high dudgeon.

Quite late in the afternoon, someone else knocked. "Dear Lila, do let me in," I heard Alastair say. "I must see for myself you are making a complete recovery."

"Beggin' your pardon, sir, no one is allowed to see Miss Lila," Polly told him, her tone deferential to one so high in the *ton*.

"Oh, do relax your guard, woman," came Alastair's weary reply. "Here I have struggled down this terribly long corridor and you forbid me entrance? I can tell you, King is weary of holding me up. And if you don't let me in, I shall probably expire here. Do you want that on your conscience? Who would set fashion then? Who give Prinny an example to aspire to? Who pass judgment on a new lapel, a daring waistcoat, the resurgence of clocked hose? Oh, I am feeling quite, quite faint."

"Let him in, Polly," I said as I adjusted the shawl I wore over my nightrail. "He won't go away, you know."

Mr. King did look weary as he helped Alastair to a chair by my bed. I thought my cousin probably regretted leaving his own bed, for he was frowning and grimacing from the pain. Still, he dismissed his servant brusquely, and he looked at Polly so pointedly she curtsied and went to the dressing room without a word of protest.

"That's better," he said as he tried to make himself more comfortable. "What's all this about being ill? You don't look it."

I spun him the tale of bad food at dinner, and when he did not accept that, mentioned I might have caught something contagious in Grimshead village. As I did so, I wondered why I did not simply tell him the truth. I knew he could not have poisoned my eggnog. Still, I worried he might let such a confidence slip. He did like to gossip and it was important for him to be ahead of the others.

"So that is why you are isolated. And here I thought it was just to avoid Sylvia lecturing you in that high, tiresome voice of hers, or little Cecilia striking poses and pouting when you did not sufficiently admire her. You will note I mention only the females. I am sure no male besides your brother has been in."

He paused, but when I had no comment, he went on, "Of course I am the exception that proves the rule, coz. But then, in my wounded condition, I must be considered harmless. Dear, dear. I am not at all sure I care to be considered harmless. Tell no one lest it get about in London and ruin my reputation."

I smiled at him. He really was ridiculous, but amusing. And even in a dressing gown and slippers, he made an elegant appearance. The silk ascot at his throat, his fawn breeches, and his carefully groomed blond hair were all perfection. I saw he was wearing a large emerald ring that exactly matched his eyes.

"I understand Lady Cecily is about to announce her heir," he said next. "I really don't understand why it has taken her so long. Surely there is only one among us worthy of the honor."

"Indeed? And who might that be?"

"Why, me, of course," he said haughtily, his eyes wide. "Do consider. The Danvers are impossible. Roger is stupid and she, a greedy harpy. As for Cecilia, she is only a female and a silly one at that. Your brother is too young and careless and you, dear, *dear* Lila, also suffer from the unfortunate failing to be the right sex. We need not regard Douglas-Moore, as he calls himself. He is a bastard. The Douglas fortune will not go to such as he. Lady Cecily is too proud for that. That leaves only Grant, and he already has a fortune of his own. He is, moreover, tied to Byford and his duties as earl. He will not put that aside for any claim of the Douglases, and the old lady is shrewd enough to know it. No, although I am sure you know how I do hate to puff myself off, I must say I am considerably better dressed and better-looking than Grant, to say nothing of having more charm, address, and wit. Don't you agree, hmm?

"All this is why I was shot by someone who was desperate to get rid of me, the forerunner. Lady Cecily and I have discussed it. She even brought that fact to my attention. I was quite elated when she did so, I can tell you."

I was impressed with the case he made for himself. It did seem to me he might inherit, and for a moment I felt a pang for my brother. Young and careless he might be, I was sure he would grow into a more worthy heir than Alastair would ever be. And he had plans to use the castle. I would be willing to wager Alastair would never set foot in it again. Indeed, it would not surprise me if he tried to sell it before our great-aunt was even cold in the ground.

He stayed with me until Polly came back and he did not protest when she said I must rest. King was summoned and he and Polly half carried Alastair back to his own room.

When Polly returned she lit some candles and closed the old draperies, for the early winter dusk was falling. The wind had risen as well. I could hear it howling around the windows it rattled, and below, the booming sound the breakers made as they attacked the ledges. I lay back on my pillow and sighed. Somehow I had been sure the earl would come back to see how I did, but he had not done so. Indeed, all day whenever I heard anyone in the corridor, I had waited in anticipation, only to be disappointed.

He did not come that evening, either, and when Polly finally left me for the night, locking the door securely behind her, I told myself once again Alastair must have been mistaken. Annoyed, I pushed my pillows into a more comfortable position. I was about to blow out my candle when I heard a noise at the door. Fascinated, I watched as the door handle was jiggled. The door did not open, of course, but still my heart began to pound in my chest. Had the poisoner returned to finish the job, I wondered? Had he or she come to smother me in my sleep? Thank God no one could gain entrance!

It was then I heard a key in the lock, saw the handle turn. I sat there in bed frozen with fear as I clutched the covers. As the door opened slowly, I called myself every kind of fool for not jumping from bed when I had the chance to get the poker so I could at least try and defend myself. Can you imagine the relief I felt when Byford put his head around the door, then stepped in and closed it, his finger to his lips?

That relief was short-lived. In its wake came a surge of anger so fierce I shook with it, anger that this man who had ignored me the entire day could just arrive late and let himself into my room, thereby scaring me half to death.

"You!" I said. "How dare you frighten me so? Have you no compassion at all? Didn't you even think about how I would feel when I saw the door handle turning?"

"No, I expected you to show the good sense I know you have in such abundance," he replied as he came closer. "And so you did for you didn't faint and you didn't scream, now did you?"

"I am angry enough to scream now," I told him. Then I saw the key in his hand. "Where did you get that key? Not from Polly, I swear. Are there any others in existence that I should worry about?"

"No, this is the only one. Buttles found it for me on the housekeeper's key ring. That is still kept in the room that would be hers if Grimshead boasted such a person. Better in my possession than another's, don't you agree?

"How are you feeling?"

I was taking deep, steadying breaths, trying to calm myself and I did not answer immediately. At last I managed to tell him I was quite well, thank you, in a tight little voice. He grinned as he sat down on the bed to study my face.

"I understand you had a visitor this afternoon," he said. I wondered at the change in his face—his voice.

"Yes, Alastair came. I refused everyone else, but I could not refuse him."

"No, of course not," he said grimly, going to stoke the fire.

"Why have you come here now?" I asked his back. "Why didn't you come earlier?"

"Because I didn't want anyone to see me, and wonder," he said over his shoulder. "We are trying to catch a would-be murderer. We must be careful."

"Did you notice anything today? Did anyone seem surprised that I was still alive?"

"They wouldn't be likely to show it, even if they were," he said wryly as he returned to perch on the bed. "No, there were no obvious signs of agitation. Everyone voiced their regret you had been taken ill. Sylvia was quite vocal about ill-advised jaunts. Lord, you would have thought Scotland awash in disease to hear her attack the village. As you might suspect, Roger had several instructive tales to tell us.

"I did not see Cecilia until dinnertime. She claimed she had spent a miserable day, and she was sure she was about to fall victim to whatever malady you were suffering. It goes without saying hers would be much worse. Sylvia put her in her place. Douglas-Moore, on the other hand, asked me to tell you if I should chance to see you, that he was praying for you. As for Robert, I finally had to take him aside and tell him his frosty silence and suspicious glares were enough to give the game away. Did you by chance have any revelations about who the guilty party might be?"

I admitted I had not a little absentmindedly, for I was acutely aware that Byford should not be sitting on my bed late at night, not even if all we were doing was discussing possible villains. Even putting aside my mother's and Polly's distress, my reputation would be ruined if it were to become known.

"You shouldn't be here," I blurted out. "You should not have come."

He looked at me long and hard. "I know that," he said. "I could not help myself."

"Why?" I whispered.

He did not answer. Instead, almost leisurely, he leaned forward and bent to kiss me. Only his lips touched mine. I could have escaped that kiss. All I had to do was lean back on my pillows. When I did not, his arms came around me and he gathered me close. Once again I felt the surge of emotion and longing and hunger he had shown me before. It took my breath away.

When he stopped kissing me many moments later, he did not let me go. Instead, he put his hard cheek against mine. I closed my eyes as he said, "I will not apologize this time. I think I began wanting to kiss you again as soon as our first kiss ended. I know I am mad. I know you are in love with Alastair. But even knowing that couldn't keep me from falling in love with you. I knew it the night I found you with the pistol and accused you of being the guilty one. I told myself I would make you love me, somehow. Then, after we found Robert safe, and I kissed you—do you remember how you kissed me in return? I knew then it would not do for you were only grateful to me. You kept telling me of that gratitude, and I told myself I didn't want you that way. But I was wrong. That is why I came tonight, to tell you I will take you any way I can get you. And if gratitude is all you can feel for me, well then, that will have to suffice."

"I don't love Alastair," I whispered.

He leaned back then so he could look into my face. I cannot imagine what he saw there. I was confused, dizzy even, with his kiss, the things he had told me, his seductive nearness.

"You don't have to lie to me, Lila," he said. "I could tell from the first time I saw you in the library the night you arrived, that you adored him. It was how you looked at him . . ."

"Yes, I thought I loved him then. But since we have been here, I've come to see what I felt was only infatuation. I don't love him, not now. But I don't understand. I tried so hard not to show my feelings."

"You were not obvious about it. You are too much the lady for that. I'm sure no one else ever suspected. Are you *sure* it was only infatuation? Very sure?"

I nodded. It was all I could do. I wanted to tell him I loved him but he did not give me the chance. At last he said, "How strange this is, this love. I have never felt anything like it before. Oh, I'll not lie to you. I had my calf love, my affairs. But even in the heat of passion, I knew it would not last. This time, this time it will. Your mother named you truly. You are Delilah. You must be to bewitch me so."

"You are mad," I breathed. "I am so ordinary. And I'm too tall, and I'm not at all beauti—"

I was not allowed to finish, for he was kissing me again—all over my face, my throat, my mouth—while his hands caressed me until there wasn't a coherent thought in my head.

"Never let me hear you say anything so silly again," he growled in my ear. "You are beautiful, oh, not to the *ton*'s specifications perhaps, but the *ton* is fickle. Last year wasn't it brunettes who were admired? This year it will probably be blondes. Pocket Venuses have recently been held up as perfection; can statuesque women be far behind? I see you, that lovely skin, your seductive body, your laughing eyes and tempting mouth, and I am determined to have you. Alastair be damned!"

"Alastair be damned indeed," I agreed, happiness welling up to engulf me.

"What? Do you mean it? Truly?"

Now it was my turn to reach for him. It was a long time before we were able to return to even the semblance of proper behavior.

"Delilah," he said, lingering over every syllable.

"I think I should tell you I don't answer to that name, and haven't since I was ten," I told him. "If you want to get my attention, you must call me Lila."

He drew back to smile at me. "In public, if I am not calling you countess, why, of course I will. But when we are alone together after we marry, you will always be Delilah to me. And although I hate to contradict you, love, you do so answer to that name. Why, haven't you just done so, tonight?"

Chapter Seventeen

He must have been right, for it was very late before he finally left me, telling me to get some sleep during what was left of the happiest night of my life. I don't know if I slept with a smile on my face. I certainly woke up with one.

Before we parted, Grant and I talked about what was to be done. There seemed little chance we could discover the poisoner now. We decided I might as well rejoin the company, coming down after luncheon so it would not seem as if I had made too quick a recovery. And as Grant pointed out, I was probably safer eating the food prepared for the entire party, than that which Polly brought for me alone.

I spent the morning pacing my room, impatient to see him again, even if it could only be discreetly, for we had also decided to keep our love a secret, at least for now.

"When this is over, when I have you safe away, love, then it will be time to tell the world. Do you agree?"

I almost laughed at seeing this tall, powerful man, so used to giving orders and getting his own way in everything, humbly asking for my opinion. It was then, I think, I began to believe he truly did love me. But after Polly had escorted me to the library and I was greeted by the others, I wondered if I would not have been better off alone in my room after all. For although she professed relief I had recovered so quickly, Sylvia took me to task for coming among them when I might still be contagious. She begged me to take a seat apart and proceeded to spend most of the afternoon with her face hidden in a handkerchief. It made me feel quite the outcast. Roger, although he nodded at his wife's speech—and when did he not, poor man?—was quick to tell me how well I looked, unsettling me considerably. "Blooming, you are, coz," he beamed. "I had not thought to see you looking so—so bright-eyed and blushing."

I thanked him, careful not to look at Grant. He was seated at the desk with a book I was sure he was just pretending to read.

"It must be due to all the time she has spent in bed. Bed rest is so beneficial," he murmured as he turned a page. Silently I vowed he would pay for that remark, sometime soon.

"Glad it was nae worse, lass," Douglas-Moore said with a smile on his ugly face. I smiled back as I thanked him for his concern.

Robert continued to scowl at everyone. I sent him a warning glance as Cecilia joined us. Polly had told me that morning that she had taken to her own bed and did not intend to get up all day. I was sure learning I had had changed her mind.

"What is all the bustle about?" she asked after the subject of her precarious health had been thoroughly explored. "The hall is full of servants coming and going, and for once they are moving rapidly. I don't understand."

"Lady Cecily has decided to join us for dinner tonight," Douglas-Moore told her as he turned the page of his newspaper. "She told Crowell so and that doctor chappie agreed it would do her no harm.

"Didn't she say as much to you, m'lord?" he added, turning to Grant. "I saw you coming from her room earlier."

Grant nodded absently, but he did not reveal the purpose of his meeting with our hostess.

"I hope she is going to tell us who she has chosen to inherit," Sylvia remarked, forgetting her handkerchief for a moment. "I shall tell Harley to begin packing. We may well be able to leave here tomorrow."

The thought seemed to cheer her considerably, and Cecilia as well. She was so happy the ordeal of her visit was almost at an end, she became quite gay, flirting impartially with both Robert and Grant, teasing them about the Season and London, and how she would be looking out for them when she came to town. After one particularly leading remark, accompanied as it was by a delicate blush, Sylvia took her sharply to task. "This is not at all becoming, Cecilia," she said. "Your behavior is such that any decent woman must blush for you. And do not think to excuse yourself by pointing out the gentlemen are relatives. That does not excuse your wanton behavior, not at all. You should strive for a more modest, retiring nature if you know what's good for your reputation."

Cecy tossed her chestnut curls and looked rebellious. I knew she was bored. Besides, she could no more stop flirting when there were gentlemen about than she could stop breathing.

"I do not have to listen to you, Sylvia," she said pertly. "You are not my mother, why, we are practically of an age! And you are not even a relative, except by marriage. I shall do just as I please."

"I should be very sorry to have to write and inform your mother of your behavior and insolence to me," Sylvia said in an awful voice. "Then she would know there never was any chance of you being named the heiress, after what you have done. I am sure she would be very cross to hear such bad news, don't you agree?"

"Oh, leave her alone," Robert surprised me by saying. "She doesn't mean anything by it and all this squabbling is so tiresome. Aren't things here bad enough without that?"

Sylvia looked aghast, her mouth opening and closing in her astonishment at being taken to task by my generally sunny brother. It must be that my experience, added to his own, had affected him even more deeply than I had thought.

"Come on, lad, I challenge you to a rematch," Grant said, indicating the chess board nearby as he closed his book.

"No, thank you, sir," Robert said, scowling impartially at us all. "I think I'll take a long walk."

"Take Henry with you," I called to his back as he went to the door. His only reply was an impatient shrug. I looked at Grant then, imploring him to do something. His steady gaze reassured me somehow. And it was true, Robert was probably safer outside.

Cecilia sighed and went to the window. "The fog has lifted," she announced, as if no one but herself had the wits to observe it. I was glad Alastair was still in his room. Such an inane comment would have called for a suitably sarcastic, cutting reply from him and hurt Cecy badly.

It was a very long afternoon.

When the first dressing bell rang at last, I was quick to put my needlework away to go upstairs with the others. I felt unsettled, deprived even, for Grant and I had been able to exchange only that one quick glance when Robert left us. It had been so hard! I wanted to stare at him, drink him in, memorize him even. And I wanted to remember how it had felt to be in his arms, the touch of his mouth on mine. All afternoon my nerves had been taut with yearning. The sewing I had done would have to be picked out, for it was not even as good as a seven-year-old's, toiling over her first sampler.

I decided to wear my brown velvet gown to dinner. I knew it was stunning. Hadn't Alastair admired it the first time I had worn it? I wondered if Grant thought it became me.

Polly seemed strangely silent this evening, I thought as she hooked me up. I wondered if she suspected I had had a late-night visitor, and who it had been. Perhaps she had heard the housekeeper's key was missing—but no, if that had been the case, she would have come to me at once, full of her concern. Somehow I did not like to ask her about her silence. I suppose I was afraid all my love for Grant would come tumbling out, in spite of our decision to keep it secret. Besides, I wanted to hug that secret alone for a while longer.

Seated at the dressing table, I asked Polly to put my hair up and curl it. As she began to brush it, I told her about Lady Cecily's sudden decision to join us for dinner. When my hair was done I had her fasten on my pearls and arrange the lace ruffles at the bodice of my gown once more before we went downstairs together.

Halfway down the flight I heard Lady Cecily scolding someone and I hurried my steps. She was standing before the fire, leaning on Grant's arm, and issuing a stream of orders to the servants nearby.

"Crowell, have this fire built up at once. It is freezing here in the hall! Whatever were you thinking to allow such a puny blaze? You know my father always insisted on a roaring fire here on cold nights. And you there, Agnes, bring more candles, and none of these smelly tallow ones, either! How are we expected to see in this gloom?"

The servants hurried to do her bidding as we all stood dumb-founded and Grant led her to a chair by the fireplace. "I have been informed by the cook there will be a slight delay with dinner," she said next, looking around at us impartially. We were all there, with the exception of Alastair. "If dinner is anything like the disorder I have found here in the hall, I can well understand it. Why did none of you think to mention the conditions prevailing outside my room?"

"Perhaps it was because we assumed life at Grimshead was always like this. Small or nonexistent fires, poor, sparse meals, few candles, and dusty neglected rooms," Grant said, smiling down at her. I thought he looked wonderful, so tall and hand-some in his well-cut evening clothes. I wished he were smiling at me. And then I remembered the silent Polly beside me, and dismissed her in a whisper, telling her not to wait up.

Lady Cecily looked so angry at his remark that Cecilia came over to me and tried to hide behind my skirts. As I watched, I saw our great-aunt draw a deep breath before she returned Grant's smile. "Dear boy," she said warmly, "how naughty of you especially not to tell me. Spenser! Where are you, woman?"

Her companion hurried forward, looking not only horrified, but distressed. I saw she had on yet another black gown this evening. This one sported a tiny frill of lace at the collar.

"This is all your doing, Spenser, with your parsimonious ways," the old lady said. "I shall deal with you later."

"Yes, m'lady," poor Miss Spenser breathed. I did not envy her the coming encounter.

When Crowell announced dinner, Roger, prompted by his
wife's firm hand on his back, hurried forward to beg the honor
of leading his great-aunt in to dinner.

"Certainly not," she snapped. "My dear Byford will take me
in. He is much the best of you, and I feel safe on his strong
arm."

Sylvia Danvers frowned, Roger bowed in defeat and retreated, and the rest of us looked amazed at this sudden affec-
tion that seemed to have sprung up between our hostess and her
eldest great-nephew. I saw Robert and Cecilia exchange
glances as Grant bent to whisper something to the old lady. She
laughed and rapped his knuckles with her fan. Together they
advanced toward the dining room as we all fell in behind. Even
Miss Spenser came with us, blushing on the doctor's arm.

The table was set very differently from all our previous
evenings here, and I was not the only one who gasped in surprise. There was a tremendous amount of crystal and plate laid
out, as well as an elaborate silver and gold epergne covered
with nymphs and cupids at play. Also displayed were three silver candelabra set at intervals down the table.

I heard Douglas-Moore's sniff of disapproval for the wealth
before us, as Lady Cecily took her seat at the head. "You must
take the place of honor opposite me, Grant," she commanded.
"The rest of you sort yourselves out as you wish. We will not
stand on ceremony."

Another well-placed shove propelled Roger Danvers to the
seat to Lady Cecily's right. Next to him, Robert placed Cecilia, leaving Sylvia to sit next to Grant. Lady Cecily asked
me to sit on her other side. Her glare in Roger's direction
seemed to say she would not be deprived of some intelligent
conversation. The doctor sat next to me, with Miss Spenser
beside him. Douglas-Moore sat to the earl's right.

The dinner we were served was vastly different from anything we had been treated to before during our stay at Grimshead
and it was served not only by Crowell and the elderly footman
with the sniff, but by three others as well, all of them done up
in their finest livery. From the amount of food brought in, every

one of them was necessary. When Roger exclaimed over the huge saddle of beef, the pigeon pie, and the cold salmon in aspic, and rhapsodized about the platter of lobster fritters and a delicious cream soup, Lady Cecily looked amazed.

"Well, of course. I do not keep a French chef, but Mrs. MacKay is a good, plain cook. Grant," she said, her voice raised to reach the other end of the table, "do try the haggis. If there is still anything of Scotland in you, you will enjoy the haggis. Crowell, more wine for the earl."

I stole a look down the table to where Grant was nobly helping himself to the haggis and did not envy him. I wondered why Lady Cecily was making such a fuss over him, and I saw from Sylvia Danvers' frown, she wondered, too. I could hear Mr. Douglas-Moore attempting a conversation with Miss Spenser, so I turned to the doctor and asked him if he thought the roads were clear enough for travel.

"I believe so. I know you must be anxious to return to your home in England. It is too bad you had to first see Scotland in February, when the wind howls so over the North Sea. We do have some wonderful sunny days in the summer. Somehow they seem twice as beautiful because we have to wait for them so long."

He turned as Crowell offered him more wine and I took a moment to observe Lady Cecily. This evening she was wearing another outdated gown; this one a blue satin worn open over a lace petticoat and huge hoops. On her head was her powdered wig, this evening embellished with jeweled combs and plumes. Her neck and arms and fingers were covered with jewels, and they sparkled in the candlelight. I had to smile to myself. Lady Cecily was eccentric, that was true, but there was an air of gallantry about her, a willingness to face whatever life had to offer without whimpering. I felt suddenly as if I were being stared at, and looked down the table to see Grant regarding me. He lifted his glass to me in a silent toast, and I felt myself begin to blush.

We spent almost two hours at the table, but after the last course and the several removes that accompanied it had been served, Lady Cecily rapped on her goblet to gain everyone's attention. Motioning to Crowell, who immediately left the room, she waited until there was complete silence.

"My *dear* relatives," she said, staring at each and every one of us in turn, "I have an important announcement to make, for at long last I have decided who will inherit the Douglas fortune."

She paused and smiled. I could see everyone was behaving predictably. Robert and Cecilia had their heads together, whispering excitedly, Sylvia Danvers was leaning forward, her face avid and the remains of her dinner forgotten, while her husband wiped his perspiring face with his napkin. Miss Spenser was shrinking back in her chair, one hand to her mouth, and I wondered why Douglas-Moore looked so secretly amused. Only Grant and the doctor seemed perfectly at ease.

The butler and footmen returned to the dining room bearing champagne and some beautiful old cut-crystal stems and went around the table serving us. When this had been accomplished, our hostess rapped for attention once again. Struggling to her feet, she raised her glass and said, "Let us drink to my heir, Grant St. Williams, Earl of Byford."

After the initial excitement, I saw my brother congratulate Grant while Roger nervously crushed his napkin as he peeked down the table at his wife. I saw he had reason to be nervous, for she was very pale and her brows were drawn together in a frown. Mr. Douglas-Moore beamed as he studied her—I wished he would not be quite so obvious in his glee at her disappointment. Now Cecilia was wishing Grant well, and trying to hide her apprehension about how her mother would take the news. I did not look at Grant. To be honest, I was disappointed Robert had not been Lady Cecily's choice, and I was afraid he would see it.

"But . . . but he has no need for the money," Sylvia sputtered, echoing my thoughts. "He is as rich as a nabob already."

"Yes, that is true," Lady Cecily said as she signaled the butler to refill her glass, ignoring the doctor's frown. "But he is the eldest among you, and he has certainly shown me he has the most sense. I have also been impressed with his character and intelligence. The Douglas fortune will be safest in his hands. But come, drink up! This is an evening of celebration!"

She turned to me and whispered, "If looks could kill, the earl would come into his new wealth this minute. Do observe Lady Danvers, my dear. I have not been so amused for years."

I stole a look at the lady in question, her face purple now with indignation, and tried not to smile.

"Why did you announce the heir tonight, ma'am?" I asked. "Surely it puts Byford in great danger, does it not?"

I thought she looked at me strangely. "Why, yes, I suppose it does," she said slowly. "But you must all leave Grimshead soon. I cannot tell you how distressed I was when I learned of that poisoned eggnog. I see you suffered no ill effects from it however. You look beautiful tonight.

"That new attempt prompted me to bring this to an end by naming Grant, however. You are a good lass, Lila; do not worry about the earl. He is very capable of defending himself."

Our party concluded in a somewhat somber mood, the air full of unspoken disappointment and chagrin. Grant himself had little to say after he had thanked Lady Cecily and proposed a toast to her continued good health.

Before she gave the signal for the ladies to withdraw, she asked the gentlemen to join them in the drawing room after they had had their port, announcing that Alastair, who had dined in his room, would be carried down to join them. Two footmen, one on either side, helped her to her feet and assisted her from the dining room. The rest of us ladies followed her.

I thought I had never seen such an air of excitement and delight as rested on our great-aunt's face, and I realized that of everyone present, she was the only person who was enjoying herself to the fullest. And then, as I walked with the others down the hall in her wake, I wondered what other surprises she had in mind for the evening.

Chapter Eighteen

Alastair was already established on the chaise in the drawing room. Lady Cecily greeted him, and then as she went slowly to her wing chair near the fire, instructed one of the footmen to serve him some port. "For," she said with a huge smile, "in spite of being forced to endure only our female company, you shall not be denied your wine, sir." Alastair thanked her. I noticed he took the glass with his left hand, so I knew he had not abandoned his pistol. Somehow it made me feel better and I went to ask him how he did. I admit that ever since Lady Cecily had made her startling announcement, I had not been able to shake off a mounting sense of unease. To know Alastair was armed, as I sincerely hoped Grant was, was reassuring.

As I took a seat beside my cousin, I also tried to stifle the unworthy feeling of regret Robert was not the heir. My father, although possessed of a comfortable fortune, was nowhere near as well-to-do as the Earl of Byford, or even Alastair or the Danvers. Robert would have only a modest inheritance, while my portion was no more than respectable. Still, it was our great-aunt's privilege to dispose of her wealth any way she wanted, and no one should have counted on being the recipient of her largesse. And, I admitted to myself as I took the cup of tea Miss Spenser was handing me, I certainly had to agree with Lady Cecily's assessment. Grant was the best among us in my eyes, too, and certainly more sensible and mature than my twenty-one-year-old brother.

"Spenser, have Crowell bring up the last bottle of Napoleon brandy from the cellars," our hostess ordered. "I regret I cannot offer it to anyone but Grant, for there is little left, but I want him to enjoy it on this most important evening."

"And what is this?" Alastair whispered to me, his brows raised.

I told him what had happened in the dining room and was surprised to see his face pale. Then, as if he saw my confusion, he laughed lightly.

"So, to the wealthiest go the spoils, eh? Life is definitely unfair, don't you agree, my dear? I myself would have been delighted to be named heir, but since it is not to be, I shall have to struggle on with what is left of a constantly diminishing fortune until I can find a wealthy heiress. What a shame you are not such a one, Lila, for we deal extremely well with each other. And if I have to marry someone, I wish it might be you. At least you have some conversation."

He sighed and looked so glum I laughed at him. "But I have heard it said, sir, that all heiresses are beautiful," I could not resist reminding him.

"And beauty is in the eye of the beholder, and handsome is as handsome does, and money cannot buy happiness," he replied, shaking his head. "I know all those old chestnuts, and not a one o' them is true. In my experience, the heiresses I have known have all been distressingly ugly; squinty, obese, with shrill voices and red hands. Well, I daresay I shall become accustomed."

I chuckled again as I pictured my elegant relative beside such a vision as he had painted. Then I promised him I would be on the lookout for as handsome an heiress as I could find, to whom I would praise him to the skies while sending him an urgent message to come immediately. I spoke lightly, of course, for I knew he was only funning.

He grinned at me. "And how was dinner, coz? Lord, I wish I might have been there to see the fun. Did La Danvers cut up royally? I can see from her expression she is not best pleased with the results of her stay at Grimshead."

I looked to where Sylvia, although supposedly attending to a conversation between Lady Cecily and Cecilia, was not contributing a word. Her lips were compressed in a thin, disapproving line, and her eyes were cold. As I watched, Crowell came in behind Miss Spenser, bearing an old bottle of brandy on a silver tray. He brought it to Lady Cecily and presented it reverently.

"Yes, that's the one. Put it over there on the drinks table, but mind you place it somewhat apart from the other bottles. That is ambrosia, not meant for mere mortals."

Crowell obeyed and after adding some more coals to the already blazing fire, bowed himself out. Miss Spenser took up her usual position behind her mistress's chair.

"Lila? I asked you a question," Alastair said, his voice petulant. "It does seem to me you might be more attentive, especially since I am wounded. It has not been at all amusing for me, you know, lying on my bed of pain alone. And now I find out Grant is to inherit, well, I am quite cut up. Come, tell me of the dinner and everyone's reactions, to cheer me up."

Obediently, I amused him with a quick account of the party, not forgetting to mention the lavish food accompanied by no less than four wines, the elaborate table decor, and Lady Cecily's unholy delight at the mischief she had stirred up. He was still chuckling at my description of Sylvia's alarming changes of complexion, when the other gentlemen came in. My gaze went immediately to Grant, and I was pleased he was looking at me in the same searching way.

"Ah, there you are," Lady Cecily said. "Do make yourselves comfortable. I have always hated that custom that requires women to leave the gentlemen alone after dinner. I am sure we miss the most interesting conversations and all the best jokes. So unfair!"

Roger Danvers hurried to his wife's side and, taking the seat beside her, bent over to whisper in her ear. Sylvia did not seem to hear him or even notice he had taken her hand and was patting it gently. For a moment, there was some confusion as the

three men took their seats. Lady Cecily ordered her companion
to bring her a glass of port.

"I know, Doctor, I know, but you must permit me to indulge
this evening. It is not every day one names one's heir, after all.
Grant, my dear, I have had what is left of the last bottle of good
brandy my father laid down years ago brought up from the cellars especially for you. You will find it there on the table. Now,
now, Doctor, not a word."

Dr. Ward subsided, shaking his head, as Grant inspected the
old bottle with the same reverence Crowell had shown. He
poured a generous measure into a snifter that stood nearby, then
turned the glass slowly between his hands to warm it before he
raised it to inhale its aroma. Thanking Lady Cecily for her kindness, he strolled over to where I was sitting beside Alastair to
ask about his health. We all listened while Alastair said he was
gaining strength every day. "I know you must be anxious to return to town, Grant, but do not desert me, I beg of you. I am
sure I will be able to travel within the week. Isn't that so, Doctor?"

"Indeed, sir," the doctor said. "In fact, I am a little surprised
you do not feel better than you do, for the wound is healing
more rapidly than I had expected."

Alastair smiled faintly, and conversation became general.
Lady Cecily drank her port and talked to Mr. Douglas-Moore,
while the Danvers still kept to themselves. Cecilia had taken a
chair next to Robert's and the doctor's, and Grant and Alastair
exchanged a few words. I stared into the fire, a little uneasy for
some reason I could not name. And why was that, I wondered.
It was only an ordinary evening with everyone replete after a
magnificent dinner. Still, I could not help my apprehension. I
shook my head when Robert went to the drinks table. All those
wines at dinner, then champagne, now port. Robert would be
sorry tomorrow but at least there was no chance he would be
lured out in the cold again. Not tonight, he wouldn't.

Grant stood on the opposite side of Alastair's chaise, still
holding the snifter of old brandy in both hands. I looked around
the room until my glance alighted on Miss Spenser. She was

standing once again behind Lady Cecily's chair, but now I saw she was leaning forward eagerly, her eyes wide with excitement behind her thick glasses as she stared straight at Grant. Her mouth was open slightly, and I saw she was gripping the top of the wing chair so tightly her knuckles were white. I turned just as Grant raised the snifter to his lips.

"No, no!" I cried, rising to go to him. "Do not drink it, my dear. I fear it is poisoned!"

As he put the snifter down on a table nearby, he smiled at me warmly. "I suspected as much, Lila. That is why I only pretended to drink. But how did you guess?"

I hesitated. I did not have a single bit of evidence, only the strange way Miss Spenser had looked. How could I accuse her? It was so unbelievable she was the guilty one. I saw Grant was staring past me at Lady Cecily's companion, his gaze intent and somber now, and I looked behind me and gasped. Miss Spenser had moved away from the chair to level a pistol at the company, every one of whom appeared frozen with horror.

"Do not move," she commanded in a high voice that cracked with nervousness. "Mr. Russell, throw that gun you are holding under the blanket on the floor behind you." Alastair hesitated and she pointed her pistol at his heart. "Do as I say or I will shoot. I can hardly miss at this range, sir."

It only took Alastair one quick look at the woman's gray eyes, shining with fanatic intent, to make him obey. I watched with dismay as his pistol skittered away across the carpet.

"Spenser?" Lady Cecily asked in a faint, disbelieving voice. "So it was you after all."

"Yes, m'lady," she replied, her gaze moving rapidly over the group to make sure no one moved. "Yes, it was I, a stupid, silly widgeon, as you have called me so often, fit only to pass the plates and pour the tea. *I* planned it all. *I* carried it out."

"But why? I do not understand," the old lady asked, sounding completely bewildered.

Miss Spenser laughed, a shrill, bitter travesty of amusement. Some of her hair had escaped her tight bun and was straggling around a face mottled with red blotches. I saw she was panting in her excitement, her hurried breathing perfectly audible in the room's stunned silence. Now she nodded and laughed again, and I shivered in fear, she sounded so mad.

"You don't understand?" she screamed, and Lady Cecily shrank back in her chair. "I did it because the Douglas legacy is mine. Do you hear me, all of you? *Mine!* What right have any of you to come here after so many years of neglect and take it from me? Eating and drinking so much, and burning candles and coal without counting the cost. All these years I have been so frugal, for when you died, m'lady, Grimshead would belong to me. Oh, I was upset when you said your father's money would never go to a bastard, but then I remembered I am of legal birth. It was my mother who was illegitimate. Still, she was your father's daughter and your half-sister as well. Of course the money is mine. None of the rest of you were going to have it if I had to kill every one of you."

Her voice had risen to a shriek and I wondered if perhaps one of the servants might not come in to investigate. Then I remembered their age and decrepitude, and prayed they would not. I looked at Grant. He was staring at Miss Spenser, his eyes narrowed and intent, and his body so tense I knew he was only waiting for the right time to try to disarm her, and I prayed for him as well. Prayed he would not attempt anything for it was plain Miss Spenser was quite, quite mad. Quickly, I glanced around at the rest of the party.

Cecilia had fallen against the back of her chair as if in a faint, and the Danvers sat close together, clutching each other's hands and looking like a parody of the nursery rhyme pair Lady Cecily had named them. Alastair and Robert were motionless, a still-life portrait, and even Mr. Douglas-Moore's mouth hung open in shock. Don't move, Robert, I ordered him silently. Don't move!

"My dear Miss Spenser, you are distraught and you do not know what you are saying," Dr. Ward said calmly as her shriek died away to silence. "Come, give me the pistol before you hurt yourself with it. Let me help you."

She smiled at him, a coquettish simper that did not sit well on her faded, wrinkled face. "Of course you would want to help me, dear Matthew," she said softly in a coy, girlish voice. "You know very well that after *she* dies, and Grimshead and all the money are mine, we can be married at last. How long we have waited, my dearest, but it will not be long now, I promise you."

The doctor stared at her, and the hand he had been holding out for the pistol, dropped to his side.

"Marry you?" he asked in complete incredulity. "I have no intention of marrying you; wherever did you get such an idea?"

For a moment, Miss Spenser frowned, but then she tossed her head and smiled at him again, her eyes glittering. "It is like you to pretend, sir, but I have known all along of your feelings for me, in spite of the way you tried to hide them. Those tender smiles, the way you always took my hand and asked so carefully about my health. In the beginning, I could not really believe it, for it was like a dream come true—all those horrible years that I slaved away here alone, taking care of a nasty old woman, but now my reward—and yours, too, my darling—is at hand. Why should I allow strangers to take my money? I earned it, and I have waited patiently such a long time. Do you remember how long, Matthew? Twenty-seven years of devotion and hard work it has been. And now I was supposed to sit quietly and watch it being given to another? Never!"

"Why did you kill Excalibur?" Lady Cecily demanded. She looked quite fierce. I wondered if she even realized the danger we were all in.

"I never meant to kill your doggie, m'lady," Spenser said, sounding more like her subservient self. "No, indeed. I poisoned the comfit to get rid of *her*."

"Me?" Sylvia Danvers asked, horrified, as Miss Spenser waved the pistol in her direction. "But why?"

"Why, Lady Greedy-Grab? Because I watched you the first afternoon as I took you around the castle, eyeing all the valuable antiques and silver. I could tell you wanted that gold salver especially. That was my Grandfather Douglas's salver! And you are not even a relation! But I knew you would steal as many things as you could, even if m'lady did not choose your husband as her heir. So I had to kill you so that not a single thing that belongs here at Grimshead should be taken away. It is all mine. Everything here is mine!"

Sylvia Danvers sank back in her chair as Miss Spenser laughed and aimed the pistol at her. I was afraid she might fire and I spoke up in what I hoped was a normal tone of voice.

"Did you also cut the hole in the library wall?" I asked.

"Oh, yes, and I poisoned your eggnog, too. I was shocked when I returned here the other day to see Lady Cecily kissing you and calling you her 'dear girl.' She has never called *me* that," she added, sounding grim again. "The eggnog did not work either—I have had the most unfortunate run of luck, when you come to think of it; so unfair!—but my plan this evening was to dispose of your brother, and you, too, Miss Douglas. I went to fetch more of the poison from where I had hidden it in my room this afternoon after I heard Lady Cecily tell Matthew she was determined to leave everything to you and your brother. When or why she changed her mind in favor of the earl, I have no idea, but after the announcement at dinner, it was a simple matter to change the victim and put the poison in the brandy meant only for Lord Byford. When Crowell brought the bottle up from the cellars, I told him to fetch another glass, for the snifter he had put on the tray was spotted. His eyesight is so bad he couldn't tell whether I was speaking the truth or not, and while he went back to his pantry to get one, I put all the poison in the bottle and recorked it. You have had a narrow escape, Miss Douglas, you and that handsome scamp of a brother of yours. This was his second escape, too. My, he does lead a charmed life, doesn't he? Anyone else would surely have frozen to death, locked in the shed. That was a clever idea for a stupid, silly widgeon, now wasn't it?"

She giggled and looked to the doctor as if for approval, and remembering how she had handed me a cup of tea, and how I had drunk it down, I shuddered. How easy it would have been for her to poison the cup while she was puttering around the tea tray readying things.

Lady Cecily, who had been sitting upright in the wing chair

listening intently, now spoke. "You have not been as clever as you suppose, woman. And it was all for nothing anyway. I never intended you to have Grimshead—the very idea! And the only money I was going to leave you was the pension due any faithful servant. But now I shall have to summon the law and charge you with all these crimes. Give me the pistol. You cannot shoot us all, so what is the point in shooting anyone? Do you want to hang?"

Spenser turned to her and I held my breath, wishing Lady Cecily had not been quite so blunt.

"What can you mean, ma'am?" she asked, sounding genuinely puzzled. "You know very well that until these others came, you were going to leave the money to me. Why, I have always counted on it. It is just that these London society people have turned your head. But when they are gone, you'll come to your senses and remember who has always had your best interests and your well-being most to heart.

"Matthew?" she pleaded, turning in his direction. "You knew she meant to leave me everything, didn't you? I know you will help me convince her of my rightful claim, for then we can be married just as I planned. And I will still help you with your patients. You need not fear I intend to waste the fortune playing lady of the manor, dear Matthew. Not I!"

Dr. Ward shook his head. "I fear you have been suffering delusions, Miss Spenser. Lady Cecily never mentioned such a plan to me. I am her doctor, concerned only with her physical condition. We did not discuss anything else. As for marrying you, I have no such inclination. It was only ordinary kindness that made me inquire for your health. I fear you have been imagining any warmer regard."

"But . . . but you love me, dear Matthew! I know you do!"

Her voice cracked with her intensity and in spite of my fears, I felt sorry for the woman. Mad she surely was, but she had been building her castles in the air for all these years, fancying herself a great heiress and loved by Matthew Ward as well. How shattering for her to discover none of it was true.

She began to weep, heavy sobs racking her thin body. The

pistol she was holding fell to her side and Grant made a move as if he intended to go and try to take it from her.

"No, m'lord, I'll get it," the doctor whispered, edging toward her, his eyes never leaving her face.

"I cannot bear it, no, no, I cannot," she cried out in a despairing voice. "To think it was all for nothing, all of it! And I have worked so hard, made so many wonderful plans, and now, when my dreams were finally about to come true, they have been denied me. Oh, cruel, cruel!"

She wiped the tears from her face with the back of her forearm. Then, seeing the doctor and the earl moving toward her, she crouched and raised the pistol again.

"Get back! Everyone stay exactly where you are!" she ordered. Although her voice shook, it was firm with resolve again. The men stopped and she went on, "I'll not hang, nor will I go to prison. There is another way out for me and I intend to take it."

Chapter Nineteen

I saw Miss Spenser glance at the snifter of poisoned brandy where it sat apart from its fellows on the drinks table. I knew she intended to drink that brandy, kill herself, and my hands flew to my heart in horror. But as she rushed by the wing chair, Lady Cecily thrust out her silver-headed cane and tripped her. She went down in a heap of tangled black skirts. Instantly, Grant was upon her to wrest the pistol from her grasp. The doctor was right behind him. At this last failure, the ending of her own life, all the woman's wits seemed to leave her, and she began to scream at the top of her lungs, spewing demented ravings and curses as she struggled with the two men trying to subdue her.

I was glad they had been able to move; I felt incapable of it myself, and I suspected all the others were in like state. Miss Spenser was kicking and scratching now. Her hair had escaped from its tight bun and it whipped around her contorted face. She had not ceased her keening when Mr. Douglas-Moore took a hand. Waiting until her face was turned toward him briefly, he hit her sharply on the jaw with his fist and she sagged unconscious in the doctor's arms.

"I suggest ye take her away an' tie an' drug her, Doctor," he said, his voice rough. "I'll help ye. Yon woman's mad. She belongs in a lunatic asylum."

The doctor nodded, although I saw his eyes were grim, and between them they carried Miss Spenser out of the room.

Everyone was silent until the sound of their footsteps died away.

"I really do think that I shall be forced to leave Grimshead whether my wounds are healed or not," Alastair said softly as he shifted to a more comfortable position on the chaise. "One must think of one's nerves, after all."

We all stared at him, still speechless, as he bowed to Lady Cecily. "My compliments, m'lady. That was surely an act of genius to trip the lady with your cane. I doubt if any of the rest of us would have thought so quickly or acted so decisively. Or if we would have wanted to," he added, almost as an afterthought.

Our hostess had sunk back against the squabs of her chair, the hand that shielded her eyes, shaking. At his words, she raised her head and nodded. "I admit I was so angry, sir, I did not think of anything but stopping her."

"Yes, it was very bad, was it not? All that poisoning?" he murmured. "She is truly insane."

"Well, yes, there is that, too," Lady Cecily agreed, her voice gaining strength. "But at the time, what really made me cross was that she had poisoned the last bottle of good brandy."

Grant shook his head, but I saw the tears on the old lady's cheeks and I knew she was not so heedless of her companion's fate as she pretended to be.

"Would you like us to leave you now, m'lady?" I asked, going to kneel before her to offer her my handkerchief. "This has been so upsetting for you."

"You're a good lass, Lila. I have always thought so," she said, mopping her cheeks and trying to smile. "Please do not go. I am so wrought up I would never be able to sleep. Grant, a snifter of brandy, if you please, before Dr. Ward comes back and forbids it."

Grant moved to do her bidding. I wished we were alone together, just the two of us, so I could run into his arms and be comforted by his strength. Last night seemed an age away. Suddenly Robert, who all this time had been standing perfectly still holding his glass, gulped the contents as if he had just remembered he had it. He joined Grant at the table, asking Alastair in a hushed voice what he could get for him. Lady Cecily reached up to pat my cheek as she said, "Best you see to Cecilia, dear. I think she has fainted, and who can blame her?"

I went to my cousin and was glad to see that, outside of her pallor and shallow breathing, she was conscious, for she had begun to quiver and moan. I saw that Sylvia was staring straight ahead, her face still white, and her husband, his pale blue eyes popping in amazement, tottered over to fetch her some brandy from the bottle he had used earlier. I wished Grant had not put the poisoned bottle on the mantel to get it out of everyone's way, for it seemed to loom over us there, reminding us of his narrow escape and Spenser's thwarted suicide.

"I seem to have made the most frightful mull of things," Lady Cecily remarked after a sip of brandy. "My father would be ashamed of me. But thank heavens you came to see me this afternoon, Grant, and convinced me that naming Lila and Robert as my heirs was putting them in danger."

"And he, of course, was perfectly willing to brave that danger, if he could be named the Douglas heir instead," Sylvia said, speaking for the first time, her breast heaving in indignation at Grant's cleverness.

Lady Cecily sent her a glance of complete disdain. "That was only playacting for this evening. The earl was sure the murderer would make a move after I announced my heir. He was on guard for it, which neither of the Douglases would have been."

I stared at Grant in wonder. He had put himself in danger for me, and for Robert. And we were to be her heirs? I could not seem to take it in, and a quick glance showed my brother was just as confused.

"M'lady makes me seem foolishly courageous, but in truth there was little danger," Grant explained. "After discussing the situation and pooling our knowledge, we devised a trap, using the Napoleon brandy as bait. You see, I was almost sure the culprit had to have been Miss Spenser, even though Lady Cecily had a hard time agreeing. With Alastair wounded and Robert's life attempted as well, there were only three suspects left." He bowed to the Danvers and to Cecilia. "It could not have been

Lila. She found the pistol after it disappeared when Alastair was shot. And while we were, er, discussing this in the dining room, someone took that pistol away."

I saw he was careful not to look at me as he recited this pale, edited description of what had happened between us.

"That left only you, Cecilia, the Danvers, or Miss Spenser, and seriously, I could not believe you three could be murderers. In any case, none of you could have been the spy in the priest hole."

"Thank you," Sylvia said sarcastically, but Roger bowed in his ponderous way and thanked m'lord for his compliment in all seriousness.

Grant continued as if he had not been interrupted. "Only Miss Spenser could have been the owner of that mysterious eye. Since she was so seldom in our company, the priest hole was the perfect means to keep abreast of our activities and conversations. But even knowing that, we could not just accuse her without proof. Of course neither Lady Cecily nor myself had the slightest idea the woman expected to inherit, and was mad as well, or that she would carry a pistol with her this evening. I would never have placed you all in jeopardy that way, believe me."

Everyone was silent for a moment, remembering that madness and what might have resulted from it.

"But, Byford, you have forgotten Douglas-Moore," Alastair reminded him.

"Oh, Douglas-Moore was never in the lists and he knew it," Lady Cecily was quick to say. "I asked him here because I like his spirit, and to add spice to the mix. Besides, he certainly doesn't need the money. Haven't any of you heard of the Moore reaper? And the new loom he invented some years past? He's made a fortune from them. I expect he has more money than any of us."

We were all talking about these extraordinary things when the doctor and the wealthy inventor rejoined us. I looked at Mr. Douglas-Moore in amazement, trying to reconcile this broad,

plain-faced, ordinary man in his rough clothes, with a fortune.
It was difficult to do so.

I saw Robert go to Lady Cecily and bow, and I hoped he
would not act inappropriately, knowing as he did now how
wealthy he was soon to be, but there I wronged him. He only
thanked her and told her he would do his best to be worthy of
her trust and the Douglas name, when the time came for it, of
course, which he hoped would not be for a long time yet, 'pon
his soul, he did. He was quite red when he finished but she only
smiled at him for his tangled speech.

Cecy came to me to exclaim about my good luck, and
Robert's too. I could see she was well pleased and wondered at
it until it occurred to me that although she had not been named
heir, she would still have good news for her mother about how
close she and Robert had become here at Grimshead. I could
practically see my Aunt Mary beaming as she began to plan the
wedding and hoped my brother would do his best to avoid that
particular parson's mousetrap.

Alastair beckoned to me and I went to see what I could do for
him. "My dear, dear Lila," he said, taking my hand in both of
his and pressing it. "How fortunate you heard my proposal before I learned you would inherit. Now you, and all the world,
cannot accuse me of any mercenary intent. Say you will consider it, there's a good girl, for I would find it tedious to have
to court another not half as charming as you are yourself. In
fact, I refuse to even contemplate such a course; I am sure it
would bore me, and you know how I abhor boredom."

He looked up at me, his beautiful green eyes sparkling with
mischief, and a smile transforming his handsome face. I remembered how a year ago I would have given almost anything
to hear him make me a proposal. Now I did not feel a single
pang of either yearning or regret.

"Ladies and gentlemen, if you please," Dr. Ward said. "We
must allow Lady Cecily to get to bed. This has been a long
evening for her, and one filled with the kind of excitement I
cannot recommend for one suffering her serious health problems. She needs her rest."

"No, no one must leave just yet," the lady said as she put her empty glass down on the table beside her. "We are not finished here, not a bit of it, sir. Can it be you have all forgotten Spenser never said anything about wounding Alastair? She only admitted to shutting Robert in the shed and trying to poison Lady Danvers and Lila. Oh, and cutting that spy hole, of course."

She looked at Grant as if to beg him to take the lead. "We must discover who is responsible for that if we are to sleep well."

"Well, of course she had to have shot Alastair, too," Sylvia said in her positive way. "Who else could it have been?"

"I doubt she did," Lady Cecily said dryly. "In spite of waving that pistol in such a threatening way, I am quite sure Spenser has never fired a weapon in her life. She probably stole that one from the gun room. It looked very like a pistol I used to carry years ago. But stay! Do you accuse her, ma'am, because you are the guilty one and think to foist the blame on a madwoman who cannot defend herself?"

"Roger! Did you hear what that woman had the nerve to say to me?" Sylvia asked indignantly. Her voice was high and hurried, and I could not help but think it might have been better for Lady Cecily to have put it another, gentler way.

"Do something! Don't just sit there like a lump of coal! Take her to task, tell her there are such things as laws against libel. Why, she has defamed me, *me*, your beloved wife! Do something, I say, and at once!"

"Perhaps he might be able to if you would just be quiet, ma'am," Alastair remarked, staring at her as he might stare at a bug that had fallen into his wineglass. Sylvia gulped for breath, her face scarlet. I knew how distressed she was. I even found it possible to feel for her. She had come out of this evening with hardly any shreds of dignity left. Accused of greed she could not deny by Miss Spenser, then only excused as a suspect by the earl because she could not have managed the priest hole, and now accused by Lady Cecily of the direst crime—how must she feel? Roger made no move to take his great-aunt to task for insulting his wife. I thought him a spineless man, weak and ineffectual behind his facade of jovial good fellowship.

I caught Grant's eye, wondering why he had not contributed to the conversation, if you could call it that. What was he waiting for?

"There is another reason Alastair's misfortune cannot be laid to Spenser's account," Lady Cecily went on, as if she had not been interrupted at all. "She doesn't have the wits to have planned anything so involved, nor the nerve to manage the shooting, hiding the gun, and then disappearing. Just consider how all her other attempts failed. No, she would have gone all to pieces and we would have caught her at it."

"Then who *did* do it?" Cecilia asked plaintively. "Someone had to."

We all looked around at each other in confusion. That there had been a murderer in our midst we had come to accept, but *two*? No one spoke, and in the silence, Alastair's sigh was clearly heard. "Oh, very well," he said, at his most worldweary. "I see there is nothing for it but to confess. If I do not, Byford is poised to accuse me, aren't you, dear fellow? I saw you pocket my pistol after Spenser was taken away. When did you begin to suspect me?"

"After I asked Dr. Ward about your condition," Grant told him, taking that pistol out to hold it carelessly ready. I was having trouble catching my breath. Alastair had shot *himself*? But that didn't make any sense! I would have said so except Grant went on, "He could not understand why it was taking you so long to regain your strength from what was little more than a deep flesh wound. And I knew you were perfectly capable of following Robert from the castle and locking him in the shed. After, of course, you dangled the glory of solving the crime under his impressionable nose. Now I know you are not guilty of that, but there is still the mystery of your shooting to be solved. How did you manage it, sir?"

"I cannot tell you how you have wounded me to even *think* I might have plotted young Robert's demise," Alastair complained. "Not that it wasn't a fiendishly clever idea, and entirely worthy of someone of my intelligence. But as you admit, I had no hand in it. I am only guilty of my own misfortune."

We all stared at him, too busy trying to understand what he meant by that impossible statement, to speak. He reveled in the attention for a long theatrical moment before he began to enlighten us.

"You see, after the dog died of the poisoned comfit, and Cecilia found the hole in the library wall, it occurred to me I might use what was happening for my own benefit. I knew after my interview with Lady Cecily I had made a good impression on her. It was not difficult. Most old ladies find me charming, if you will forgive me for saying so, ma'am?"

He paused and waited for her nod before he went on, "But I also knew there were others she might find charming as well, and I could not take a chance on that. After thinking it over carefully, I came to the conclusion that if I were shot at, ma'am, you would be so sympathetic, so horrified it had happened here at Grimshead, you would be swayed to make me your heir. Not very gentlemanly of me, to be sure, but I do need the money most dreadfully."

He paused again as if to give us a chance to comment. There was not a sound in the drawing room, and no one's eyes had strayed from his face. Well satisfied with the attention he was receiving, he went on, "I convinced King—my valet, you know—to shoot at me in the hall when we would be quite alone. He was not supposed to *hit* me, you understand, only aim for the wall behind and to one side of me. Then he was to drop the pistol into that ugly Chinese vase on the table where the bedroom candles are kept, and run up the back stairs while I called for help and pretended horror at my narrow escape."

He sighed again and held out his hands palms up. "It was too bad he didn't think to admit he was such a bad shot. I do not intend to let him forget that, after all the needless pain I have suffered. No, I expect he will be paying for it—indefinitely."

"How despicable you are, Russell," Lady Cecily remarked.

Alastair paled a little, although he attempted a chuckle. "A man does what he has to when the devil drives, ma'am," he said.

"Would it be possible for Mr. Russell to travel by coach as far as Newcastle tomorrow, Doctor?" Grant asked, never taking his eyes from his recumbent cousin.

"Yes, I am sure he would come to no harm," the doctor said in a voice full of distaste.

"Summon the footmen, if you please, Lady Cecily. I think it wise to have Alastair carried to his room now. He should get a good night's sleep. My coach will convey you to the port before returning here, sir. You can make arrangements to take ship from there to London."

As the footmen entered the room, he indicated the chaise.

"Oh, I say, there's no need to get miffy about it," Alastair protested. "Of course I suppose it was bad of me to try and delude Lady Cecily and I do beg your pardon for that, ma'am. But surely there is no need to take my little plot so seriously. I don't, and *I'm* the one who was hurt. Why don't we all just forget it and cry friends?"

"Don't you have any idea what you have put everyone through, especially the ladies? No remorse for it? Cry friends indeed! You would be wise to hold your tongue, sir," Grant told him. "My temper is on a very short leash, and so, I imagine, are the tempers of everyone else.

"Take him to his room. Tell his valet they leave at dawn. I'll notify the stables.

"No, Alastair, not another word. Take him away."

We all stood like statues until the footmen disappeared into the hall with their now silent burden. I could hear their footsteps echoing in that vast space as they crossed it to the stairs. Alastair Russell, I thought bleakly. The man I had thought I loved to distraction.

"Ye handled that well, m'lord," Douglas-Moore remarked. "I dinna think I've ever seen a nastier piece o' work than that cousin o' yours."

Grant tried to smile. "Unfortunately I must remind you, sir, you are also related to him. In a way."

Both men ignored Sylvia's outraged hiss as Douglas-Moore said, "Half-related, wouldn't that be? First time I've ever found being a bastard had any advantages, but I'm glad 'tis so."

Chapter Twenty

We were in a subdued mood when we all retired to bed shortly thereafter. I was glad I had told Polly not to wait up to put me to bed, for I did not think I could bear to go over everything that had happened this evening with her. She would hear about it soon enough from the other servants in any case.

I did not undress. Although he had not even hinted at it when he bade me good night with the others, I knew Grant would come to my room. I added more coal to the fire before I washed my face and sat down to wait for him. I felt drained, limp, and when I heard his key in the lock, I did not even get up from my chair.

He locked the door behind him before he came and drew me up into his arms. He did not kiss me. Instead, for the longest time we only stood together like frightened children, holding on to each other tightly. Grant had removed his evening jacket and his cravat, and I buried my face in his linen shirt to breathe in the scent of him as deeply as I could.

"I meant to get whoever attempted to murder Robert for you, Lila," he said at last. "But Miss Spenser is mad. She cannot be tried for the offense."

I leaned back in his arms to study his face. He looked very tired and the sculpted planes of his face were set in harsh lines. I reached up to try and smooth them away.

"Never mind," I told him. "Robert is alive. That is all that is important. But Alastair! I am still having trouble believing what he did, and all for an inheritance. And this from a man that last Season I considered a god. Prayed he would notice me, come to love me."

I shivered thinking of my own escape and Grant picked me up and settled down in the old wing chair with me in his lap. When he kissed me, it was easy to forget my former love. Forget everything.

We talked of many things that night. How soon we could be married, whether we would live mainly in town or at Byford Court in Dorset, where we would travel as soon as Napoleon was vanquished, even the children we might have. When he left me, I fell asleep the minute I got under the covers, for the first time feeling so easy at Grimshead that the sound of the breakers against the ledges was as soothing as a lullaby.

I was late to breakfast the next morning, and relieved when Crowell told me Alastair had left hours before. I had been dreading having to see him. I was also relieved to hear Dr. Ward had taken Miss Spenser away; a calm, docile Miss Spenser who behaved as if she were going on her wedding journey, even to throwing an imaginary bouquet from the gig as it pulled away from the front steps and waving her hands to the crowds of well-wishers and servants that only she could see. Poor Miss Spenser.

Roger and Sylvia also left later that day, taking Cecilia with them. Cecy was anxious to begin preparations for the coming London Season, and Lady Cecily had asked both Robert and me to remain at Grimshead awhile longer. My brother, still dazed by his good fortune, quickly agreed. "Happy to stay as long as you like, ma'am," he said, grinning expansively. I was just as agreeable, for Grant was also to remain.

I had to smile when I saw Cecy's effusive leave-taking of Robert, the way she wheedled a promise from him that he would not fail to call on her during the Season. It was obvious she had already chosen the wealthy gentleman she was going to marry. It occurred to me she would have a lot of competition, once the name of the Douglas heir became known. Sylvia stiffened when Cecy kissed Robert good-bye so warmly, blushing adorably as she did so. I could tell she was soon to be treated to a lecture on the proper behavior of young misses of the *haut ton,* one that would last at least until the coach reached the English border. I was very glad I was not a member of *that* traveling party.

Sylvia's good-byes were brief and coldly formal, although Roger acted as if he had had the most pleasant sojourn possible in Scotland. He was still extolling the healthful benefits of the bracing salt air and extending his compliments to one and all when his wife pulled him into the coach.

Mr. Douglas-Moore was not far behind them. He told Lady Cecily he had been away from his business too long as it was. As he took his leave, he pressed a Methodist tract into Robert's hands, which my brother was astonished to discover was all about the evils of drink and loose living, and how difficult it was for a rich man to enter the kingdom of heaven.

"Something insane about a camel going through the eye of a needle," he told us that evening at dinner. "And what has that to say to anything, I should like to know? We have no camels in England, except possibly at the Royal Enclosure, and I am not such a flat that I would try to put one through the eye of a needle in any case. Such stuff!"

Lady Cecily laughed so hard I thought she might choke on her dinner. Grant laughed, too, to Robert's indignant confusion.

In the days that followed, we were very busy. Both Robert and the earl spent a great deal of time with Lady Cecily's man of business and her agent, riding about the snow-covered property to note improvements that were long overdue. I set myself to putting the castle in better order, persuading Lady Cecily to pension some of the older servants off, and hiring new ones. We acquired a housekeeper, and a strong, calm widow from the neighborhood to serve as Lady Cecily's nurse and companion. The Douglas lawyer came and went after drawing up the new will, and in the evenings we all adjourned to our great-aunt's room to listen to stories of the past and the family. I was glad to see Lady Cecily seemed much better now, and less often in pain, although I did not delude myself she had very long to live.

The doctor told me that on one of his calls. He also told me
Miss Spenser was under the care of a family nearby. She was
happy enough as long as she could see Matthew Ward every so
often, or even just catch sight of him making his rounds in the
gig.

Still, in spite of how well everything was progressing, I resented the fact I never had a chance to be alone with Grant. We
had broken the news of our coming marriage when the lawyer
was at Grimshead, for Lady Cecily was determined to leave me
a large sum since, as she said, I might well decide to remain a
spinster like herself. She was pleased at the news, and took my
advice and left some of her fortune to Cecilia, the rest to a
school for orphans that her mother had founded years before.
She was adamant Alastair Russell get nothing, and the Danvers
only the gold salver Sylvia had coveted. She was also adamant
that I have some of her jewels, most notably a handsome dia-
mond and sapphire set complete with tiara, and a double rope
of rare pink pearls. She gave Robert her father's favorite ring,
a huge ruby solitaire that covered his finger to the first knuckle.
I knew he considered it hideous, although he thanked her gra-
ciously.

One afternoon when the sun was shining brightly and a warm
wind from the south began to melt even the thickest drifts,
Grant and I set out to walk the drive as we had done before. It
took us a long time; I am sure you will understand why.

"I have been reading my Old Testament," he told me as we
skirted a puddle. "Judges is such an interesting book."

I smiled to myself. "Indeed, sir? And did you acquire any
new knowledge from it?"

"I discovered your namesake was not a very nice woman.
The way she conspired with the Philistines against Samson—
deplorable!"

"He was not very nice either," I reminded him. "All those
harlots, to say nothing of the wife he discarded. Still, he was in-
fatuated with Delilah although I agree she could not have loved
him. But to think after they caught him in his weakened condition, they put out his eyes. What an awful thing to do!"

"I see you have also read Judges."

"When I was young," I confessed. "In fact it was right after my mother forbade me to do so, saying it was not at all suitable for a young girl."

He chuckled and pressed my hand where it rested so casually on his arm. I thought how innocent we would look to any passerby, two people taking the air and walking slowly down a drive, arm in arm. How little did our demeanor show the carefully leashed passion we hid under our polite facades. Or how anxious we were to discard those facades.

We had reached the gatehouse. There were plans afoot to make it habitable again and repair the gates, but no work was to be done until spring. As we turned to walk back, Grant said, "I have learned two important things recently. The first is that if I want any happiness and harmony in our marriage, I would do well not to spit anywhere in your vicinity, ma'am."

I began to laugh, recalling that day on the beach and my furious denunciation of men and all their faults.

"The other is straight from Judges, my darling Delilah," he went on smoothly, looking straight ahead now, "and that is that I had better begin to worry the first time you suggest I need a haircut."

We were married in April, just as soon as the banns could be called in the village church near my home in Oxfordshire. My mother was upset by the haste. She called it unseemly, but I suspect the real reason she did not like it was because it gave her so little time to arrange things and to gloat over the splendid match her too tall, plain, twenty-four-year-old daughter was making.

It is said that happy is the bride the sun shines upon, but that cannot be true, for it rained hard on my wedding day, with the windowpanes streaming, the downspouts gurgling, and puddles of gargantuan size forming everywhere. I did not notice. When I walked down the aisle to meet Grant where he waited for me at the altar, why, surely no bride could have been more ecstatic than I.

And later, when Sylvia Danvers wished me happy, and called me Delilah, I laughed. Laughed, because with Grant's arm tight around me and his eyes full of love as he smiled down at me, I felt like Delilah indeed.

Scandalous Secrets by Patricia Oliver

Years ago, Lady Francesca St. Ives was divorced, and cast out of her family amid scandalous rumors. Now, she has returned home to make a new life for herself—without the aid of a man. But a little girl who needs her help—and the child's handsome, intriguing father—may slightly alter the lady's plans...and her heart....

0-451-19886-7/$4.99

The Barbarian Earl by Nadine Miller

The unscrupulous Earl of Stratham has offered his illegitimate son Liam a generous inheritance—if Liam marries the noble Lady Alexandra Henning. But an arranged marriage is an affront to Alexandra's romantic sensibilities—unless Liam can find the way to her heart—and perhaps open his own as well....

0-451-19887-5/$4.99

To order call: 1-800-788-6262

Coming in January

The Sentimental Soldier by April Kihlstrom

Amid the intrigue and espionage of wartime France, a British Colonel posing as a priest, and an adventurous young lady masquerading as a prince make reluctant allies—and unlikely lovers....

0-451-19898-0/$4.99

The Dangerous Baron Leigh by Emily Hendrickson

Since the death of her fiance, Lady Jocelyn Robards has been in seclusion, refusing all suitors. Many assume she is deeply in mourning. But in truth she is haunted be a long-ago affair, the flames of which still passionately flicker in her heart—and are about to ignite once again....

0-451-19929-4/$4.99

Second Chances by Andrea Pickens

For Allegra Proctor, tutoring the Earl of Wrexham's son has its disadvantages—namely, the arrogant earl himself. But Allegra has her reasons for staying on. And when the earl discovers them, both are plunged into a delicious scheme of revenge, intrigue, and a passion they'd never dreamed possible....

0-451-19821-2/$4.99

To order call: 1-800-788-6262